JANE

JAMEY GITTINGS

Jane by Jamey Gittings

Published by Attila Press

ISBN: 979-8-9921827-0-5

The title tells who.
The story tells only part of why.

CONTENTS

THE BEGINNING 9
    Foolscap and the Girl with the Dog 13
    Pablo's Cock 17
    Ice Cream Parlor and a Lighthouse 19
    Bolstered by Stories of French Romance 23
    Karen & the Irony of Status 25
    Surfin' Safari 28
    The Island Beach 30
    Roger and the Most Beautiful Woman in the World 32
    Goofy Foot 35
    Sand-handled 38
    Over as a Whole Unit 41
    Eddie and Jill 45

THE MIDDLE 51
    Interrogation 53
    White Lotus and The Child Buyer 57
    Full Moon or Spotlight 61
    Twerp Defined 64
    Cat's Bathroom 70
    Axiomatic Surfing 76
    Keep it loose 78
    Bubbles in my Blood 85
    Paramour and Too Clever 90
    Pineys and Fessing Up 94
    Mother Leeds and Her Spawn 99
    It All Begins with Hips 103
    Shuffleboard, Lost Botany Students, and the Jersey Devil 107

It was a Great Blue Heron...Probably 119

She Must Like Me 123

Squirrels vs Ducks 128

Fish Food. 131

Cleverness Redux. 135

Cardboard, a Linebacker, and Holes in the Sand 139

Four Holes, Four Wheels 147

Up and Down the Lifeguard Wire 150

End of a Good Day with Nothing to Add 152

Lifter's Meeting. 154

An Island Tradition. 160

Watershed. 162

A Pretty Mature Approach 166

A Scream From the Outhouse. 169

Driving With Mother Leeds 179

The Difference Between Have and Make 183

When a Choice Is Not a Choice 186

More Bubbles and Hansel & Gretel 190

Flaccid vs Irony. 194

Duplicity 197

THE END 199

Ghost 201

Gertrude Stein vs Aunt Clair 203

Out of the Twin Sisters 205

A Bathroom Made of Glass 208

Line of Demarcation. 214

Redemption 216

The Oblation 219

Two in One. 223

Jim Makes His Appearance 226

Jim's Worth 230

Poetic Justice 236

The Resurrection of Pablo 242

Skinny Dippin' & Birthdays 244

True 248

Authenticity vs. Integrity 251

An Ugly but Honest VW 254

Pablo's Authenticity 259

Hurricane Watch 261

Summer Dress in a Hurricane 267

Piña Coladas. 269

Amazing. 271

Puzzle Pieces. 273

The Benefits of a Good High School 278

Caterpillars. 281

Reification 284

Omnipresence of Metaphor 286

Jim Again 289

Another Picnic. 291

Lifeguard Games and Ball 294

Two Days Before Not Yet. 296

Happy Birthday. 301

Nothing More to Write 305

Note to the Reader

No story can exist apart from the collective experiences and relationships of its author. Many of the characters herein were inspired by real people, some represent composites of real people, others are complete creations. All characters should be read within the context fiction for that's where they reside. Where memoir creeps in, whether as a character or in a situation, it is filtered both through the haze of time and turbulence of imagination (stole that last image from Mittelhotzer's Shadows...). All are fabrications of fiction.

The Author

Her name was Jane Deriksson, and I was in love with her. She was my girlfriend's mother, and I had just turned nineteen. That's the end of my story. It was summer 1967 in New Jersey, at a place called Long Beach Island. I had just graduated from high school and had accompanied my father back east on a trip to visit his two sisters, Clair and Isobel. That's the beginning. But there's a lot in the middle.

THE BEGINNING

1

It All Began with Huckleberry

Ever since my father had read me *Huckleberry Finn* when I was six or seven, I'd always wanted to be a writer. Indeed, from that time on, I felt myself to be a writer. I viewed the world as a writer, but with the disdain of Hemingway, Steinbeck, and Salinger, that I co-opted as my own. Despite this, I wrote almost nothing.

Graduation from high school was not the usual rite of passage but the result of a benevolence wrought of the school's wish to be shed of me for good and all. Up to the end, the outcome was in doubt, so no word went out from my parents to other family members about the upcoming event. As such, nobody but my parents attended, and I received no cards of congratulations with checks or cash enclosed. The graduation was a pretty anonymous affair. I did, however, bask in the knowledge that quick thinking on my part had fanned the flames of distaste that brought me over the line. The light under the door was not enough to rival a firefly.

I'll tell the whole story later. But after being caught ditching the majority of my classes for almost a month in the last half of my senior year, I was brought into the office of the boys' dean along with the counselor. The purpose of the meeting was to restructure my academic schedule in light of my recent truancy. With the quiet smile of the operator of a guillotine, the dean informed me that even with the present adjustments I would come up a credit short of graduation, and I would therefore have to return the next year for a final semester. The news chilled me, my body went zero to the bone (got that from Emily Dickinson). Still, thinking fast and uncharacteristically keeping my cool, I said casually that this was OK by me. Perhaps I could get a class just before noon and stay for lunch. "Could I still play football?" I asked.

Thinking only punitively, the boys' dean had not stopped to consider *his* cost. Additional time with me would punish him as well as he would have to deal with me for an added semester. Looking as if he'd just bitten into a rotten piece of fruit with nowhere to spit, he made a U-turn from revenge to self-interest. The two men quickly arrived at a solution—a variable-unit course could add the extra credit, and Latin American History did the trick. I could complete my studies before the graduation deadline. This remains the only distinguished accomplishment of my four years there. I was prouder than the valedictorian.

2

Foolscap and the Girl with the Dog

S o I was ready for the trip back east with my father. We flew out of Arizona to Philadelphia. There, we were picked up by Aunt Clair and driven the seventy miles to Long Beach Island, New Jersey. My father was the youngest of a brood of five and the darling of his two sisters. By proxy, I was a darling, too. It was quickly decided that I would spend my summer on the island. High school was just a memory of a stubbed toe. I was eighteen, and ready for adventures that would be transformed into prose.

Long Beach Island is a spit of land eighteen miles long and four blocks at its widest, connected to the mainland by a three-quarter mile causeway that controlled all traffic in and out. The island has a gentle crescent-moon shape, its outer curve facing eighteen miles of open ocean, while the inner one embraced eighteen miles of bay facing the Jersey coast. Thirty-six miles of sand and foam (got that from Khalil Gibran).

For the week and a half that my father was there, we visited friends of my aunts, ate at seafood restaurants and spent time at the beach. When he left, it was time to establish some justification for my visit. I'd heard that the township was hiring lifeguards. What with thirty-six miles of beach, the openings seemed promising. I was told by someone at the township building that I should see Hart

Lifter, the head of lifeguards. I liked the name, and took note of it for future use in literary endeavors. I asked his whereabouts from a few people in the building and was directed to his location in the basement, and told that his name was, in fact, Art Lifter. I liked Hart better and kept it intact for my purposes. Thus instructed, I found him in his basement office. His persona lived up to his name, for Mr. Lifter was tall, tanned, muscular, middle-aged, and bald, he looked like a weightlifter. I wondered briefly if I'd look as good in thirty years. I decided I would certainly never cross him.

After a short interview, and a look at my senior lifesaving card, he hired me. I was given a red jersey with white short sleeves, *LifeGuard L. B. I.* splashed across the front in yellow, blue swim trunks, a white pith helmet, and a silver whistle to be worn round my neck. I left with the first real job of my life, the best job of my life (but that's material for a different story).

Long Beach Island sported 500 year-round residents, including my aunts, but during the summer, the population swelled to 10,000, nearly all of them needing lifeguard protection. Ten thousand stories all waiting to be melded into fiction. Ten thousand souls, and I knew only two. The summer was yet to start, at least as lifeguards were concerned, for another week. I knew no one and was white as a sheet of foolscap. When I learned the word for the particular size of paper, though it was slightly larger than a standard typing sheet, I took it as a general term for typing paper. I liked the name. When I would look at a blank sheet of paper before I got to writing anything, I imagined it a mirror in which I was reflected—a comment on me and a metaphor of writing fiction.

I took on *foolscap* as a nickname, and I set off to appropriate some color. I established a three-hour schedule of lying on a beach towel, and a regimen of turning over at roughly twenty-minute intervals. The melanin gods had been stingy with me and color came slowly, but the foolscap changed slowly to just fool—not good, but better. Borderline acceptable for a beach town, I told myself as I marinated in suntan oil, looking much like a chicken basting on a rotisserie. I spent my time at the beach observing people and trying to fashion stories about them.

I became fascinated by a young woman with a physical disability who moved awkwardly and spoke haltingly. She spent time chasing a small black-and-white dog across the sand. This seemed to make her happy and she laughed a lot. I placed my towel at an oblique angle to better observe her and her interactions. Well within earshot, I tried to decipher her language. After much effort, I had decoded only the name of the dog, Beverly. I was proud of my progress, however, but thought Spot would have been a more efficient name. Her family, at least that was my assumption, seemed to understand everything she said.

In addition to the young woman, there were five. An older middle-aged couple I took to be her parents, and three younger people spanning a range between late teens and early thirties: a boy of about fifteen, and a man and a woman in their twenties or early thirties. I took all three to be siblings. The man and woman could have been husband and wife, though I saw no overt signs of intimacy. It was difficult to judge the age of the young woman as her features were distorted by her speech and frequent laughter. I placed her somewhere between the teenager and the other two. Probably she was my age. It was evident that she was a young woman rather than a girl, as demonstrated by her attractive breasts. The shoulder straps of her one-piece black bathing suit were tied together below her neck in the back, securing decorum. The need for this added security made me sad.

Periodically, she would lumber to the surf and enter the ocean. In this she was usually accompanied by a family member, most often the teenaged boy, who seemed to have the closest relationship with her. Once in the water, she became almost graceful in her movements and her face relaxed as she bobbed up and down as she employed a kind of sidestroke. This always made me happy. Through their conversations I learned all their names but little more. I concocted the outline of a story in which the young woman was not disabled at all but an author doing research for a book about how random beachgoers would react to someone out of the ordinary. But that's as far as I got. I tried to summon the courage to introduce myself to her but never succeeded in that that, either.

My academic record may not have been distinguished, but that didn't mean I was uneducated. I had supplemented the public-school curriculum with paperback books, novels mostly, which I read tucked behind more substantial textbooks, as my teachers prattled on. Through the four years, I had amassed a sizable literary history and a decent vocabulary. If the authors I read contributed to a skeptical and ironic view of the world—Hemingway's built-in crap detector, Holden Caulfield's take on phonies, Huck Finn's reluctant and introspective battle with convention— they all convinced me I was on the right track. Besides, it was the '60s.

Along with my sunning schedule, I had set aside a time for writing. This was after my nightly dinners with Aunt Isobel, which included a number of martinis liberally made from her favorite Beefeater's Gin. The fact that I was a little tipsy when I sat down in front of my father's old Underwood portable only confirmed that I was a real writer. I had just finished a short story, my first mature story, I told myself, called *Pablo's Cock*.

3

Pablo's Cock

The dialogue was mostly purloined (a word stolen from Poe) from Steinbeck's *Tortilla Flat,* and it told the story of a poor man in a border town who was not without ambition. Pablo becomes enamored after seeing a cockfight and sets out optimistically to find a fighting cock of his own. It's a story of pursuing fame and fortune. After several failed attempts, Pablo finds that fighting cocks are expensive, and his dream begins to dull until he runs into the widow Peralta. In a forlorn conversation about poultry, Pablo tells her of his troubles in finding a fighting bird. The widow then relates a story about a hen that routinely abuses her rooster. "I think if I don't get rid of her she'll kill him," she tells him. Pablo's a poor man but not without imagination, and he offers to buy the chicken for a small price, solving the widow's problem.

The number one fighting cock of the town is El Rey del Piratas, the king of the pirates, and he has remained undefeated over the past year. He is owned by the brother of the proprietor of the local cantina. The two brothers hate each other after a rift over a woman who is now the wife of El Rey's owner. Pablo arranges for a competition between the Pirate king and his bird, which he has kept secretly at his modest dwelling. He then goes to the owner of the cantina, reveals his plan, and secures the funding for a pair of fighting spurs and a loan of money to wager. The day arrives, and Pablo brings his bird, hooded to disguise that she is not a rooster at all.

The whole town is present at the fighting ring. It's been difficult to find opponents for El Rey del Piratas. People are skeptical, but excited, as Pablo brings his chicken into the ring. The two combatants face each other, and as El Rey is set free, Pablo unmasks his bird that he calls Hijo de Peralta (child of Peralta), honoring the widow. Few spectators initially realize the sex difference. However, El Rey is not only a champion but also a gentleman, and recognizing the gender disparity, he refuses to attack a lady and allows himself to be beaten by the redoubtable female. He bleeds to death on the sawdust floor of the fighting arena to the cheers of onlookers, who remain ignorant of the rooster's gallantry. The owner of the cantina is beside himself with the joy of revenge. Pablo is a hero.

I left the story there, after debating whether Pablo is allowed to profit from his chicanery or is deemed a cheat. I would decide later. I pulled the last page from the typewriter pretty well satisfied, as excess flakes of whiteout drifted off the page like so much dandruff.

The next night, I read my story to Aunt Isobel over martinis. She loved it, like she loved everything about me. Still, I was heartened by my first serious writing since a story about killing my grandmother that I had written early in my senior year during a particularly boring week in American Problems. More on that later. (Spoiler alert: it's no big deal.)

4

Ice Cream Parlor and a Lighthouse

T hough I had written a story that I thought had promise, I had made no friends. My routine at the beach had spawned no social activities. My relationship with the disabled young woman went only one way. Undaunted by my previous cowardice, I set out to become a part of the island. The island is structured into a number of incorporated small polities: Holgate was on the southern tip. Moving north, like pearls on a string, was Beach Haven, where my two aunts lived in separate apartments in separate buildings of the five-building brick complex. North Beach Haven was next, followed by Spray Beach, Ship Bottom, Surf City, Harvey Cedars, Loveladies, and Barnegat. Barnegat, at the far north end, was the site of an isolated lighthouse that I would soon learn was a popular make-out spot.

Beach Haven was marginally the biggest *town*. It housed a large square dominated by the Lucy Evelyn, a three-masted schooner whose bottom had been filled with gravel, leveled on land, and retrofitted as a gift shop with a wide front door cut into its side. Bordered by the ocean, a number of other less dramatic shops ringed the square, a bookshop, a candy store, and an ice cream parlor among them.

The summer was just getting started, but plenty of people moved through Schooner's Wharf, as the square was called. I went into the ice cream shop, and despite the crowds outside, few people were buying ice cream. A girl stood behind a phalanx of buckets with multicolored contents. I bought a sugar cone of rocky road, and given the lack of other costumers, I lingered to talk. Her name was Pam, and she was from Havertown, Pennsylvania. "It's close to Haverford. My parents spend their summers on the island, and I thought it was time for me to start paying my way. It's boring, but I do get to meet people." She smiled sweetly at me as a few costumers entered the store. The smile encouraged me, and with chocolate dripping from my fingers, I waited for them to leave.

Pam told me she had just graduated from high school. "What now?" I asked her.

"A small college," she said, "and a major in English." I told her I was a writer, and she seemed impressed. "Listen," I get out of here in twenty minutes. Want to get something to eat?" I left the shop as more costumers entered, washed the chocolate off my sticky fingers in a drinking fountain outside, and waited for her. Although it was nearing six o'clock, the sun was still high in the sky, and more people seemed to be entering the square.

At the appointed hour, she exited, spotted me, and walked over and took my hand. As she seemed to know where she was going, I remained in tow. After a few blocks, she stopped next to a new white convertible Mustang with a red interior. "My parents' graduation present." I noticed the statement was made with neither embarrassment nor pride. I admired her flat style.

"Paying your way may be a steep curve," I said as she took down the top. "Looks like a lot of ice cream needs to go over the counter."

She laughed. "Yeah, well, it's mostly symbolic."

"Where do you want to eat?" I asked.

"Let's get a couple of sandwiches at the market and go for a drive."

Two crab salad sandwiches, a bottle of sparkling cider, and we were headed up north. I didn't ask about a destination.

"So what do you write?" she asked.

A few days earlier, I would have been hard-pressed for an answer, the only option being the death of my grandmother, which was a story taken from my experience of living with a bedridden grandmother who needed periodic injections to keep her heart going. I had practiced giving injections to a grapefruit in case I were ever needed. The occasion never presented itself in real life. But during a particular series of mind-numbing lectures on dams and roadways of the Southwest, I resurrected the experience in fiction. The class was eponymously named American Problems; I took it personally, as it was certainly a problem to me. The teacher took my furious writing as paying attention, as I seemed to be taking copious notes. He was confused when I miserably failed the test on the material a week later. Anyway, when the time comes to give the injection, the antihero of the story fails to muster the courage; his hands shake, and his nerve abandons him. My grandmother dies. I was certainly the model for the character, I never shared the story with family. *Killing Grandma* was an attempt at dark humor spawned by the dams and roadways of the West.

But with Pam, I could answer that my latest work was a short story called *Pablo's Cock*. I hastened to assure her it was not a pornographic tale.

"Tell me about it," she said. "If it's any good, I'll read it later." I give her a synopsis. She was quiet as she thought it over. "It's pretty good. I like that it's about *woman power*," she said, reading into it something I hadn't intended.

"Yeah," I said, not about to muddy a compliment. The telling of *Pablo's Cock* took up a good deal of time, and I noticed we'd driven a distance from Beach Haven. I didn't yet know the lay of the Island, so I had no landmarks to orient me when a giant brown-and-white-striped tower appeared in front of us.

"What's that?" I asked.

"Barnegat light. It's a good place for a picnic." She took out a blanket from the Mustang's trunk and spread it out over the seagrass that surrounded the lighthouse. I could hear the crash of unseen waves hidden by the vegetation. "Bring the cider and the sandwiches," she called to me over the sound of the ocean. I obediently complied.

We sat on the blanket, ate our crab salad, as Pam opened the cider by screwing off the cap. "I usually like wine when I come here, but I didn't plan for this. I usually get someone to buy it for me."

"You've been here before, I take it."

"Only since junior high," she said, smiling.

I looked at her closely now for the first time since my sugar cone purchase. Short brown hair surrounded exposed ears. Her eyes were large, green, and wide apart; her nose was uncommonly broad and flared the distance between her eyes. I found this feature particularly attractive. The corners of her mouth curled up in a perpetual smile. The total effect was quite exciting to a young writer.

Throughout our drive Pam had periodically reached over to take my hand. Now I took her hand. Moving closer, she leaned her face toward me, and we kissed. She wrapped her arm around my back and pulled me to lay flat on her, and we kissed for a while. Opening my eyes, I turned my head to see the giant phallus of Barnegat light. Struck by the symbolism, I moved my hand from a position, referred to by my peers as second base, to a spot between her legs thinking *this could be the day*. Hope was dashed in a simple shake of her head, and I retreated like the turning of a high tide. The kissing and petting, however, continued. I thought to ask, "Are there any people in the lighthouse?"

Pam laughed. "No, you're all right, buddy." She laughed again.

She now reached between my legs and deflated the lighthouse. I may be the writer, but clearly Pam controlled this narrative.

5

Bolstered by Stories of French Romance

The sun had sunk beneath the Jersey horizon, and a cool breeze blew in from the shore, dark and getting cooler. "Perhaps we should be moving on," said Pam, rubbing her bare arms. Neither of us had brought a sweater.

"Shit! Ejaculated the Apeman." (Got that from Burroughs and Tarzan). Pam stopped rubbing her arms and turned sharply.

"My aunt. I'm supposed to have dinner with her."

She relaxed with the information. "What time?"

"Sometime after eight."

We took off. The clock in the Mustang said 8:30. During the fifteen-mile drive, I explained my relationship with my aunts, and Pam did me the courtesy of speeding. "They adore my father, and me by extension. They love, but don't especially like, each other. That's why they live in separate apartments, in separate buildings, in the same complex. I live with my Aunt Clair and eat dinner with Aunt Isobel."

"Sounds complicated."

"Not really. It's a functional compromise between love and dislike," I said as Pam pulled next to the apartment buildings.

I asked if I could see her again, and she said to just drop by the Ice cream store. It was not the answer I was looking for from one who had just neutralized a guy's lighthouse, but I took what I could get, and ran, nearly an hour late, to my aunt's upstairs apartment.

Aunt Isobel was gracious with my tardy arrival and excited about the news that I had met a girl. Over martinis and rewarmed spaghetti, I described Pam, our meeting at the ice cream parlor, her Mustang, our crab salad sandwiches, and our drive up the coast. I stopped our travels short of Barnegat and its lighthouse. I thought I might stammer and blush. So, I moved the blanket to the beach and brought the waves into view. Most of the narrative was fiction, the bits of truth only served to add substance to the story. I drank three martinis as Isobel ate up the story. In her mid-seventies, she had remained unmarried but not without her beaus. As a younger woman, along with Aunt Clair, their mother, and my father, she had lived in France, both Paris and the Riviera. It was her greatest pleasure to talk of these times, and now primed by my escapade, she recounted romantic stories and perhaps a little fiction of her own. Fiction or not, I loved these stories, especially as they related to my father, who was not only beloved of the family but also its black sheep and the hero of many colorful stories. I fully expected to relocate to the Riviera sometime soon and write novels of international intrigue, channeling Eric Ambler. I left Isobel that night somewhat unsteady on my feet but well satisfied with the day.

6

Karen & the Irony of Status

It was still just short of a week before I would report for my lifeguard duties. Pam's casual remark to *just come by* the ice cream store seemed to me a little blasé and spoke to me of little interest, so I didn't present myself at the ice cream counter for a few days. The week stretched out in front of me with as much promise as a dead-end road. I spent time further exploring the island with nowhere near the result of the first day. I did. however, find a record store and bought a few albums, though I had nothing to play them on. *Sgt. Pepper's Lonely Hearts Club Band* and *Ray Charles Invites You to Listen*. I went back to the beach, but the young disabled woman and her family had gone. I tried hard to buffer my failure to introduce myself, but it still came through as abject cowardice. I went home, pulled my outline of Karen's story, for that was the young woman's name. I experimented with making her into an undercover detective, but got nowhere. Without her image in front of me, the ideas stopped. *Maybe with a little distance*, I lied to myself.

Other than staring at a blank white page, I spent the bulk of the next two days arguing with Aunt Clair over the use of her car, which she denied me. I should have known better, since her intractability and prowess in an argument were the stuff of family legend. Family history told of an argument she had with Gertrude Stein in Paris over the meaning of a Picasso painting. She had no limits. Still, I persisted. Over the next two days I was eroded, through a deluge of humor and conviction, into silence and failure. My time on the island would remain peripatetic. I went back to the beach on a second day and Karen was still gone, and the sadness that came of it was a great surprise.

OK, two days gone by. Pam had suffered enough. I presented myself before the ice cream counter. To boost my confidence, I'd donned the red jersey with white sleeves and *LifeGuard LBI* emblazoned in yellow. I hadn't stopped to think that at least one out of every two young men on the island would wind up as a lifeguard. I thought the jersey would provide me some distinction. Ill-conceived though it was, it seemed to work. Pam greeted me with "You're a lifeguard?" She seemed impressed.

"Yes," I said modestly, as I ordered a sugar cone of something pink called bubblegum. She gave me a double take but produced the cone.

"You really a lifeguard?" she repeated for a confirmation. I wondered briefly what it was about me that prompted her skepticism. I guessed that she accorded the position with a certain romance and status. I would soon find out that the garbage men who emptied the fifty-five-gallon steel drums that lined the beach assumed the highest rung on the status ladder. They were paid more, but as it turned out, they maintained an identifiable odor and so leveled their status with the more dramatic lifeguards. Isn't life funny?

"I thought that I'd see you sooner," she said.

"Sorry, but I've been working on a new story."

"Really?" she asked. More skepticism, I thought. "What's this one about?"

She seemed to ask this with genuine interest, and I gave her an exaggerated account of the outline of the Karen detective story, barely wincing at the resurrection.

"Interesting," she said as costumers entered the shop. She attended to those in front of her and returned to where I nibbled at my cone.

"This is really shit," I said, struggling to swallow my last bite.

She laughed. "Yeah, bubblegum is really the worst, and I've tried them all." She reached over the counter, took the cone, and tossed it in the garbage. "Want to try something else? It's on the house." She smiled. I shook my head. "Want to take a ride?" she asked, and I nodded. A young woman had just entered the store, moved behind the counter, and donned an apron. "My replacement, Judy," Pam said. Judy and I nodded to each other. I'd selected my time as thoughtfully as I had my shirt. Pam removed and stashed her apron, then took my hand.

7

Surfin' Safari

Top down. "Where to?" I asked.

"I'd like to drive to the southern tip of the island and watch the surfers for a little while," she said. I had to admit to myself that I was a bit relieved not to return to Barnegat Light. I asked myself why but didn't answer.

"OK by me," I said, relaxing into the red leather of the seat.

Pam drove to Holgate, the southernmost community, which was primarily populated by sand dunes. She wound her way between several cedar sand fences and stopped on top of one overlooking the open ocean. "I haven't changed my snow tires—better for the sand," she said. The position did give us a spectacular view of the shore and about twenty surfers riding the substantial waves. "We're a good half mile from the Jersey coast so we get some bigger waves."

Coming from Arizona, I had little knowledge of surfing, save for Beach Boys songs. I broke into a high-pitched version of the first stanza of "Surfin' Safari,", ending with an elongated "meee." Pam looked at me in amazement.

Embarrassed at my falsetto outburst, I tried to suppress a blush. It's impossible to suppress a blush, however. "Do you surf?" I asked her, to take the heat off me.

Regaining her equilibrium, she stopped laughing. "No, I don't, but I love to watch. It's freedom. I'm not very athletic, I'm afraid."

"Did you ever try it?"

"Once. I almost killed myself. I'm just content to watch it." We sat back and watched the athletic people surf. Pam opened the trunk and returned with two tepid beers. "I replenished my stock since Barnegat," she said.

The surfers were indeed impressive. Pam knew the names of many of them, both men and women. "I'm a surfing groupie for sure." She then adopted a running monologue, identifying individual surfers and their moves. Between the beer and the surfers, I was having lots of fun.

There was one surfer who seemed to outclass the others. Even at the distance, I could tell by her bathing suit she was a woman. I called Pam's attention to her. "That's Jill. She's the best surfer on the island, male or female," she said.

"She's even better than Roger, who is the best male surfer. Even though she's only sixteen, she's been written up in *Surfing* magazine."

Aside from her superior surfing, Jill was identifiable by her platinum blonde hair, which was cut short above her shoulders. "If you want a closer look, there're binoculars in the glove compartment," Pam told me. I extracted them, stood up above the windshield, and viewed the surfers close-up. I tried to appear casual, as if focusing on the surfers on the whole, but I concentrated on Jill. Unlike many of the other surfers, she seemed to talk to the others as she negotiated the waves. I thought that she laughed a lot. She seemed to surf with a joy the others lacked.

"Had enough?" Pam asked.

"Sure," I said, hoping I didn't sound reluctant. I could have watched Jill till dark.

8

The Island Beach

I didn't ask where we were going next, thinking it better to be surprised. We drove a short distance, probably still in Holgate, to a weathered, three-story wooden building that leaned slightly akimbo. Island Beach Hotel was announced in enormous letters that filled the solid windowless wall constituting the south end of the building.

"It looks like a large piece of driftwood washed up by the sea," I said.

Pam laughed. "It's got good bar, though. Don't check IDs. I know them." We entered the bar, empty save for one couple who sat before the bartender at a long wooden counter. Pam sat down at a table. "Hi, Shirley," she said to the waitress who approached. I tested the veracity of Pam's claim and ordered a martini, Pam ordered a Seagram's and Coke, and Shirley batted not an eye. I was impressed.

Our drinks came with a bowl of peanuts salted in the shell. "I wasn't entirely honest with you the other day," Pam said.

"About what?" I reflected that honesty is not synonymous with integrity, at least for us writers.

"About why I work at the ice cream shop." This seemed a minor lie to me, but I waited for more. "Also, that my parents gave me the Mustang as a present for graduation. It was a kind of bribe."

"A bribe?"

"They bought me the Mustang, provided I get a job this summer and began to assume responsibility for my life. So, the ice cream, it wasn't my idea."

"I think that all parents, in one way or another, bribe their children," I said. "And far as I can see, nobody takes responsibility for their life."

"It's more than just the job. I barely graduated."

"Welcome to the club," I said. "I had to trick the administration into coming up with an extra unit to be rid of me. I think of *barely* graduating as a feather in my cap. An accomplishment greater than the honor roll. And I'm thankful to your parents for forcing you to work in the ice cream store."

The jukebox came on with Procol Harum, *Whiter Shade of Pale*. I broke into song once more. I sang it, this time, in a low, quavering, sexy voice that tried to matched the singer. Pam, who had been taking a sip at the start, had Seagram's dribbling out of her nose by the end as she laughed uncontrollably.

"You *are* terribly sweet," she said between her hiccups and snorts.

"Now that we've met each other," I said, "let's meet here, rather than the ice cream store."

"OK," she said and saluted me with what was left of her Seagram's.

"Just make sure you introduce me before we leave."

"They all know me. Mention my name if you have trouble. You haven't understood, though, what I've been trying to tell you. It's I'm not a *nice* girl. I was arrested for drugs. I *should have* been valedictorian, but I just didn't care. If my father wasn't who he was, I would have been in deep trouble—so, the ice cream parlor." It seemed like a pretty light sentence to me.

"A bad girl, eh?" I tried to say it as a gangster. "I'm a bad boy, too, see. I like bad girls, see," I said in my best Edward G. Robinson.

"No," she said. "You're not." What writer likes to be told he's not a bad boy? I was slightly offended.

"Well, let's just play it out for a while. OK?" I said.

"Another round?" she asked.

9

Roger and the Most Beautiful Woman in the World

I wasn't to start my lifeguard job for another two days. I'd spent some time working on my Karen story, but after several attempts I'd still produced nothing that was any good. I went down to the beach, and over next days, Karen never showed. After one more swipe at the story, I put it away in a folder euphemistically titled *Maybe Later*. I tried hard not to think of my failure to introduce myself. I filled in time with walking down the beach to Holgate and watch the surfing close-up, thinking I might write something about it. I followed my surfing research, as I thought of it, with meeting up with Pam after work at the Island Beach Hotel. We would take drives, hold hands and kiss, but we never returned to the lighthouse. I suggested that on Sunday, Pam's day off, we take a picnic to Holgate and watch the surfers.

Although I had a few of their names from our first observation, I hadn't yet talked to any of them. (Good researcher, eh?)

Pam set out our beach towels and a picnic basket at the shore. She had packed the basket with all it contained. Other than the suggestion, I had contributed nothing. I had never been so close to the action, so shyly I'd kept my distance. With Pam's placement, the waves occasionally reached our toes and the edges of the towels. Pam responded to my concerned look. "Don't worry, tide's going out."

As a part of my *research*, I had experimented with language, mostly terms for angles I would apply to describe the ways boards cut across the waves. Acute, obtuse, oblique, orthogonal, and 360 were all candidates. I realized that I had not given a thought to tides, or any other ocean or wave terminology, not surprising from a guy from Arizona, but embarrassing to a writer. I made it a point to get a book on the ocean, tidal forces, wave nomenclature, stuff like that to augment my descriptions.

During my ruminations about nautical vocabulary, Pam unpacked her sizable picnic basket that had been filled to the gills. *Gills!* I thought. That's an ocean term, at least a fish term. (Close.) She had stacks of sandwiches, bags of potato chips, a good two six-packs of beer, small plastic bottles of water, a loaf of bread, a jar of peanut butter, and a large jar of grape jelly. Some of the surfers exited the ocean and meandered over. Laying their boards down, they sat around our beach towels and exposed fare.

Pam greeted them by name and introduced me to each. I was already familiar with some of them, at least their names, but introduced myself for the first time. She gestured to the food and drinks and said to *dig in.* She turned to me and said, "I told you I was a surfing groupie."

There seemed no dietary difference between male and female surfers, and the sandwiches and the beer were most popular. The beer was quickly gone, and Pam pulled out more sandwiches and beer from the veritable clown car that was the picnic basket. There had to be close to a case of beer in there.

The crowd had reached about ten, and I was talking to Andy and his girl, Sarah, about surfing. How, coming from Arizona, I was interested in learning but knew nothing. "I'll give you a lesson a little later," Andy said as he reached for a beer. The group of surfers shifted as one so that Andy and Sarah left an empty space beside me.

I noticed a man I knew to be Roger approaching us. Simply the most beautiful woman I'd ever seen walked at his side. Roger carried a surfboard, but the woman seemed not to be a surfer and was dry in her black bikini. They sat down beside me, and Pam introduced me, saying to Roger that I was also a writer. "What do you write?" he asked.

"Mostly fiction. I'm working on a novel," I said as I elevated the sterile outline of Karen to a novel. *I'm getting better at lying*, I thought. I didn't blush.

"What do you write?" I asked Roger.

"I'm not a real writer," he said modestly, a tact I'd yet to learn. "When I do write, I do it as a journalist. I've written some articles for *Surfing* magazine, some for newspapers, I've got one now in the local rag on buying a board. Nothing serious." More self-deprecation. "I'm really a surf bum. The articles just keep me in beer money." I really liked this guy. He reached over and grabbed two beers and gave one to the beauty by his side. "This is Jane. Sorry," he said to her. "We got involved in talking shop."

She smiled gorgeously, a radiance that extended all the way to her eyes. "What else is new?" she said evenly.

"Are you a surfer?" I asked.

"No. My sister surfs. Like you, I'm a watcher. I've seen you here before," she said in answering my quizzical look.

"Yes, you are observant. Pam first introduced me to this, and I thought I'd like to write something about it."

"Do you know anything about surfing?" Jane asked.

"Not a thing," I answered. It felt so good to say something truthful about my writing.

Roger expelled an explosive laugh and slapped me on the shoulder. "Well, that can only be a benefit, and we can change that. Come to think of it, I've always thought an article written from the perspective of newbie about learning to surf would be worthwhile. Maybe we can work on that together."

10

Goofy Foot

The picnic couldn't have gone any better, save for the absence of Jill, the platinum blonde best surfer on the island. Andy, from behind me, said, "Let's get you started." I stood and looked down at Roger.

"Go on. I'll catch up to you later."

I knew Andy to be a good surfer from previous observations, and he set out to find me a board from one of the sedentary surfers around the picnic. One of the girls offered up hers. "Don't worry, it's long enough for you," Andy said. "Anyway, it's easier to start out a little short." With that caveat, and a borrowed board underneath my arm, I followed Andy into the ocean. I peeked over my shoulder to see if Pam was watching—she was not. I looked to the breaking waves, which appeared to be larger than before. I imagined myself standing on the board, knees bent, in the tuck of the curl, riding smoothly toward the shore. I was trudging through the surf when Andy stopped me. "Let's stay in the whitewater for a while and get you used to balancing on the board. Put your board into the water but hang onto it."

I placed my board in the roiling surf, holding the sides so it didn't slip away. It took more strength than I would have imagined.

"Now, lower yourself on the top." Andy held onto the rear end of the board. I tried to stabilize myself on the board that now rocked in the relentless surf. "You got it?" he asked. It was obviously a rhetorical question. He released his hold on the board, and I floated off to the shore prone on the surfboard, whitewater swirling around my ears. The board and I moved gracefully, if without drama, to rest on the sand. I was up quickly, board in hand and moved out to where Andy stood, clapping. "Good first ride. Do it again." We repeated the process, me laying belly down on the board, Andy holding the back of the board by its rear fin, which I soon learned is called a skag. What I thought would be an intrepid escapade turned out to be a lesson on a bicycle with training wheels.

The fourth time I beached myself, Roger was there to greet me. "Good so far?"

I wasn't sure if he was teasing me, so I uttered a noncommittal "Yeah."

"It's good to get a little balance before you begin," he said. "Thanks for starting us out," he said to Andy, thereby taking command of my tutelage. Andy moved back to the picnic group, and I gave him a wave.

"We'll get you into the water, but first I want to go over some things on land." So saying, he took my board up on to the beach and set it in the sand. "Stand on the board the way you would riding a wave." I stepped onto the board hesitatingly and positioned myself toward the rear of the board, one foot in front of the other, the way I thought I'd seen the surfers do it.

"OK, you're a goofy footer." That didn't sound promising.

"What's that?" I asked.

"It's where you put your right foot in front. It's not the most common style, but it's OK, used mostly by left-handers. You left-handed?"

"No."

"That's OK," he said again. "It's important to listen to your body. If it tells you to put your right foot first, put it first. At least for the start—you can always change it up later. Let your body move into the wave, until the two of you fuse into one—the two of you breathing together. When you can do that, you're a surfer. That's your first lesson, by the way."

"Goofy foot it is," I said.

Roger laughed and slapped me on the shoulder. "Goofy foot it is. Next thing, you're standing too far back. Move up to just a little behind the middle."

I shuffled slowly up the board and stopped where Roger told me. "I've watched the other surfers, and they always seem to be at the rear of the board," I said.

"That's because they're experienced. The back of the board is how you change direction. Right now, all we want you to do is ride straight in. This area of the board is the most stable." I acknowledged the logic with a simple grunt, and Roger laughed. *I really like this guy*, I thought.

"One more thing is your stance. Both of your feet are pointing forward. Only the front foot should be pointing forward. The rear foot should be about ninety degrees pointing sideways. That foot is where you root your balance—it's your connection to the wave—to the ocean."

I moved my feet into position. Roger grabbed his board. "Good," he said. "Now let's go surfing." Boards under our arms, I walked out into the ocean with Roger Axxst, the best surfer on the island—the best male surfer, that is.

11

Sand-handled

We paddled out across the whitewater, and I had to concede that my time with Andy was not wasted. I felt balanced on the moving strip of fiberglass resin and wax. We got to the breaking waves, and to Roger's instructions, I tried to dip the nose of the surfboard down underneath the breaking curl. I tried twice, three times, to duck under the curl only to be caught by it and thrown back toward shore. But Roger was patient and sat on his board on the calm side of the swell and repeated his instructions. The fourth time, I ducked under the wave to find myself astride Roger.

"Second lesson, or third, I've lost track," he said, "is how to get from a prone position to a standing one. Push the board down into the water from about the middle of the board—don't want to dump the nose—with a push from your arms, move from a crouching position onto your feet, then stand up. Some people go from their knees to their feet, some directly with a push of their hands. Sorry, I can't be any more help than that. You just have to get the hang of it. Once you're on your feet, you're on your own." With that, Roger nosed over the crest of a wave and was gone in a long, fluid ride into the shore.

Left alone, I tried to repeat Roger's move, but the waves continually slipped underneath, leaving me behind the curl that would carry me across the ocean to the shore. Not having Roger's timing, I positioned myself in front of the swell where the wave would break. Still, I managed to elude the waves with my frantic paddling. Finally, I inserted myself into the curl of the wave, but too soon. The wave crashed down on me, I let go of the board that was now positioned on top of me, and I was manhandled by foam and sand, like a T-shirt in the cycle of a washing machine—*sand-handled,* as it were. I came to the surface sputtering like a swamped motorboat to see my board upside down on the beach a good thirty yards away.

The only good thing: I was now in water shallow enough to stand up. The surf now pearled around me, and I used it to wash off the sand that stuck to me. Expelling the saltwater from my nose and mouth, I regained my equilibrium, as I trudged the considerable distance to recover my board. I dared not look to the picnic, but I quickly retrieved my board and set out for another try. This time, I managed to duck my board under the breaking wave and was on the calm side of the swell, where I found Roger sitting on his board. "Good first try," he said. I thought he might just be making fun, but he flashed me a hand signal that I'd seen surfers use with a fist, thumb and little finger extended to the side.

"Not so fucking good," I said, smiling.

"No," Roger said, "you don't get crushed, you don't learn to surf." With that, he dipped over the crown of an approaching wave, gliding obliquely on another perfect ride.

Heartened by his words, I positioned myself under the curl of oncoming waves, and after one, two, third time's the charm, the board moved in toward the shore with me on my belly, enthralled by the motion. I didn't think to stand up until toward the end of the ride, but I gave it a go. I managed to get to my feet for a good three-quarters of a second before, goofy foot and all, I was pitched over the side. The upside—the surf was shallow, I wasn't manhandled by it, and I had only fifteen yards to retrieve the board that this time rested in the sand right side up. Standing by my board was Roger clapping. "Your first ride, bravo!"

"Did it mostly on my belly."

"No matter. You gained your feet—that's the important thing." I found it impossible to suppress a goofy smile.

The rest of the next forty-five minutes was pretty much the same. Waves slipped underneath my board as I paddled frantically to catch up to them. I managed to catch some with my earlier success, only to stand up and immediately pitch off the side. Then the long trudge to the beach to retrieve it and to try again.

Throughout, Roger stuck with me. At one point, we sat together in the calm swell of the waves. At least I had mastered sitting on the board without tipping over. A particularly strong wave was coming in, and I thought *what the hell*. I dipped over its dome and found myself in the curl rocketing toward the shore. Magically, I found my feet and managed to remain upright in the middle of the board. I looked to see Roger riding alongside. I became terrified that I would pitch over in front of him, causing him to *wipe out*. It was the only surfing lingo I had before that day, gained from a Ventures guitar instrumental. I managed to fall off just before the end of the ride, but it was on the side away from Roger. But the fact was that Roger and the Newbie surfed into shore together.

12

Over as a Whole Unit

I walked with Roger back to our picnic spot, boards under our arms like *two* real surfers. Andy came over and slapped me on the shoulder. Pam clapped and said bravo. The praise seemed excessive for what I felt was a pitiful performance—I'd ridden only one wave, and fell off that before the end of the ride, which struck me as a metaphor for my writing, much ado about little. I made up my mind to take a more substantial approach to my endeavors—both the surfing and the writing. I returned my borrowed surfboard to the lender, thanking the young woman called Debbie, who responded with, "Any time." Roger and I sat down in our previous spots, he beside the most beautiful woman in the world, me beside the picnic basket. I reached into it for a beer but found it as empty as the eyes of a serial killer.

"Let's go to the Island Beach," someone said. This was enthusiastically seconded by a number of now sedentary surfers. Both Roger and Andy along with Debbie, who had been deprived of her board, said they would stay and surf a little longer—obviously taking a *substantial* approach to their surfing. *Let that be a lesson to ya*, I thought in support of my previous resolution.

"I'll meet you a little later," Roger said, slapping me on the arm. I took it as the confirmation of an emerging friendship. The group moved off in various vehicles to reassemble at the Island Beach. Declining offers of a ride, Pam and I chose to walk the half-mile to the hotel.

Among the last to arrive, we joined the surfers who had pushed tables together and sat around with their drinks—beer, mostly. They laughed and talked loudly. The few other costumers looked as if they had been washed to the periphery, while we occupied the center of the room. It was a formidable group. Pam and I took a seat at the mosaic of tables toward the outer edge.

I noticed that Jane, the most beautiful woman in the world, sat in the middle of the crowd, a ways away and across from where we sat. I looked at her and wondered what it was about her that made her the most beautiful woman in the world. I mentally detached from the group to think about it. Her shape definitely contributed, and first seeing her in a black bikini didn't hurt. She was taller than average, perhaps five-foot-eleven. Her shapely curves and full breasts were both accentuated by her bikini. But many girls and women had comparable bodies and shapes; it couldn't be just that. She had dark brown hair, pulled back so it draped down over her shoulders—attractive—but not that, either. Her features were regular, her brown eyes enormous, but it was her smile extending to those gorgeous eyes that bathed her presence in a golden light (closer). Still, I wondered what transformed her into the most beautiful woman in the world. I was puzzled, and I continued my internal inquiry. I looked at her from across the logjam of tables. Her bikini was now totally covered by a chambiras shirt, but still she radiated charm as she laughed and conversed with those around her. I remembered a remark about Gregor Mendel that said his genius was to understand that genes went over as a whole unit and kept their integrity, not blending with, or diluted by others throughout the generations of the inheritance process. *Perhaps,* I thought, *beauty is the same way, only going over as a total—it makes no sense to pick it apart into components.* Sitting there, it made sense to me—Jane's beauty went over as a whole unit. That was just the way it was. I was there not to ramify, only to apprehend it.

I turned my attention back to Pam, who was talking to other stragglers who had joined us. When she turned back to me, I asked, "Is Jane Roger's girlfriend?"

"No, she used to be, but they broke up several years ago. She's married now, but they still pal around together when she's back on the island. She's a stewardess on American Airlines and visits her family here." *A stewardess,* I thought, and had to fight down the urge to buy a ticket somewhere.

We *shot the shit,* as they say, for a good hour or so. It was nice to begin to make some friends. Roger came in with Andy and Debbie, and our being on the periphery, they sat next to us. Roger kept an empty seat beside me. He motioned for Jane to join him, and just like that I was sitting next to the most beautiful woman in the world. "Excuse me" was the extent of our communication as she took her seat. Her chambiras shirt did nothing to cover her legs, and it was an act of considerable discipline for me to keep from looking down. The torture was ended when Jane, tired of our talking around her, exchanged seats with Roger. We talked about writing some more, and at his insistence I told him the tale of *Pablo's Cock.* He laughed and nodded in all the right places, slapped me on the shoulder, and said he would like to read it.

"Were you serious about writing an article with me about a newbie's take on learning to surf?" I asked.

"Yeah, I think we could sell it, if not to *Surfing* magazine, at least to the local rag." That was the second time he'd talked about the local rag, and I asked him about it.

"I don't mean it any disrespect. It's called the *Islander,* and it keeps me in beer money."

"I'll work on today's experiences, and when I've got something I'll show it to you," I said. "Hey, how do I get in touch with you?"

"I have a room here at the Island Beach, number 305, but it's only to crash. I'm mostly at Jane's house. Actually, it's her family's house. It's at the 29th Street beach. Here, I'll write down the address on a napkin. I don't have a telephone. Just drop by, and if I'm not there they'll know where to find me."

He handed me the napkin, and I looked at it. The numbered streets, I knew, ran horizontally the length of the island. The address was on the main thoroughfare, 2930.

"We also need to keep up with your surfing," he said. "I have a number of boards, so that won't be a problem."

"I should be getting along," I said, not wanting to push my incredible luck. "I get my assignment as a lifeguard tomorrow and start work. About time."

I said goodbye to the group, to Jane, and made a date to meet up with Pam at the Island Beach after our mutual work ended the next day. The Island Beach Hotel was turning out to be the hub of my universe.

"Lifeguard, eh?" Roger said. "Your starting to blend in with the island." I hoped that was true. I noticed that Pam took my seat next to Roger as I left. I spent the rest of my night writing my first accounts of surfing, feeling like Jack London writing a first draft of *To Build a Fire*—that after dinner with Aunt Isobel, of course.

13

Eddie and Jill

After waking up early the next morning, I donned my lifeguard uniform, put on my blue trunks and my red, white, and yellow jersey with *LifeGuard LBI* on its front. No question who I was. I finished with my white pith helmet before I remembered the silver whistle. One of the few useful things I learned in math class was the importance of an *ordered sequence*. Putting on your socks was not an ordered sequence, but putting on your socks and shoes was. Putting on your pith helmet and your whistle, as it turned out, also was. I tried to violate the principle of ordered sequence and put on my whistle over my pith helmet, but after a few tries I gave up. I took off the helmet, placed the whistle around my neck, then replaced it. Fully garbed, I looked at myself in the bathroom mirror and smiled.

I had been directed at my interview to assemble at the township building at nine o'clock. The building was about a twenty-minute walk away. It was just about eight o'clock, so I walked slowly but still got there early. I joined the few other early birds, both male and female, all sporting lifeguard uniforms. The males all wore outfits identical to mine, the females wore a red one-piece bathing suit with the same stenciling as the boys, with *LifeGuard* etc. also splashed across their front. We all shuffled around each other like novice square dancers. As I knew no one, I waited at the outer edge.

The deck began to fill up. Most seemed to know each other, and they talked excitedly. Art Lifter made his appearance along with a woman I didn't know, and the group became quiet.

"Welcome all, nice to see so many familiar faces," Mr. Lifter said as we moved to surround him. "Mrs. Brown will meet with the woman over there. Men, stay here with me." The women shuffled off to follow Mrs. Brown. With the separation of sexes, we looked even more like a beginning square dance.

"What's with the separation?" I asked a lifeguard next to me.

"The girls are the lifeguards on the bay side, and we guard the ocean side," he answered curtly, as if it was obvious. I was reminded of the Mort Sahl's line that "a woman's place is in the stove." I guess *a female lifeguard's place is in the bay.*

Lifter continued: "Most of you know the routine, so I'll just give you your assignments. Newbies are linked up with an experienced guard." That was the second time I'd been called that. "They can tell you how things are done." *A man of few words who didn't mind delegation.* Art Lifter took out a sheet of paper from the back pocket of his shorts and read off pairs of names and the name of a street. "Edwards and Ball: 3rd Street beach. 6th Street: Shapiro and Koseff." Art Lifter moved north up the shore in roughly three-block increments, until he got to 29th Street, where I was assigned with someone called Lambert. That was where Roger stayed, at least hangs out at his girlfriend's house. His ex-girlfriend, that was. What a coincidence. Lifter continued until he exhausted his sheet. "If I haven't called your name, come and see me."

When nobody approached him, I went and asked him to point out Lambert. "I changed your assignment," he said. "I had a request from Roger Axxst for you to be placed at 29th, says he's teaching you to surf. Roger was one of my best lifeguards. I'm linking you up with Eddie Lambert. He's a veteran. I think it's a good match, and he can show you the ropes. He's over there." Lifter pointed to a tall guy with a large nose talking with a couple of female lifeguards.

Lifter now spoke to all assembled. "Find your partner and move to your beach. You're on the clock." I walked over to Eddie Lambert and introduced myself. He seemed affable enough. I followed him to his Volkswagen, and we drove the short distance to 29th Street. There was little traffic on the island, and we parked along the main street a half-block away. On the way, we talked about ourselves. Eddie said at the end of the summer he was going into the Navy. He was nineteen and had been a lifeguard for three years. I told him I was a writer from Arizona and was spending the summer with my father's sisters.

The beach was defined as the distance between two long stone jetties. In the center was a wooden lifeguard stand resting on its side. Eddie and I righted the stand and moved it closer to the surf. There were a few surfers out in the water, and Lambert blew two short blasts of his whistle and waved the surfers in. "There's no surfing between the jetties during the hours of nine and five while we're on duty." He explained that there were beaches designated for surfing, but after five you could surf anywhere on the island. We took our seats on the stand.

"You ever lifeguard before?" Eddie asked me.

"No," I said. "Just got my lifesaving card in a P.E. class in high school." Since it wasn't a question about my writing, I answered truthfully.

"Well it's not that hard, but you have to be vigilant, watch for anything unusual, someone swimming into shore but not gaining any ground, somebody gulping air, a head bobbing in and out of the water. Don't be afraid to make a run, even if it turns out not to be needed."

"Run?" I asked.

"When you go in after somebody, a rescue. Occasionally, someone will wave to you that they need help, but that's not usual. Most people don't know they're in trouble until they're already in it. You've got to anticipate. You'll learn the signs pretty quick. Watch the children the closest. Parents often don't."

It was clear that Eddie Lambert was an experienced and conscientious lifeguard. With those simple instructions, my tenure as lifeguard began. More people had entered the beach, popping up on the white sand like pimples on an adolescent. Most stayed on beach towels in the sand, and those who entered the water mostly stayed in the surf or close by. "We try to keep swimmers between the flags to limit what we have to keep track of."

"Flags?"

"Red flags on wooden poles, two of 'em. They'll deliver them to us this afternoon. After that, I'll keep 'em with me and we'll set 'em up in the morning when we get here. For now, just observe what's out there."

Eddie blew the whistle at a couple of boys walking out on the jetty. "We keep people off the jetties, especially children. They tend to slip off and hurt themselves. The whole idea is to prevent things before they happen. Makes things easier."

Things were pretty uneventful, with no runs necessary as Eddie played the role of traffic cop. He instructed me on what to look for, cautioning me not to invent more problems than there were, as I voiced improbable scenarios to things I was seeing. Sometime in the late afternoon a green four-wheel-drive Scout drove up to the lifeguard stand and a young man got out. He wore similar attire to us but with the word *Supervisor* stenciled on the front of his jersey. He didn't say anything right away, just gave the beach an extended scrutiny. "Those swimmers are out a little wide, don't you think, Lambert?" he said, as if a drill instructor commenting on poorly polished shoes.

"It didn't seem fair to subject them to rules that were not yet in place. We've been expecting the flags—thought you'd be here sooner," Eddie replied. With that remark, my previously positive opinion of Eddie Lambert turned into admiration that I hoped would morph into friendship.

The young man, who looked to be a few years our senior (college sophomore, perhaps), stood no taller than five-foot-five, with two days' worth of dark shadow on his face, said nothing. He pulled a pair of wooden poles from the back of his vehicle and laid them beside the stand. Going back to the Scout, he pulled out a lifebuoy, threw it down in front of Eddie, and left without a word. He spun his wheels in the sand and drove off a bit too fast.

Eddie looked over at me and smiled. "Chris Mackee's a real asshole. You'll come to hate him."

"I already hate him," I said. Eddie chuckled and slapped me on the arm. Must be an island thing.

We jumped down from the stand. Eddie handed me a pole with a red flag on it. "Go stick this in the sand about the same distance from our stand that I do. Just make sure everyone that's swimming now is inside of it. We'll adjust them to the proper distance tomorrow. Asshole," he said under his breath.

Toward the end of the afternoon I felt another slap on my shoulder. I turned around to see Roger, smiling. "Good to see you made it to the 29th."

"I hear you had something to do with that."

"Just asked a favor, that's all," he said. "It'll make surfing easier for us if you're already here. We can surf any time after five."

"So I've been told," I said. "Tonight?"

"Can't tonight. Jane and I have a dinner date, but drop by. You have the address. We just came out for a short swim." Roger moved out to the front from behind the stand, and I now saw Jane, the most beautiful woman in the world. She nodded and touched me on the knee.

Remembering my name, she introduced me to her sister. "Jill, this is Jimmy. Jimmy, my sister, Jill." Before me stood the platinum blond best surfer on the island. I had no good words. "I've seen you surf," I said lamely.

"I know, I've seen you sitting on the beach. Roger says he's teaching you to surf." To Roger, she said, "And you don't teach anyone to surf." With that, she said, "I'm going for a swim. Drop by the house when you're finished here." She ran into the ocean. Roger followed. Jane was content to enter only thigh-deep.

Eddie, from his patrol along the shore, returned to the stand. "You know Roger Axxst?"

"Yeah, he's teaching me to surf."

"That's why Lifter made the change. I was set to partner with someone else. You know Jill, too?"

"No, but I hope to. I know her sister, Jane, just a little, from Roger."

"Impressive. Roger doesn't like to teach. How'd you manage that?"

"He's a writer, I'm a writer. We might write something together."

"I'm impressed," Eddie said.

Our first day ended. "You need a ride?" Eddie asked.

"No thanks, but thanks," I said. "I'm going over to see Roger at Jane's. By the way, what's their last name, Jane and Jill's, I mean."

"I don't know what Jane's new name is, she just got married, but Jill's is Deriksson."

Jill Deriksson.

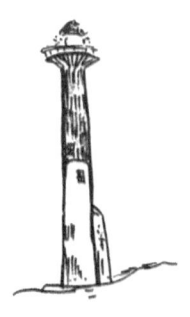

THE MIDDLE

14

Interrogation

The address was 2930 Beach. Beach Avenue was the imaginatively named main road running the length of the island, ocean on one side, bay on the other, with its segregated genders of lifeguards, respectively. Along the bay side of the road was an unbroken string of bungalows, not like a string of pearls but more like a row of jagged tombstones in an English churchyard. Some dazzling, some rotting, all about the same architecturally—two- to four-bedroom, two-story wooden structures, with a small space between them. On the other side of the road, the really big houses occupied the beach overlooking the open ocean. The Deriksson home was neither dazzling nor rotting, neither large nor small. It folded into its neighbors like a kissing cousin. It had a doorbell, and I pushed it. The first to meet me was a large orange cat, who meowed a cordial greeting. The cat was followed by a middle-aged woman with a hairstyle that reminded me of a Bob Dylan poster that was popular. She wore a formless, loose-fitting beach dress that I thought was called a muumuu.

Her smile was radiant and welcoming. "You're Jimmy. I'm Jane, Jane and Jill's mother," she said in an accent I couldn't quite place, kind of like a New York one but not quite. She opened the screen door and stepped aside for me to enter. From the screened porch, she directed me into the house proper. The ground floor was made up of a large living room contiguous with a small dining room and a long, narrow kitchen. The rooms were casual, with the disorder and litter of living but also clean. "Would you like a glass of cream sherry?" she asked. "It's pretty much all I drink these days, but there's also beer." I told her I would love a glass of cream sherry, never having heard of it.

In the large living room sat Roger and Jane, still in their bathing suits, sitting in opposite corners of the room. They looked relaxed, with legs crossed, and each held a drink.

Jane motioned me to sit on a wicker couch, as she handed me my first glass of cream sherry. It was sweeter and stronger than I expected. *Like martinis*, I thought, *it would taste better the more of it you drank.* "Roger tells me you're a writer," she said.

Roger saved me from prevarication by saying, "Jimmy related a story that he'd recently written. I thought it was very interesting and want to read it in original copy. We're also going to write an article about learning to surf." I thought how nice it was when someone else, a writer at that, perpetuates your myth.

"Um," Jane said, sitting against the wall between her daughter and Roger and thinking it over. *I also have a novel about a disabled young woman who's an undercover detective on the beach that's going absolutely nowhere*, I thought but didn't say. There are limits even to myths.

"Who do you read? Who's your favorite?" she asked in the manner of: "Where were you on the night of the 25th?"

I knew I was being interrogated and considered my answer carefully, thinking this family might become important to me. Faulkner might be a more erudite choice, but in the end, I answered truthfully. "Steinbeck."

"What's the last Steinbeck you read? Not your favorite, only the last book of his you read."

That was an easy one. "*To a God Unknown.*" I'd finished it on my plane trip east. *This telling-the-truth thing is pretty good stuff,* I thought.

"What did you think the tree represented?" More interrogation. I was just glad my answers weren't Faulkner and *The Sound and the Fury,* and hers wasn't, "What did Quintin's muddy drawers represent?"

I didn't answer immediately, but thought about it for a while, probably a minute or two, but sitting there as I stared into my cream sherry glass, it seemed a lot longer.

Tentatively, I said "I think it stood for people's fear, people's feelings of inferiority and lack of confidence, and a reluctance or unwillingness to understand..." I ground to a stop.

"Unwillingness to understand what?"

"Anything. Anything different. Anything challenging. Anything awkward." I found myself thinking about Karen and the story I had struggled with. *Maybe Karen was the tree in my story?*

Jane flashed me a warm simile that embraced her eyes, and from then on, we were connected. I could see where Jane, the daughter, owed her beauty.

"I guess you do have the makings of a writer," she said.

"Jeez, Mom, I thought you were going to shine a bright light into his eyes," said Jane.

Jane, the mother, got up and refilled my sherry glass. I hadn't noticed, but I'd been sipping pretty heavy.

"You should get ready," said Roger, who had been listening silently to the interrogation.

"Yeah," said Jane, the daughter. "If we don't act quickly Charles might call." She gave a coquettish little wriggle and a restrained but glittering laugh. "I'll go upstairs and change." Roger twisted uncomfortably in his chair.

"You ready to go surfing tomorrow?" Roger asked me, to find a different subject, I thought.

"Absolutely," I said.

"I have a couple of boards in the back and we can choose one for you."

"I'll bring my short story tomorrow for you and Mrs. Deriksson, along with the notes I've worked up about our first surfing lesson."

"Jane," Mrs. Deriksson said. And thereafter it *was* Jane.

"It's not a lesson," Roger said. "We're just going surfing together."

"Right," I said. "Should I put that in my notes?" Roger laughed, the talk of Charles forgotten. I would never meet Charles, though he was as much a persona in the household as any of us.

Jill came down the stairs. "Sorry, you guys, I had to take a shower. Have you been entertaining Jimmy?"

"Grilling him's more like it," Jane said as she passed her sister.

Jill bounced over to the couch and sat beside me. "They've been treating you harshly, have they?"

15

White Lotus and The Child Buyer

It was the first time I had really looked at Jill, up close that is. Dominated by her platinum blonde hair cut short just below her ears, it was the first thing that engaged your eye. Her platinum corona framed large green eyes that were set wide apart. She was built according to a whole different body plan than her sister. Unlike her shapely sister, Jill's figure was athletic and solid, slim but substantial, with broad shoulders. She was shorter than her sister by a few inches, but still tall. A moderate suntan spoke of a Scandinavian heritage that her last name implied. Her smile, rather than radiant, like her mother's or sister's, was ironic and was applied skeptically with an inner humor, as if she were aware of some inner joke of which others were ignorant. Despite these qualities, it was warm, even accepting. She had a substantial bosom that seemed to function as her body's center of gravity.

"Learning to surf, eh?" she said. "You look like a California surfer, blond, not much of a tan. You from California?"

"Arizona."

"Arizona?"

"Yeah, I'm a pretty unlikely student."

"Good thing he's not taking lessons, eh, Roger?" She demonstrated the irony I'd seen in her smile. She raised a platinum eyebrow and emitted a suppressed chuckle. Roger smiled but remained silent, and I perceived a history of teasing between the two.

Jill also spoke with a slight accent like her mother's. However, she alternatively slid in and out of it. It was strongest when she was teasing. She seemed to lap up the last words of her sentence with her tongue covering the middle of her upper lip and front teeth. It was a characteristic that I found irresistibly attractive. I would soon realize that what I perceived in Jill and her mother was a Jersey accent. I would come to describe it in my writing as "like a New York accent, but softer, and spoken with a greater sardonic conviction," but that would come later. For Jill, when the accent appeared, it signaled playfulness.

Jane came down now dressed in a flower print summer dress and sandals, the dress swirled around her at mid-calf like palm fronds in the breeze. Her brown hair was pulled to the side and cascaded over her right shoulder, and from her exposed left ear a single silver earring dangled. The effect—though casual—was stunning. I thought briefly, *how the hell did you, Roger, let her get away?* Though she hadn't seemed to get too far.

"Jane told me that you might be a good candidate for a boyfriend," Jill said in her Jersey accent, lapping up the final word *boyfriend* with her ironic smile.

"I don't think I said it *quite* that way sister." It was obvious that this was a household of banter, and I liked it.

Jane, the mother, who had been working in the kitchen, took her previous seat between her daughter and Roger, facing Jill and me on the wicker couch.

"Who is your favorite writer?" I asked her.

"I do like Steinbeck. He's been a favorite of mine in the past. At the moment, however, my favorite is John Hersey." I nodded, having a decision to make. Do I respond honestly, or like cream sherry, do

I keep secret that I'd never heard of him, or continue with honesty?

In the end, I compromised. "I don't know much about him."

Jane's smile told me she'd identified the subterfuge of my statement, but she went on. "He's a journalist turned novelist, wrote *Hiroshima* and *The Wall* pretty much as a journalist, but after that wrote quite a lot of fiction. One I've particularly admired is *The Child Buyer*, a dystopian account of a congressional hearing called to approve the sale of a bright child to a corporation. It's chilling. The last book of his I read was *White Lotus*." She mirrored tit for tat her earlier interrogation of me. "It's a fable of an American young woman who is taken as a slave and brought to China after a war won by China against America. She's from Arizona, by the way. Some say it provides a parallel to the American slave system. Provocative, and a good read."

The room remained quiet through her narration, but at its end Roger stood and said, "We better be going. We have a reservation at Le Champignon Rouge at seven."

"You're not going to change?" said Jane's mother. It was more of a statement than a question.

"They know me at the Rouge, I'll be fine in trunks and T-shirt." Jane smiled and gave a shrug. As it turned out, Le Champignon Rouge was owned by a friend of my Aunt Clair, and I had eaten there several times with my father and aunts when he was here.

"Would you like to eat with us, Jimmy?" asked the mother.

"No, thanks," I said. "I'd like to, but I can't. I have to eat with my aunt. She looks forward to it." Jane smiled her approval.

"You want a ride?" the younger Jane asked. "You live in Beach Haven, don't you? We're going that way."

I said that would be great.

"I want to go, too," Jill said. "I'll walk back." Nobody seemed to think this was odd.

Before we left the house, Jane handed me two books, *The Child*

Buyer and *White Lotus*. "Return them when you're finished." As it turned out, I would return only one.

We drove to the apartment complex in Roger's battered VW. Unlike Eddie Lambert's, it was a convertible and seemed spacious under the setting sun, the sounds of the surf were audible. Jill and I got out in front of my aunt's complex, and the couple drove to their dinner. Jill gave me a little hug, then turned for home.

"Wait a second," I said. I ran upstairs to tell Aunt Isobel that I'd be about an hour late. To her puzzled look I said, "It's a matter of gallantry." Respecting gallantry, she asked no questions, nodded her head, and indicated that she would wait for the explanation. Jill was waiting at the curb.

"I'll walk you home," I said.

"Walk me home," she said, laughing. "What about dinner? That's crazy." Her tongue lapped her teeth and upper lip as it surrounded the word crazy. In the fading light she flashed me an ironic smile.

16

Full Moon or Spotlight

We walked along the beach, our feet in the water, getting to know a little about each other on the way. It was dark now and a full moon came out (perhaps I made that up, but it should have). Jill's hair shone like a halo in the moonlight (maybe it was just by the spotlights of the beach houses aimed at the ocean).

She said she had one more year of high school, she was just about seventeen, and lived in Bethlehem, Pennsylvania, where her father ran a records office for a steel company. "He comes down on weekends and holidays in the summer." I asked how they came to be on the island.

"My mother's a Jersey girl who always dreamed of living on the island. So, when my father's business began to take off, they bought the house we're in. There weren't that many people here back then, and things were reasonable." I told her my aunts were among the few year-rounders, and she said she was impressed. "My mother spends all the time she can here, even comes down here in the winter. We've spent a couple of Christmases here, and even had to evacuate a hurricane on one of her trips. If it wasn't for my little brother, Jan—he's twelve—she'd probably be a year-rounder. Will be, too, once Jan is able to take care of himself. They bought the place when my sister was two. I've never been around when we haven't lived here. Grew up on the beach."

"Tell me about surfing. Pam tells me you're the best surfer on the beach, Roger included."

"Pam?"

"Yeah," I said, and sensing some animosity I chose my words carefully. "Just a girl I met at the ice cream store. She's the one who first introduced me to surfing. To the surfers, that is."

"Pam McCready! The one with the Mustang? She doesn't know anything about surfing," More antagonism. I thought I'd *stepped in some shit*.

"She just introduced me to some of the surfers at Holgate, including Roger and your sister. She called herself a surfing groupie."

"My sister's not a surfer, and not a surfing groupie, either."

Deciding to face the bull head-on, I said, "Do I sense some dislike here?"

"No, not really, we just move in different circles." She backed off a bit.

"So," I said, expelling a deep breath I'd been holding in, "tell me about surfing."

Calm now, Jill got into it. "I can't remember a time when I didn't surf. Family legend has it as a toddler I used to watch the surfers from the shore. Once, when I was about two, a surfboard washed in at my feet and I tried to stand up on it as it rocked in the surf. When I refused to relinquish it, the young surfer whose board it was asked my parents if he could give me a ride in the shallow water. Story was that I rode the gentle surf into shore without falling off. I don't remember it. It might be apocryphal, but after that my father had a small surfboard made, stood out in the ocean, and taught me how to surf. My memories all have boards and surfing attached to them.

Apocryphal? I thought liking the word. This was indeed a family to contend with.

Jill alerted me that we were at the entrance of the 29th Street beach, and we walked to her house. At the door she said, "I haven't found out anything about you."

"We have lots more time," I said.

Jill hugged me and stepped through the open screen door. She didn't kiss me, though, but a perfect day has to end perfectly.

17

Twerp Defined

I walked the twenty minutes back to Isobel and dinner inter-ruptus. Just before I arrived, it stuck me that I had stood up Pam at the Island Beach. I was supposed to meet her after my first day. I reviewed the mitigating factors. I didn't know where she lived, didn't have her telephone number, and didn't know any of her close friends, and I had a lesson, a date, at least, to surf after work with Roger. Still, I had stood her up. Pam wouldn't start at the ice cream store until I was already lifeguarding. She did work an hour later, but I had surfing. What to do? I left the action hanging as I arrived for dinner.

Over martinis, I told my aunt of my gallantry. She was a sucker for gallantry. Told her I was set to start surfing lessons in the afternoon after work and asked her if we could start dinner later than our normal eight o'clock. She immediately reverted to a former life, saying, "We never ate earlier than ten in France." That seemed to seal the deal, and we agreed to begin dinner between nine and ten.

Still, what to do about Pam? Despite the *perfect day*, I slept poorly. I woke up early, made coffee, and ate a bagel with cream cheese and lox, an eastern innovation I'd recently discovered. On my walk, I decided to push back my surfing the hour it would take to walk to the ice cream store, suck-back to Pam, then walk back. I felt a little better doing what I thought was the right thing. (What else is a guy to do?)

I was early at the beach, but Eddie was earlier, and he introduced me to a lifeguard tradition whereby we did a practice run. We had moved the lifeguard stand, close to the water and placed the lifebuoy out in front. The buoy was an elongated hexagon about three feet long and one and a half feet in width. It had a rope attached at one end and ended in a loop at the other. The drill: One lifeguard goes out into the ocean maybe thirty yards, the lifeguard making the run starts out sitting on the stand. The run starts when the rescuer jumps off the stand, picks up the buoy, places the loop of the rope around his neck and shoulder, and enters the ocean swimming with the buoy trailing behind. When you reach the faux drowning man, you grab his wrist, turn him around and either place him on the buoy or put him in a carry, depending on how much resistance the runee employs, and tow him back to shore.

Eddie went first. Moving like a cat, he jettisoned his whistle. In his jump down, he grabbed the buoy and placed the rope around his neck in one move as I bobbed in the waves. I offered little force, allowing myself to be towed into shore. "Next time give me some resistance," he said good-naturedly.

My turn. I jumped down, and stumbling slightly, grabbed the buoy by its handle that stuck stiffly to the top of the buoy. I lost hold of it as the buoy slid into the surf. It took two hands to free the handle. I moved into the ocean before I realized that I had not put the loop around my neck and shoulder. Losing what inertia I had, I corrected my omission. Eddie chose to give me some resistance, serving to provide a more realistic condition to the drill, and fought my attempts to grab his wrist. I was getting pissed, and I grabbed his wrist with more force than necessary and turned him aggressively around. I slapped my arm around his chest and towed him to shore, as he allowed himself to ride docilely on my hip. We stumbled out of the surf with Eddie laughing, me still slightly pissed. "Good going," he said. "You finished well. Don't worry about the buoy—we rarely use it, only if someone is far out. When the buoy is new the handles stick to the side. Doesn't matter anyway, just grab the whole buoy, it's only three inches wide. But a good run all in all. I think we'll get along fine. And next time get rid of your whistle."

We set out the wooden poles a little over half a football field apart, defining the extent of the beach for swimming. No longer upset, I moved to the stand and sat next to Eddie Lambert like I belonged there.

The day passed without incident. Eddie used his whistle to keep people between the flags and from going too far out. With each action, Eddie passed on a new rule. He knew everyone on the beach and seemed to be well-liked. People kept coming to the stand to say hello. Eddie introduced me to about 200 people. Many of them were quite attractive girls whose names I tended to remember better than the others. I'm a three-trial learner when it came to names. Unless I'm intimately involved with someone, I need at least three times before I can remember.

At about four o'clock, Chris Mackee drove his green Scout behind the stand. Approaching from behind, he looked at me as if I were a caterpillar he'd just stepped on and was looking for a place to scrape it off his shoe. He said nothing to my "How you doin'?" To Eddie, he said, "Any runs?" It was stated as a question, a mere formality to a needless interaction.

"Nope," Eddie said, not taking his eyes off the swimmers. At Eddie's height on the stand, and the diminutive Mackee, the word fell like an anvil on Wile E. Coyote's head.

Not having a quick comeback for "nope," the supervisor took a long look at the beach, seeing nothing out of line and said, "At least you got the flags right today."

"Yeah," Eddie said, "We checked the manual three times."

"The manual?"

"Yeah, the manual. Don't tell me you haven't read it," Eddie said, not taking his eyes from the ocean.

Chris Mackee at least had the character to know when he was defeated in a skirmish. He entered his Scout, and with spinning wheels, left. He would, however, live to fight another day, and as it would turn out, so would we.

It was my turn to slap Eddie on the arm. "Artful," I said.

"I really hate the little twerp. Don't know how he got to be Lifter's little darling."

Eddie didn't know that I knew the actual meaning of the word twerp. Kurt Vonnegut told me in a book of his, don't remember which. A twerp is someone who bites the bubbles when he farts in the bathtub. I'd tell him later, but then, I was just content to sit beside my new hero and wait for the workday to expire.

I had told Roger that I'd meet him at the Deriksson's, at Jane's, and we'd select one of his boards for whatever these sessions were. Roger didn't want it out that he gave lessons, and I would respect that. I walked over and saw his car out front and went around the path to the backyard where Roger stood reviewing the boards laid out before him like recruits standing at attention. He introduced me to each board, with a precis of the pros and cons. Then he pointed to the longest board in the assemblage. "I think that this is the best for you. It's called a cat, and it has a hollow nose, so it's really not as long as it looks." He seemed to be explaining the benefits more to himself than to me. "Anyway, let's start with that."

He went to pick up his board, and I stopped him, telling him of my situation with Pam. With no way to contact her, I needed to meet her at the ice cream shop and explain things, to apologize.

"Stood her up? I feel for you, buddy. I'll take your board to the beach." Then he said, "Say, do you want a ride to ice cream store? It's a ways."

"Thanks," I said, "but I think this is something I need to do myself."

He winked, then slapped me on the arm (*one more time I think and we'll be going steady*, I thought). "Go pay your dues."

Before I left, I gave him a brown folder, the one with a flap that you tie up with string. I'd kept it wrapped up in my towel underneath the lifeguard stand since morning. In it was my *Pablo's Cock* story, and the notes of my surfing debut, newly titled: *It's not a lesson.*

I handed it to Roger, who said he'd leave it with Jane, the mother, for safekeeping.

Paying my dues, I walked the twenty minutes to the ice cream store. *Penitence?* I was certainly feeling penitent as I entered the coolness of the shop. Pam was behind the counter, and I was grateful there were no other costumers in the store. No costumers at all, save only the one penitent. I imagined walking on my knees, over Mexican cobblestone streets, on a trek to pay homage to a patron saint. (I saw that once in Mexico. People in the crowd would take off their coats and lay them in front of the supplicant, providing a feeble cushion from the cobblestones.)

There was no one providing a coat, and I was not really on my knees, but the image powered me to the counter. Pam pretended to be busy with other activities and did not turn to me until I spoke her name. She approached me with a face about as warm as one of her ice cream tubs.

I started apologizing immediately. "Pam, I'm so, so sorry," I began lamely. "I know I said I would meet you at Island Beach, but I forgot." (Not really an improvement.) "I really intended to go, but at the end my day Roger sought me out, and we began a program of surfing lessons" (why not use the term here?) "and I just forgot." The ice cream began to melt a little around the edges. The eyes, however, remained cold.

"Roger?" she repeated the operative word. "You went surfing with Roger?" The thawing progressed.

"No," I fessed up. This honesty was becoming an annoying habit. I could see the ice returning to the edge of the pond (sorry to change metaphors in midstream). "But we talked about it and came up with a plan."

"A plan?" she repeated vaguely.

"Yeah, we'll meet every day after work. We're also working on an article together about a newbie learning to surf."

"When do you start? With the lessons, I mean."

"We started today."

"Today? Why are you here now?"

"We met after work, and he selected one of his boards for me. A cat," I threw that in for authenticity. "I told him I had to see you to apologize, he understood, and we agreed to meet in an hour." I could see all the ice melt, with the pond glittering in the sunlight of her smile.

"How did you get here?" she asked.

"Walked." Her smile got larger. Still, no costumers. Her replacement, Judy, had just entered the store.

"Judy, do you mind if I take off a little early? It's been slow." Judy said it was fine. "Come on," Pam said, "I'll take you there." As we left the store, she held my hand, and the ice cream settled in their tubs in a puddle of liquid (original metaphor restored).

On our drive over, Pam asked me where Roger and I met to come up with our surfing plan. The ghost of honesty again asserted itself. I admitted that the conversation took place at Roger's ex-girlfriend's house. I mentioned Jane's mother. I didn't know why, but I said nothing about Jill—actually, I did know why.

18

Cat's Bathroom

Pam parked her car on the street and put up the top. The beach was now peopled by surfers, their cars lining the entrance to the beach in an assemblage of old Volkswagens and battered, rusted station wagons. The white Mustang with red leather interior shone like a diamond in a beggar's ear (modified that one from Shakespeare).

The car caught a few looks from passers-by as we moved onto the beach. I saw Jane on the sand, sitting on a beach towel. She spied us and waved us over. "Roger's out there in the middle of the pack. What's new?" She gave a little chuckle, and she and Pam exchanged greetings. Next to Jane rested the cat. "Roger says when you got here to take your board and paddle out." Jane moved over on her beach towel and gestured for Pam to sit.

"Is Jill here?" Pam asked.

"No," Jane said. "She's at Holgate. Went there with Fast Eddie."

I'd been scanning the line of surfers futilely looking for her, and I was relieved that she wasn't here. This realization came with a twinge of guilt—why? I know why—and who was Fast Eddie?

Anyway, I grabbed my board and paddled out to Roger, who seemed to be waiting for me. "Looks like you patched things up," he said.

"Yeah, I guess," I said, thinking about dripping ice cream.

"You remember the golden rule of surfing?" he asked me with a smile.

"Keep my back foot at a ninety-degree angle?"

"Nope." He shook his head.

"Position myself near the middle of the board for stability?"

"Nope." He laughed. "All important, but not the primary rule. If you don't like rules, substitute principle," he said, demonstrating an insight to my basic character. "It's to anchor yourself to the ocean. If you were on land, it would be to root yourself to the earth." His words approaching poetry. "Don't ever forget that. Everything else in surfing is just little tricks you add to that principle." With that, he dipped over an oncoming swell and glided to the sand.

Left alone, I tried to internalize the meaning of Roger's axiom—to transform it into action. Imbued with conviction, I placed myself in front of an oncoming wave. I still didn't have the skill to attempt to nose over a swell. I caught the wave, stood up, and was immediately pitched off the side. As I took the long trek to retrieve my board, I thought it would take a lot more than conviction to a principle to ride a wave. I'll reminded myself to remember that for my notes on the article. I picked up my board without a look to the towel where Jane and Pam sat, and paddled back to where Roger waited. "Too short a root, too light an anchor," I said preemptively. Roger saluted me as he caught the next wave.

The rest of my session (not a lesson) went about the same, with conviction ceding to short roots and light anchors, though I did manage to squeeze in a few respectable rides. On my last trudge to recover my board, Roger waved me in, giving me permission to dismount the pummeling.

I dragged the cat over to Jane's beach towel, where Roger and Jill stood behind Jane and Pam, who were still sitting. Along with them was a young man I assumed was Fast Eddie.

"Good job," Pam said. "You're making progress." I was unable to resist a smile at the compliment.

"Jimmy, this is Eddie," Jill said. I was glad that she didn't provide any other identifying information. Eddie and I exchanged nods.

Jane stood and invited the group to her house. I was happy when Pam and Eddie opted out. We walked with our boards to Jane's house. This would become the routine after our surfing sessions. Jane, the mother, greeted us at the screen porch and ushered us into the living room. She held the brown folder I had given to Roger earlier, the one with my writing.

Roger sat in the same chair as the previous night. Jane, the daughter, mixed them drinks, giving one to her former boyfriend, and she, too, took her seat. I sat down on the wicker couch. Jill had gone upstairs, probably showering again. Jane, the mother, asked me what I was having, and I said cream sherry. She poured us each a jelly glass full, handed one to me, and took her seat between her daughter and Roger. It was a snapshot of the previous evening.

"You've finally got a partner for your cream sherry, Mom," Jane said.

Jane ignored her daughter. "I read your short story," she said, still holding the brown folder.

"What did you think?" I asked, girding myself for another accounting.

"I don't want to say anything until Roger reads it." She passed the folder to Roger. "Read it, so we can talk," she ordered.

Roger shuffled through the pages. "Good title," he said with a chuckle.

"Which one?" I asked, knowing the folder also held my surfing notes.

"Both," he said. "Now don't bother me. I'm reading."

We talked in low tones as Roger read. Jane, the mother, asked me how I was adjusting to life on the East Coast and whether I missed anything from home.

"The only thing I miss is Mexican food," I found myself saying. I hadn't thought of this before, but I realized the truth of the statement. "I haven't seen one Mexican restaurant since I've been here."

Jane offered an answer. "No, not any. You know what I do when I want Mexican food? I buy a Mexican TV dinner." While this was not the Mexican food I was craving, I filed the strategy away for future use.

"Done," Roger said after a time, looking around at us and taking a drink from his cocktail.

"And?" I asked despite myself.

"Great story, and good writing, though you have a bit of a comma problem." This was not the first time I'd heard this criticism.

"Yeah, I'm not good with rules; commas have a lot of rules," I pleaded.

"Don't worry, we can take care of it at the editing stage, but good writing, like I said, a creative story." He'd actually had said *great* before, but *creative* was just as good. And it did blunt the comma criticism.

"It's not a bad thing for a writer to have problems with rules, especially rules about writing, even grammar," Jane said now, freed to speak after Roger's reading. "Hemingway had one, and so did Faulkner just to name two. Hemingway solved it by rewriting the rules, Faulkner by adhering to them, then rubbing your face in them. You got a problem with commas—rewrite the rules. I read your story and didn't notice. That says something, at least to me." She finished with a dry laugh.

It struck me how much I liked being defended by Jane—thrilled even. *What is that all about?* I thought.

"I felt it was right out of Steinbeck's *Tortilla Flat*." She said this with a smile that indicated her awareness of the theft.

"You liked it, then, Jane?" I said. It was not the first time I had called her by name, but the first time I had said it naturally as if between friends, the first time I had said it without italics.

"I liked it very much. A very fine effort for a young writer."

Even with the caveat, I took a disproportionate pleasure from the remark.

Jill came down from the stairs with a loud final jump, still a little red from her shower, glowing like Eve's apple. "You all look so serious," she said, licking the top of her teeth.

"We've just been discussing Jimmy's story," her mother said.

"I want to read it," Jill said as she sat down next to me. Roger got up and handed her the folder.

"Aren't you going to read the notes about surfing?" I asked.

"Already have," Roger said. "Read it before I gave the folder to Jane."

"Well, what did you think?" Jill asked.

"I think we have something." He said nothing more. An awkward silence followed. When we realized nothing more was forthcoming, Jane, the daughter, broke the silence with a provocative question.

"Jimmy, what did you think of Jill's boyfriend, Fast Eddie?" Jill's rosey glow turned a deeper red.

"He's not my boyfriend!"

"Well what is he then, sister?"

"He's, just a, a surfing buddy," Jill answered.

"Oh, so when you go out together at night you change into your suits secretly and go surfing." Jill looked down into her lap. The phone rang, rescuing her.

"It's Charles calling," Jill said brightly. "Keep up the silence, Roger."

"Hi, Charles," she yelled.

Jane lowered her voice and took the phone through a narrow door opposite the stairs to a room I hadn't noticed before. From across the room, Jane, the mother, noticed my puzzled look. "It's the cat's bathroom, where we keep the litter box. Nobody goes in there except Jane when she talks to Charles."

"And the cat of course," said a giggling Jill. Roger remained silent, looking into his glass.

Jane exited the cat's bathroom. "Wrong number," she said in deadpan. The room exploded with laughter, and even Roger took part. I did love this family.

The interlude was diverting, but I still knew nothing about Fast Eddie. Why did I care? I knew why I cared.

19

Axiomatic Surfing

Again, I refused dinner, citing Aunt Isobel waiting in the wings. "Free yourself tomorrow for dinner," Jane said. Richard's coming down early this week."

"Who's Richard?" I asked.

"Richard's my husband, the father of my children," she answered.

I said I looked forward to meeting him, then walked the twenty minutes home.

Over dinner, Isobel and I discussed the French author Balzac. My aunt had said that he was one of my father's favorite authors. "At least at the time he was in France," she said. I had read little French literature—Sartre's *Nausea*, Rimbaud's *Season in Hell*, and of course, Camus' *The Stranger*. It was a rule that everyone in high school had to read *The Stranger* and *Macbeth*. It wasn't so bad, the best part of high school, actually—that is, other than getting out.

Balzac was a fact I hadn't known about my father's time in France, and I was happy for the information. I made a mental note to read some Balzac and ask my father about it. I did like the name. My father was good amateur tennis player, back when everyone was an amateur, and one of his occasional doubles partners was Somerset Maugham. I hadn't read him, either. She said one of his favorite

Balzac was one where someone was walled up in a closet, or some place. She couldn't remember which one. Maybe it was Poe's *The Black Cat.* "He also liked Poe at the time," she said. I decided I'd look into it.

Leaving Balzac and Aunt Ibby, I returned to my sleeping place to work on the surfing article. Roger had said "we had something." I wasn't sure what *something* was, but I took heart from it. I also wanted to flesh out my realization that it would take more than conviction to master surfing. I played it off, highlighting lessons as being the wrong context to address learning to surf.

I ran down the rules Roger had given me over our time together and described them. I commented that they were important only as tricks that you added to your surfing, but by themselves they weren't enough to make you a surfer. I invented a term, *axiomatic surfing*, and used it as a working title. I remembered the term from high school geometry class—axiom. A thing that could not be verified empirically. It was an assumption, a bedrock, that was the foundation for all the empirical things that were then stacked upon it—that all the little tricks owed their effectiveness to the axiom. (Maybe high school wasn't so bad.)

I went on to identify Roger's axiom as anchoring the prospective surfer to the ocean, placing yourself below the surface in the center of the wave with an anchor that kept you stuck on the surface. It was only when you were there that the *little tricks* mattered. I used Roger's metaphor of "rooted to the earth" to reinforce the concept. Then I waxed poetic on the universal utility of the axiomatic approach. On rereading this section I decided to cut out the universality, thinking it diminished the literary power of axiomatic surfing, cheapened it. I was lucky it was near the top of a sheet of paper I was typing. As I couldn't erase it, I had to rewrite the entire page.

20

Keep it loose

The next day, I made my first run, a little girl of about six who couldn't quite overcome the gentle force of the outgoing tide. I pulled her to shore, where she ran to her mother, who only noticed her daughter when the girl hugged her. Eddie was right. The children bore watching. Still, though not dramatic, it made me feel like a lifeguard. The feeling was only slightly diminished when I thought that it was Eddie who first alerted my attention to her (I would have seen her, I told myself).

The day went by without further event. At about three-thirty, Chris Mackee drove by but did not stop. Eddie gave a dismissive little laugh. "He drives too fast," I said.

"Yeah, we've all complained to Lifter, but nothing changes. Somebody said Lifter was in the Navy with his father. Anyway, it does no good to complain."

At five, Roger appeared along with Jane, who carried *my* cat. "We need to get an early start today," he said.

"My dad's coming home today. Mom's been busy making a real dinner for a change," Jane added.

I picked up the cat where Jane had let it drop and followed Roger into the ocean. I waved to Eddie, who had gathered up the red flags and was walking to his car, and yelled, "Roger and I will move the stand back when we leave." Eddie saluted me.

Out in the water, as we sat waiting for a ridable wave, Roger said to me, "You're coming along quickly."

"I've only caught a few waves," I protested while basking in the compliment.

Roger continued. "It takes most surfers a longer time to string together those few rides—to get the feel of the ocean. No, you're doing quite well." Roger seemed like he wanted to talk, and we let a number of promising waves roll beneath us.

"That's good it's coming quickly," I said. "Because I don't have a lot of patience."

"The ocean will teach you patience. I liked your writing, too. I didn't say much about it because I didn't want it open to a family discussion. Jill's a surfer, and everyone else has an opinion about surfing. But I really liked your take on the first day and the irony you injected into it. Most new surfers take it too seriously in the beginning, and if their seriousness continues, it limits their surfing. Seriousness is not good. It's why Jill's such a good surfer. Everything's somewhat of a joke to her, and her attitude translates into her smooth and artistic style. It's like writing. You approach your subject too seriously, and you cramp your style. Or worse, you come off as stiff—pompous. Keep it loose." He then nosed over a curl and glided off to shore.

I shook myself, trying to physically loosen up, and caught the next wave by dipping over the top (my first time) and managing to ride it pretty much to the shore. *Keep it loose.* I had my next focal point of my part of the article.

I was unable to repeat my success and *took my lumps* as the ocean proceeded to teach me patience. Jane waved us in as we took our last rides. I managed to ride mine in halfway before pitching off to receive a mouthful of patience.

As we moved the lifeguard stand back, I bent down and took a manila folder with my last notes, kept safely rolled up in my towel, and handed it to Roger. "The latest," I said to him.

"I'll read it tonight," he said.

"Richard's already here," said Jane, pointing to a green station wagon parked in front of the house. Roger and I went to the backyard and jettisoned our surfboards. We entered the living room through the back door. I was uncommonly nervous to meet Richard. I didn't know why—but I was just beginning to know why.

As Roger and I entered the living room a man stood up, greeted Roger, and advanced toward me with an outstretch hand. "You must be Jimmy. I've been hearing a lot about you from my family," said Richard, Jane's husband and the father of her children. We shook hands and I mumbled something I hoped was roughly translatable to *glad to meet you*. Jane sat down in her usual seat. Her mother was fussing in the kitchen. Richard went into the kitchen and mixed drinks for his daughter and Roger.

"My wife tells me you're a fellow cream sherry drinker," he said to me.

"Yes, sir," I said.

"It's Richard," he said quickly. "Always has been, the same name as my father, but I never cottoned to Dick, always Richard. Even the children call me Richard on occasion." I thought back to Jane and her use of *Richard* on the walk over.

"Jimmy's also my father's name," I said in an attempt at some kind of kinship. I had adopted my father's name only after I came to the island. Before that, I had gone by Jim to all my school friends and Jamey to my family. I guess finally shedding high school, and in a new place, I was eager for the romance of a new persona, though my aunts continued to call me Jamey.

Jill, who was not with us at the beach, sat on the wicker couch barefoot and in jeans and a sweatshirt that said *Virginia Beach*. I sat down next to her. Richard handed me a jelly glass of cream sherry

(I wonder if it was a household rule that cream sherry is only served in jelly glasses).

Anyway, I looked now at Richard. He was tall, maybe six-foot-two or a little taller, thin and angular. I could see where Jill's coloring came from. Richard was blond with thick hair and a moderate walrus mustache. He reminded me more of a Scandinavian lumberjack from Minnesota than an accountant who ran a records office in Pennsylvania. His eyes and mouth also foreshadowed the irony that resided in his daughter. It looked to me that Richard Deriksson took nothing at face value. He sat down in the chair normally occupied by Roger.

Roger, unseated like a player in a game of musical chairs, looked around the room for a place to sit. He settled on a seat on the wicker couch next to Jill, pushing her closer to me. She gave me an amused smile.

"Just one more person and I'll be sitting on your lap." She lapped up her last word and smiled.

I noticed another member of the family I hadn't seen before, a boy I knew to be twelve-year-old Jan, pronounced Yon, from my conversation with Jill on our walk. He hovered around his mother in the kitchen, dipping into the various pans on the stove. He looked at me with a quizzical gaze, and I gave him a wave and smiled. He returned it with a tentative hand motion.

"Dinner," Jane called. There was a long, narrow table fitted with a white tablecloth. The table had previously served as a barrier between the living room and the kitchen-dining area, where random meals were prepared. Now, it was set with china and wine glasses, cloth napkins, gravy boats with brown and white gravy, mashed potatoes, peas, salads on their own plates, dressing in glass bottles, two opened bottles of wine, one white and one red, and in pride of place on a silver platter, a roast dripped red. The previous casual nature of the place was all but erased. Informality was only preserved in our dress—Roger and Jan in their bathing suits, me in my lifeguard togs,

Jill in a sweatshirt and bare feet, and Jane, the chef, in her muumuu. We all stood around trying to determine where we should sit. Richard strolled over and stood at the center of the table above the roast, picked up a large knife and fork, and waited for us to find our seats. We all sat down and took turns passing him our plates.

"This dinner can't be for me," Richard said. "I think it must be for you, Jimmy." He chuckled softly and the table gave up a dry laugh. I was sure I blushed crimson.

"It's all for you, my hubby, for gracing us with your presence for more than a day and a half," his wife said.

As I regained my natural color, the dinner progressed casually, with Richard asking his family what was new in their last week. To me, he said, "Jimmy, I hear you're a writer and are learning to surf." I nodded and mumbled something. Jane saved me from further ill-formed syllables.

"Jimmy's written a good short story. Get it from Jill. He's also working on an article about learning to surf with Roger." Roger nodded his verification.

"Interesting," Richard said. To his daughter he asked, "How's Charles?"

Jane, the only one to have dressed for dinner, sat next to Roger, sipping red wine in a solid orange pastel summer dress. She answered casually. Looking flat-out radiant, she said, "Oh, he's doing fine. I'll see him when I fly back to Chicago." *Chicago? Good separation,* I thought.

I looked over to the fractured couple. Jane had done nothing to lose her place as the most beautiful woman I'd ever seen, but Roger, with a day or two shadow on his face, even in his surfing jams and sleeveless cotton shirt, also cut a striking figure. I hadn't realized until just then what a handsome specimen he was. As a couple they were well-matched. *Chicago may not be far enough for Charles' security,* I thought. I wanted to find out about Charles, but I didn't ask any questions out of what I felt was loyalty to Roger. I determined I'd ask Jill when the opportunity came.

The front door bell rang and Jill was up like a there was electricity in her seat. Though quick, Jane, the mother, beat her to the door, where there was a brief conversation. Jill was left standing awkwardly in the living room. The only word I got from the conversation at the front door was Jane's "nonsense." She returned to the living room pushing a reluctant young man from behind, her hands on his shoulders.

"Everyone, this is Eddie, Jill's friend," Jane said.

"Going surfing, little sister?" said the younger Jane, snickering.

"We're going to the movies," Eddie said, answering the hanging question. Jill hurriedly finished putting on her sandals and pushed Fast Eddie out the door.

"It was kind of mean to push him in here, but we're not big Fast Eddie fans," the mother said.

Jane and Roger went off for a walk, but I stayed on with Jane and Richard. RIchard was full of questions, and we talked a lot. About high school, growing up in Arizona, about my interests and university plans, and about my impressions of the island. About the Vietnam war. What he didn't ask me about was my writing. I wondered if that was because it was the province of his wife. He told me about his growing up in Bethlehem, about his father working in the steel mill, about being the first in his family to graduate college, becoming an accountant of sorts, and starting an information and record-keeping service for the same company where his father was a mill worker.

I told him about my father, of his time as a tennis player in France, how he was like my hero, and I opened up about how I wanted to follow in his footsteps in Europe as a writer of international intrigue. He was not judgmental and listened respectfully to this somewhat off-the-wall romantic aspiration. We talked about how Vietnam and the war delayed my pursuit of international jewel thieves, as I avoided the draft through college. I was relieved to find he shared a similar opinion of the war. He laughed at the story of how I managed to graduate from high school. He said that it would probably make a good short story.

Through it all, Jane sat in her seat and just listened. *She wasn't the only one in the family who kept records*, I thought. She seemed to enjoy that Richard and I were getting to know each other. It was getting late, and I'd been drinking more than a prudent amount of cream sherry. After thanking Jane for the amazing dinner and saying my goodbyes, I walked home along the shore.

On the walk, I had time to wonder of things from the evening. The first was the dinner itself. It seemed a bit out of place for the family's normally casual style. The formality of the dinner against the informality of our dress seemed a bit of an oxymoron. I dismissed Richard's assertion that the dinner was for me, but it indicated it was not a usual event. I finally chalked it up to a family who liked celebration but didn't take it too seriously. It was like Roger's earlier instruction to *keep it loose*.

The Derikssons were proving to be a complex family. Second, I had interpreted Richard's reticence to talk about my writing as sensitive, leaving it to his wife, but why was that sensitive? It did make me feel special, but what was its origin? Jane and Richard had obviously talked about me, and I wondered briefly if Jane had asserted some kind of territoriality. I wasn't wild about the appearance of Fast Eddie. Even if he was Jill's boyfriend, what did I have to complain about? I had my own girlfriend. Didn't I? Jane's shepherding of Fast Eddie into the living room was puzzling. She described it as mean, but was there something more? Jane didn't strike me as mean. These thoughts swirled around me, like an Arizona dust devil.

What movie were Jill and Fast Eddie watching?

21

Bubbles in my Blood

Into my first week on the job, I'd made a couple of independent runs, with no input from Eddie. Nothing dramatic, but it bolstered a feeling that I belonged. Eddie kept introducing me to the regulars on the beach, and I began to develop some relationships of my own. One was a young man of about fourteen by the name of Warren. He was outgoing and bright. I was particularly drawn to him by his vocabulary and his humorous use of it. He frequently came by the lifeguard stand to talk and was interested in all things lifeguard. He counted down the time until he would take his seat on the stand. He would borrow my pith helmet, which I never much liked, and parade around the beach and report to us minor infractions by the beachgoers and swimmers. It was not with the punitive officiousness of a Chris Mackee but with a humor that pointed out the absurdity of the operative bureaucracy. I really liked him.

Another significant beach persona was Shelly Goldberg. When I noticed her, I called Eddie's attention to her and asked who she was.

"That's Shelly. She's easy," he said.

"She's gorgeous," I shot back.

"Easy and gorgeous, it's a good combination," Eddie said. "Word is that she does modeling in Newark. She comes down here mostly on weekends."

"Newark doesn't seem like a fashion center," I said.

"Newark's a suburb of New York City," Eddie said. *I had so much to learn.*

Gap in my knowledge, or not, I became enamored of Shelly Goldberg and would find my eyes straying from the ocean and settling on her. After a few hours of this scrutiny, Shelly became aware of my periodic gaze and came over to the stand to talk with me.

Shelly was indeed gorgeous, but her beauty was 180 degrees from Jane's. Whereas Jane's was comprehensive and multidimensional, Shelly's was singular, but a singularity that was heart-stopping. Hormones bubbled in my blood like club soda in a vodka drink. After our initial introduction, she sat on the buoy in front of the stand. *Who wears pink lipstick to the beach?* Her open legs on the lifebuoy were like a magnet, so strong that I worried that my focus away from the beach would become noticeable, if not dangerous to those in the water. I looked at Eddie, who was on a routine patrol. I was relieved that he hadn't yet noticed. I tried to glue my eyes to the swimmers.

Shelly left, saying that we should get together. We made no plans, but I strongly supported the suggestion. She said she'd be around a few days more before she returned home.

Shelly moved her towel closer to the lifeguard stand. She was still in full view, as she worked on her already substantial tan. My eyes continued to drift over at regular intervals, but I managed fidelity to my responsibilities to the swimmers before me. Eddie returned to the stand and greeted me with a loaded smile, but we said nothing about Shelly. Chris Mackee showed up toward the end of the day. It was time for my patrol of the shore, so I left Chris to Eddie. On my walk, I managed a few backward glances, and their interaction seemed to be civil. Mackee left within five minutes, wheels spitting sand as usual.

At five o'clock, Jane appeared, carrying the cat, and she was followed by Jill, who was carrying her board and who, in turn, was followed by Fast Eddie.

"Roger was called to cover a surfing competition at Virginia Beach by *Surfing* magazine," Jane said.

"Yeah," Jill said. "He told me to give you a *lesssson*." She stretched out the word in parody.

Jane was quick to correct her sister, saying, "He said that you were to continue your surfing on your own. He'll be gone through the weekend. He also said to tell you he really liked your last writing, and he wants to talk to you about it when he returns."

Jill and Fast Eddie moved into the surf. I glanced over to Shelly, who maintained her place on her beach towel. She gave me a little wave, and I waved back before entering the ocean.

Despite Jill's talk of a lesson, I was alone on the water, left to employ the wisdom I'd accumulated from Roger. My mantra for the afternoon was *keep it loose*, and as I looked over to Fast Eddie, I was aware that this applied to things other than surfing. I had to admit that he was a good surfer as I watched him catch a wave and ride it adroitly into shore.

My mantra did little to affect either my surfing or my emotions. I reflected later that although passive, a better mantra would have been *patience*.

Though I surfed better than times before, I was repeatedly pitched off. *Do it loosely*, I told myself as I took the painful journeys to retrieve my board, not gazing at the observers on the sand. I tried hard to embrace Roger's caution not to take it so seriously. However, I did manage to ride a few waves to the shore. I resolved to end the session with the next good ride. The strategy turned out to be a bit presumptuous, as my next three ended with pitch-offs early in the ride. On my paddle back, I resolved that this was the last try—fourth time's the charm. Resolving to keep it loose, without believing any of it, I shook my body to loosen up and dipped off the crest of a swell. Catching the wave, I found my feet in the beginning and managed stay on them with a vision of an anchor attached to the heel of my rear foot. I shuffled back a little on the board, pressed my back foot down, and cut diagonally across the wave for the first time.

The ride did mitigate my otherwise poor performance. I held my head high as I stumbled toward the people waiting on the sand. Besides Jane, the group was made up of Jill and Shelly. I was surprised to see Pam also in the mix. Fast Eddie stood a little way apart. The women all clapped as I approached, and Fast Eddie kept his hands on his board but gave me a nod.

Three women I was attracted to, plus the most beautiful woman in the world, all clapping for me. *I guess it's like actors,* I thought. *You are only as good as your last ride.*

Thus, praised for a pretty shabby session, I turned toward how I should approach the various women in the group. Shelly was the first to greet me as I laid my board down. She was not unaware of the disapproving looks directed at her from the other woman (not for the first time, I surmised), and said, "I look forward to getting together." The club soda bubbled through my circulatory system–my veins, my arteries, my heart (ain't lust wonderful). Shelly sashayed off, giving the others in the group the predatory smile of a lioness, picked up her towel, and left the beach.

"Nice ride," Jill said

"Nice lesson," I returned. It was meant to be humorous, but it still carried an edge. Jill frowned.

Jane attempted to warm things up. "Jimmy, why don't you come over?"

Pam advanced and asked me how I knew Shelly.

I answered that we were introduced that day, by Eddie, my partner.

"And you've arranged to meet her...?"

"Nothing definite," I mumbled. And quickly followed with, "Wanna meet tomorrow at Island Beach?"

Pam hesitated.

"Usual time?" I followed.

"What about surfing?" she asked.

"Roger's away covering a surfing competition at Virginia Beach, won't be back till Monday, so we're cool."

A little more hesitation, then a nod, and she turned and walked off the beach. Eddie, Jill's titular boyfriend, stood away from the group looking as if he'd bitten into a lemon, followed her.

The safest move seemed to be to accept Jane's invitation. I'd never had to deal with a similar situation; in high school, I couldn't buy a date, so as it was, I had no chops.

On our walk to Jane and Jill's house, I noticed that Fast Eddie's old station wagon was still parked on the road, with his surfboard locked inside.

22

Paramour and Too Clever

Jill was abnormally quiet, and when we entered the house, she moved up the stairs opposite the cat's bathroom. I hoped my somewhat sarcastic remark about the lesson hadn't hurt her feelings. Jane and I entered the living room. Richard and Jane worked together in the kitchen, where they laughed a lot and seemed to be having fun. Richard greeted us with alacrity and asked if we wanted a drink. We both nodded and sat down in our usual spaces.

"Jimmy had a real good ride at the end of the day," Jane said.

"The end of an otherwise disastrous day," I added.

"Isn't that what surfing's all about?" Richard asked. "Little episodes of success embedded in a sea of failure? That's what I've noticed anyway." It was a charitable remark.

"Whatcha makin', Mom?" Jane asked.

"After last night's orgy, we're just making some plates of finger foods for all of us to pick at." Richard passed a cocktail to his daughter and the ubiquitous jelly glass of cream sherry to me.

Jane placed several plates on the defrocked narrow dining table that had resumed its function as a barrier between the kitchen and living room. A stack of small plates and pile of assorted silverware rested at one end of the table. "Dig in," she said.

We each took a plate of cut vegetables, cheese and crackers, some canapé like things of meat and mushrooms, guacamole and chips, and some pizza-like dumplings.

"I made the guacamole for you, Jimmy, and your longing for Mexican food," Jane said.

As a group, we all seemed to be a bit subdued from the previous night's excesses. We sat around looking at each other. Richard broke the ice with, "Jimmy, how do you like lifeguarding?" Jill came down the stairs before I could answer.

"He seems to be getting along just fine from what I can see," she said. She shot me an ironic smile, and I hoped I wasn't blushing. But I went with the flow.

"Yeah, things are going well. I'm taking my cues from Eddie Lambert, meeting a few people."

"And just who *are* your favorites?" Jill said, teasing.

The phone rang and her sister answered and moved into the cat's bathroom. The lethargy of the group continued, and Richard excused himself by saying he was going to read in bed. Jane exited the cat's bathroom, made her excuses, and went upstairs.

I was alone with Jill and her mother. "I have a question on your short story," Jane said as she retrieved the cream sherry bottle from the kitchen counter and filled our jars.

"I haven't finished reading it yet. I'll do that now," said Jill, leaving her mother and me alone.

"A question?" I asked.

"Yes," Jane said. "The story was well constructed, though a bit derivative, Steinbeck and all." I squirmed a little in my seat on the wicker couch as I waited for the rapier-like scrutiny of Jane's intellect. "The story ends with an implicit question that leaves the story unresolved."

More squirm. *Left unresolved?* "Unresolved," I mumbled, an implicit question.

"Yes, unresolved—unfinished, if you will. You leave the reader in ambiguity. An ambiguity that I feel is unnecessary and limits your story. That is, does Pablo profit from his albeit creative deception, or is his chicanery exposed? It has resulted in the death of a valuable fighting cock. Is he liable? Is the cheating profitable, or punished? I want to know." She looked at me flatly. "What is it that you are writing about? Bending the rules, victory for the underdog, empowering females perhaps." At this, I thought of Pam's initial take on the story "Or the nature of fairness or justice? Who or what is villain in the story? Is Pablo a hero or a scammer—is he both? The only noble character in the story is the King of the Pirates. How does the story validate him? You left it all hanging, I think you can do better, Jimmy."

I had realized that I'd left the ending hanging, promising myself I'd decide later, but that hadn't bothered me. At least until then, under Jane's scrutiny, I was vaguely aware of a moral conundrum but chose not to confront it and to delay which side of it I would come down on. If I thought of it at all, I concerned myself only with Pablo's cleverness (my cleverness). Besides, many stories ended with ambiguity, so why not Pablo's? Either way he was a hero. Wasn't he? Now, under Jane's critical eye, I wasn't so sure.

I didn't know what to say, so I remained silent and took a sip of cream sherry.

"I don't expect any answers tonight, but think about it," she said. "We've got plenty of time to talk about it." I took another sip and nodded to her. It was more of an oblation.

Jill bounded down the stairs, her old self. "Read it, pretty good. I thought it was," she said. She then hesitated a moment, before saying, "Clever." Given Jane's questions, I winced under the word. She handed me the brown folder with the string tie. "There's just your story. Roger took the surfing notes."

I stood and said that I should be heading home. Jill said, "Can I walk you home?" I looked to Jane, who smiled approval. "Sure," I said.

I thanked Jane for the finger food, cream sherry, and the food for thought and said I'd think about the things she'd raised. Jill and I left, but when we got to the screen porch, she put out an arm and stopped me. I looked outside to see a white convertible Mustang with red leather interior deliver Fast Eddie to his battered station wagon.

We walk along the shore, shoes in hand, feet in the surf. "My mother really likes you. She's never treated any of my friends like she does you."

"I really like her too," I returned.

"And Fast Eddie's not my boyfriend, not really. I just linked up with him, out of…out of convenience. Surfing's a lot about image, a girl surfer without a boy surfer is kinda the wrong image. It's shallow, I know, but there it is."

We were about halfway home and she reached out and took my hand. We walked on holding hands. Just before we left the beach I asked, "Want a real boyfriend?" Jill nodded, her platinum hair a reflection of the full moon (I'm sure I made it up this time). In front of the apartment complex, we kissed. Jill put on her sandals and walked back on the road. A new boyfriend in her wake.

It was late, and I ran upstairs to make my apologies to Aunt Isobel. She stopped me midway through my recitation. "You know, where a woman is involved, men become unreliable. Unreliable with regard to others." She smiled at my discomfort and continued: "Like your father in France. Every time he had a new paramour, you could never rely on him for anything. Used to drive our mother mad." Her eyes got that faraway look she used when she peered into her past.

Paramour? I liked it. I knew the word but had never used it. Ibby shifted gears or timeframes. "From now on, I'm going to prepare dinner in smaller portions so that I can prepare yours when, and if, you come. Are you hungry?" I did love my aunt.

23

Pineys and Fessing Up

The next day was Friday. The end of my first work week, or at least the end of a traditional work week. The beach was guarded seven days a week, and each lifeguard worked a six-day shift. Because of this staggered schedule, each lifeguard was given one day off and was replaced with a substitute. These lifeguards were usually veterans and would rotate among the various teams. My day off was Saturday, and Eddie's was Sunday.

When not monitoring the beach, a lifeguard's time was taken up primarily by drinking beer, along with dating other lifeguards and generally partying. As most lifeguards were under the drinking age, this presented a problem to be overcome. Many underaged guards had older friends who'd buy them beer. If anyone ever did a study of the contents of the fifty-five-gallon drums that served as beach garbage cans between the hours of seven p.m. and nine a.m., they would find on average eighty-five percent beer cans. Eddie's answer to the beer problem was the town of Chatsworth. Chatsworth was a small town on mainland New Jersey in an area known as the Pine Barrens, where local residents were referred to as Pineys. I knew little else about Chatsworth or the Pineys but would soon learn everybody had a story. Eddie invited me to make the forty-mile trek to Chatsworth with him the next afternoon on my day off.

I'd had little time to socialize with Eddie or other guards while being involved with Roger and the Derikssons. I was happy for the invitation and enthusiastically accepted, looking forward to some lifeguarded comradery.

Friday on the beach slipped by as seamlessly as the incoming waves. I was glad that Shelly Goldberg failed to show up. Since I had a new girlfriend and a date at the Island Beach Hotel, I had more women than I could handle. Chris Mackee showed up for his usual afternoon inspection. He walked the length between the red flags, and finding nothing he could complain about, he turned around without a word and spun off. As he rounded the jetty a young couple had to hustle to avoid his Scout. Eddie narrowed his brow as he focused on the area between the end of the jetty and the narrow patch of sand at its end.

"Isn't there's something somebody can do about that guy?" I asked.

Ed was still deep in thought. "Maybe," he said under his breath.

Eddie dropped me off at Schooner's Wharf and we made plans to meet at his house at five-thirty the next afternoon. Pam had told me that Friday was her new day off so I walked past the ice cream store. We had agreed to meet at the Island Beach after work, and that usually meant six, so I had a little time. My destination was the little bookstore on the wharf. It was a well-stocked affair with primarily paperbacks from classics to comics. I went in looking for a book about the ocean and selected one titled *Waves and Beaches: The Dynamics of the Ocean Surface*, by Willard Bascom. I'd seen many people on *my* beach reading it. I planned to use it for my surfing article with Roger, but reflected that it wouldn't hurt to inform myself as a lifeguard.

I'd not been paid yet, with payday occurring every two weeks, but I still had money my father had given me before his departure, so

I perused the walls and various isles. I picked up a book by Balzac, *Cousin Bette*, and thought I'd start my research on one of my father's favorite author, at least according to Aunt Isobel. I wanted to read a little of the author before I talked with him. Walking around the store I found a *local interest* corner, stocked with books about the area. There were several books about the Pine Barrens, and I looked through these. Most seemed to be primarily academic treatments: prehistory, geology, flora, fauna, and history. Along with the books were copies of *The New Yorker* with a cover story on the Pine Barrens displayed. The article signaled the publication of a new book, *The Pine Barrens*, by John McFee. I thumbed through the article. I liked the approach of the author and added it to my purchases. In my reconnaissance of the article, I came across a section with a provocative illustration of a gargoyle-like figure called *The Jersey Devil*. I noticed several books with similar titles and splashy covers. I chose one with a cover illustration like the one in the *New Yorker* article. I took my four purchases to the cashier, paid for them, and moved on to the Island Beach. I still had twenty-five dollars in my pocket. I'd have to be careful until payday.

The hotel was farther away than I remembered, but I still got there before Pam and was installed at a table reading about the Jersey Devil and drinking a gin and tonic when she arrived.

"Whatcha reading?" she asked me. I held up the book, "Why the Jersey Devil?"

"I'm going on a beer run with Eddie Lambert to Chatsworth. It's in the Pine Barrens. The Jersey Devil is part of the Pine Barrens' mythology," I said as if I knew my ass from my elbow, or from the Jersey Devil's.

"Why is he going to Chatsworth to buy beer? Doesn't he have friends who'd buy it for him?"

"I'm sure he does. I think it's the romance, more of a quest, and

I'm arming myself."

"Playing Ulysses to buy beer seems a bit childish, don't you think?" She asked the rhetorical question, and I saluted her with my gin and tonic.

Pam ordered a Seagram's and Coke, and said, "From what I've heard, the Devil's not just mythology, but it exists. It's creepy. Do you know anything about the Pineys?"

I had to admit that I didn't yet. "But I'm learning," I said, holding up the *New Yorker*.

Her Seagram's came and she continued. "Why is Eddie going to Chatsworth to buy beer?" she asked again. "It's a dangerous place. Pineys are like hillbillies. They'll shoot you as soon as look at you. If you have a flat tire, don't stop on the roadway to change it, just rim it into town. A number of people have been robbed or killed along the way." I was increasingly intrigued by the minute. I wasn't assured of the accuracy of Pam's information but was impressed by the drama and her passion for the subject. I couldn't wait for the trip.

Pam rolled to a halt and asked to see the other books I had at the table. "Waves and beaches," she said approvingly. I told her it was for the article I was writing with Roger and was rewarded with a smile. She assumed a faraway look that I thought was suggestive of things other than approval. "What's *Cousin Bette*?" she asked. I told her that Balzac was a favorite of my father when he was a tennis player on the French Rivera, and I received another smile.

Changing the subject again, she brought up the topic I'd been dreading. "Eddie tells me you're Jill's new boyfriend."

"Is that Fast Eddie?" I asked to distinguish him from Chatsworth Eddie.

"Who?" I realized that Fast Eddie was probably just the name the Deriksson family had bestowed on him.

"Eddie, Jill's surfing partner." I was quick to clarify.

"Yes. Eddie says *he* was Jill's boyfriend until you came along." Pam continued, "Are you Jill's boyfriend?" she asked directly.

"Yes," I answered. The conversation was awkward, but at least it was coming to the point.

"And you still kept our date?" she said.

"Yes," I said continuing my economy of response and having no real defense.

Then, thinking better, I said, "Why not? We're friends." It sounded lame even to me.

"I thought we were a bit more," Pam said.

"You wouldn't even give me your phone number, so we could arrange to meet once I started working," I countered, abandoning my economy, in what amounted to a defense.

Pam exerted her own economy to silence.

"And didn't you kiss him in your car last night when you returned him to his station wagon?" I moved from defense to accusation, trying ineffectually to look hurt. This was a risk since I had only seen the two lean their heads together.

"It was just a friendly peck," Pam said defensively, confirming the accusation. "How did you know about that anyway?"

"Saw it from Jill's house—the mustang's top was down—and how did you find about my being Jill's boyfriend? It just happened last night, and after we had agreed to meet."

"Eddie and I spent the day together. He told me at lunch." It was said with a pout and a certain aggression. A *take that*.

Between a friendly peck and an informative lunch, I no longer harbored feelings of guilt, but said, "I hope we're still friends. I do like our meetings here." (What an asshole.)

Pam received this with silence. It was all that I deserved. I wondered if Fast Eddie and Jill would still be an item on the waves.

24

Mother Leeds and Her Spawn

On my day off, I made ready for our beer odyssey to Chatsworth by reading and accumulating information about the Pine Barrens, Pineys, and the Jersey Devil. The New Jersey Pine Barrens were part of a larger ecosystem designated The Atlantic Coastal Pine Barrens Ecosystem. The land was characterized by a sandy, acidic, nutrient-poor soil. Early settlers, unable to grow their traditional crops, called the region barren, and the name stuck. Despite its inhospitable soil for agriculture, the area supported a diverse system of plant life, including orchids and carnivorous plants—a little creepy. The landscape was made up of pygmy pitch pines and scrub oak. Swampy areas of cedar forests that grew along brownish-red, iron-rich freshwater called cedar water, were common. The ecosystem, the article said, is subject to and dependent on frequent fires to maintain itself for plant species to reproduce. Despite its proximity to large urban areas, the barrens had remained largely rural, with the population of country people.

Local residents are referred to as Pineys, historically applied as a derogatory term. One source contended that Piney was now a culture demonym. I had to look that one up and found that demonym was defined as a name used to denote the inhabitants of a particular cultural area. The definition didn't seem to me much of an upgrade.

Why couldn't a demonym be used as a derogatory name? I think the statement was made to reinforce the claim that Pineys took a certain pride in the name. I didn't think demonym would go very far in modifying Pam's view of the Pineys. For a demonym could just as easily shoot you as soon as look at you, the same as a derogatorily assigned designee. Still, I filed it away in my vocabulary.

Demonym or not, living in the harsh conditions of the barrens, residents were characterized by outsiders as the dregs of society. Fugitives, poachers, moonshiners, descendants of runaway slaves, and deserting soldiers all made up popular demographic views of the Pineys. The Pineys themselves often fostered accounts of how violent and dangerous they were to discourage outsiders and lawmen from entering the barrens. Popular history included stories of notorious moonshiners, bootleggers, and robbers. Not all of the stories, it seemed, were fabrications.

Often poor, the Pineys engaged in whatever work they could find. They collected and sold sphagnum moss and pine cones (pine cones?), hunted, fished, and lived off the land. A major industry was the making of charcoal from local trees. I guessed selling beer to minors could organically be added to the sources of Piney livelihood.

If these characterizations were not enough, the Pineys were saddled with the "scientific" study of the Kallikuk family, done by the academic Henry H. Goddard and his sidekick and partner in crime, Elizabeth Kite. As bogus as the name of the family, the study was used to support the duplicitous claims of the eugenics movement, further demonizing the dwellers of the Pine Barrens as intellectually subnormal. It was then used to support the role of inheritance as the major cause of mental deficiency. It seemed sandy, acidic, and nutrient-deficient soil was not enough to denigrate the Pineys, but the deficiency should extend to their innate intelligence as well. It did not seem out of hand, to me, for the residents to do all they could to keep outsiders at bay.

All of this was interesting and set a dramatic stage for an intrepid beer run, but it was the legend of the Jersey Devil that raised the writer's hair on the back of his neck. A common description of the Jersey Devil is of a bipedal creature with hooves. The description in my book likened it to a kangaroo-like or wyvern-like creature, with a goat- or horse-like head. I had to look up wyvern, too. My research was turning into a vocabulary-building activity. A wyvern is a winged, two-legged dragon with a forked tail. I'd add it next to demonym. Other attributes of the devil include leathery bat-like wings, horns, small arms, clawed hands, cloven hooves, and a forked tail. Or should I say wyvern-like forked tail—the Jersey Devil sports a lot of hyphens. Reports of sightings also included that the creature moves quickly and emits a high-pitched, blood-curdling scream. (Would you expect anything less?)

Another term for the devil was the Leeds Devil, named after Jane Leeds, a 1700s Pine Barrens resident. As the story goes, Mother Leeds, after finding she was pregnant with her thirteenth, cursed the child and said *she* would be the devil. Some accounts identified the child as a female. Whether this was said in prophesy, or as an understandable metaphor for the unfairness of multiple pregnancies, no one said.

In 1735, Mother Leeds was in labor on a stormy night (of course it was), with villagers gathered around her. Born as a normal child, the thirteenth immediately underwent a change, morphing into a fully developed creature with cloven-hooved feet, a goat's head, bat wings, and a forked tail. After beating-up all present, the creature let out a scream, then flew up the chimney and into the surrounding pines. In some accounts, Mother leeds was supposedly a witch while the father was the devil. Long before the Goddard and Kite study, this provided the first assertion of the importance of inheritance in pine barrens descendants.

Over the years beginning in pre-independence colonial times to the present, there have been many historical, political, and cultural explanations of the Jersey Devil legend. Even the ones citing Benjamin Franklin did little to extinguish the power of the Jersey Devil in the modern mind of residents of Long Beach Island and its surroundings. There continued to be sightings.

There were many sightings in Colonial America. These tended to be attributed to the witch paranoia promoted by the clergy of the time. A wave of sightings occurred in 1909 over south Jersey and the Philadelphia area. Police in Camden, New Jersey, and Bristol, Pennsylvania, reportedly fired at a Jersey Devil-like creature, all to no effect. And in 1951, a group of boys in Gibbstown, New Jersey, claimed to have seen a monster matching the devil's description. I made a mental note that this might be good fodder for a short story, as I had with the Mother Leeds birth tale.

It took me a good half-day to compile the material, but I felt pretty well armed for the beer quest.

25

It All Begins with Hips

It was now two o'clock, and I still had three and a half hours before I had to meet Eddie Lambert. I'd not seen Jill for going on two days since we declared our boy-girl-friendship. I didn't know what a boyfriend's obligations were, as I'd never had a real girlfriend. I figured she was probably surfing at Holgate. I walked the mile and a half down the beach, and I wasn't disappointed as the platinum corona cut through the water. Fast Eddie was out there, too, but so was Pam, who was sitting on a beach towel. With my presence, the symmetry was complete. As I was coming from behind, Pam had not been aware of me until I plopped down next to her.

"What are you doing here?" There was no pleasure in her eyes as she looked at me.

"Just thought I'd watch the surfers. I have some time before I meet Eddie for our beer run to Chatsworth.

"You still going?"

"Absolutely. I spent last night and today arming myself with information that will help me survive the trip: Pineys, the Jersey Devil, the sandy acidic soil, and the pygmy pitch pines—I'm becoming an expert." I smiled.

Pam was not amused. "It's your life," she said with a shrug that said *I couldn't care less.*

Andy came into the shore to retrieve his board and waved at me. I waved back. Andy paddled out next to Jill, who sat on her board scanning the incoming swells and pointed to me. She looked over but did not return my wave. She dipped over a swell as it crested and surfed into the shore near us, picked up her board, and walked over.

Looking past Pam, she said. "What are you doing?" I think she's asking, "What are you doing sitting next to Pam on her beach towel?"

But the wordsmith answered artfully. "Whaddaya mean?"

"Why aren't you surfing?" she said.

I flushed with relief. "I don't have a board."

"Come on, I can fix that," she said, and I got up and followed.

Several surfers were sitting on the sand next to their boards. Jill walked up to a guy she called Zane, introduced us, and asked if I could borrow his board. Zane looked tentative but agreed. "If he breaks it, I'll buy you a new one," she said over her shoulder. After we'd gained a little distance, she said to me, "Don't break it, I don't have any money." Her tongue covered the word *money*.

Then she said, "I thought it was time to make good on my promise of a few days ago to give you a surfing lesson."

"How did Andy know to alert you to my being on the beach?" I asked.

"Eddie's been telling anyone who'll listen that I dumped him for you. And everybody listened. Surfers around here love gossip. Not much happens on the island," Jill said, resolving the mystery.

Jill proved an able tutor and focused on things Roger hadn't— mainly on my hips. "How you use your hips is the important thing in how you position your legs on the surfboard—it all begins with your hips. It's about stability and how you direct your board as you respond to a wave," she said. Hips: *It all begins with hips* would be my next focus in the surfing article.

Like every new revelation, this one also began with failure. I caught four or five waves, and stood up on the board, but when I focused on my hips and tried to engage them, I shimmied off the side, moving like an inept ballroom dancer.

Throughout this process, Jill sat atop the incoming swells and observed me. As I paddled out for my fifth or sixth try, she came next to me. "Did you ever play baseball?"

"Yes," I said. "I played high school baseball." The statement was true but incomplete. I had played varsity baseball as a sophomore, until I had a disagreement with the coach about how far I was allowed to play off the bag as a right-handed first baseman. It was a philosophical disagreement in which I maintained that I could play farther away from the base and still guard the line, my glove being on the hand closest to the baseline. The coach wasn't much of an innovator and felt he had already made a big concession by deploying a right-hander at first base in the first place. I continued to play off the line, and the coach continued his harangue. Even though I'd made a few plays I couldn't have made if I'd played closer to the bag and had not let anything get past me along the line, the coach told me if I continued my positioning he'd bench me. Tired of the back and forth, I told him he didn't have to bench me because I quit. That ended my baseball career. I didn't know where this reminiscence came from, or why. It took time away from my surfing education to think about, but I continued. "What about baseball?"

Jill answered, "You know you hit a baseball with your hips, if you just use your arms, you have no power? You have to get your hips into the swing. Surfing's the same. If you don't get your hips into it, you'll never harness the power of the wave. In the same way the bat's controlled by your hips, so is the surfboard. Think about the stability of your swing and the stability of the board. They're both ultimately driven by your hips."

For whatever the reason, the analogy worked. On my next ride I stood up and settled my hips as if I were swinging at a baseball and concentrated on driving the board forward. I positioned myself toward the back of the board and swiveled my hips, turning the board slightly parallel to the curl of the wave. I cut across the wave the way I'd seen Jill and Roger do it, and despite the increase of speed, I managed to remain upright into the shore. Jill caught the next wave and joined me on the shore. She didn't make a big deal about my ride.

"I think you've got it," she said as if it was nothing less than she'd expected. This made me feel better than applause. I asked her the time, and she looked at her watch and said it was four. I told her that I had to change and get to Eddie Lambert and the trip to Chatsworth. Then I had to explain about the beer run, the Jersey Devil, my research, and my pending excitement.

Jill laughed and said, "Take care, don't let the Jersey Devil get you, and don't stop along the way to pee." She laughed again. *That's what Pam said*, I thought. Fast Eddie now sat beside Pam, the nose of his board stuck majestically into the sand. I walked by them on the mile and a half back. On the way I wondered how Jill transported her board now that she wasn't Fast Eddie's partner. I imagined how Fast Eddie's surfboard would look sticking out of the Mustang convertible.

26

Shuffleboard, Lost Botany Students, and the Jersey Devil

I showed up at Eddie's at pretty much five-thirty. Eddie introduced me to a young man who was with him. "This is Mike Evers, he's our substitute guard. He'll be joining us on our trip." We shook hands and greeted each other. Evers was about my height, thin with short sandy-brown hair. He spoke with the strongest Jersey accent I'd yet heard. Ed had changed into jeans and a T-shirt, and Evers, still in his lifeguard jersey, wore a pair of blue cotton sweatpants and tennis shoes.

Ed and Mike rode in front and I sat diagonally in the backseat. We drove over the causeway and through the little town of Manahawkin on the mainland side. After a few miles, the landscape changed from the shore to hilly country covered with pines—pygmy pitch pines, I imagined. Mike Evers turned back to me and asked if I knew anything about the Pine Barrens. I pulled a moleskin notebook from the back pocket of my baggy shorts. I thumbed through the notebook where I'd written my research. I started to take them through my findings.

"Whoa! Sandy and acidic, nutrient-poor soil; pygmy pitch pines, what the hell? You take your beer trips seriously," he said in his sardonic thick Jersey accent.

"Jimmy's a writer," Eddie said.

"You going to write about the pine barrens?" Mike asked.

"I might," I said as I added a few notes about the surroundings to my book.

Eddie looked back at me and said, "It's OK to take notes in the car, but don't take out that notebook once we get there. Pineys are real suspicious about outsiders. They'd be even more touchy about an outsider taking notes."

"Understood." I continued to look out the windows at small wooden dwellings I could see through the trees.

"What you going to write about?" Mike asked.

"Short stories, background information, maybe the Jersey Devil. I think that might be an interesting story."

"Jersey Devil's creepy. I have a cousin who said he'd seen him. I don't believe him, but still it's creepy."

My interest piqued, I asked him to tell me about it. "He has family in the pines, on his mother's side, and they were visiting when Dean, that's his name, said he went for a walk at sundown and saw him in a clear-cut field. Just a lot of stumps and the Jersey Devil."

"Did he make contact with the devil?"

"No, just said he walked through the field of stumps into the woods. My cousin's not real bright—gullible. Probably gets it from his mother's side. What do you know about the Jersey Devil?"

I told him what I'd learned.

"Huh," he said. "What kind of story would you write about the Jersey Devil?"

"Oh," I said, "maybe about three guys on a trip to buy beer in the Pine Barrens. They have a flat tire." I borrowed the plot line of Pam's warning. "They get out to fix the tire and run into the devil. Only one escapes and lives to tell the story."

"What happens to the other two?"

"Nobody knows and they're never found," I said in a lowered voice.

It was still early, and the sun rode high on the horizon, but the light was blocked by the pines, surrounding the road in an ominous shade.

"Whoa, that's creepy. Let's talk about something else." Mike Evers shivered.

I heard Eddie chuckling from the front seat. "Jimmy's writing an article with Roger Axxst about a newbie learning to surf with the help of an experienced surfer."

"Roger Axxst, that's good," Mike said. The subject effectively changed, we talked about surfing until we reached a cluster of houses that indicated the outskirts of a town.

"Is this Chatsworth? I asked.

"Yep, this is it," Eddie said as he drove through the town.

There were two skeletal gas stations on either side of the road (where the three beer hunters should have rimmed their flat-tired car to), a liquor store, a sad-looking laundromat, a dry goods-hardware-grocery chimera called Baileys, and a warehouse that advertised moss, firewood, and charcoal. There were a few more anonymous structures whose functions I could only imagine. I scribbled a few notes.

Eddie drove through the town until the buildings began to dwindle. He went down a dirt road on the left and stopped in front of a barn-like, unpainted wooden building at the edge of the woods. Six-foot-high letters over the door proclaimed BEER. We had arrived.

Before we exited the car, we saw three state trooper police cars parked out front. "Maybe we shouldn't go in," I said.

"Don't worry," said Eddie, "they're all related, probably first cousins." He nodded toward the cars. "They know what's happening."

As we walked through the door, I felt that I was entering a Li'l Abner comic strip, albeit sans a Daisey Mae, as there were only men; the place could have been called forth by Kafka. There was a long bar, maybe forty feet long, made from the same planks of which the structure was built. Tables of the same lumber dotted the room around which groups of men drank beer from pitchers poured into pint Ball jars. It made me think of jelly glasses and cream sherry. The men were all dressed in a uniform of flannel shirts and slouch hats. About a third of them wore overalls, and a variety of rifles leaned up against the walls. There were no pool tables, but dartboards adorned each corner of the rectangular room. Along one wall was a shuffleboard table where four men plied chrome disks on a surface of wood and sawdust. Five state troopers stood at the bar drinking something dark that wasn't beer.

Eddie walked by the troopers and said, "Hello, Joseph," to the man behind the bar who was attending to the troopers. Joseph nodded and Eddie took a seat at a table, Mike and I followed in his wake. I was feeling a bit awkward and was trying not to imagine a sequel to the three youths with a flat tire on the road. I had to salute Pam for her most effective image. Mike Evers' eyes darted around the room as if he was trying to identify where the Jersey Devil might be hiding. Only Eddie seemed to be at ease. Joseph left his state troopers, filled a pitcher, grabbed three Ball jars, and set them on the table.

After two tentative jars, the hard edges of the room and its inhabitants began to soften, and I began to feel more at ease, and my writer's sensibilities began to return. *If you can't form a short story from this,* I thought, *you're one piece-of-shit writer.* When I thought about writing a story, I approached it as if I were adding furniture to a vacant room. Once the furniture is in, the writing is merely arranging that furniture.

Joseph was attentive and left off another pitcher. On my third jar, I was busy moving furniture into an empty room. The state troopers at the bar added color to the incubating story.

I watched the men at the shuffleboard table. The game was over and two of the players had returned to a table. The two left looked around the room for potential opponents. "Let's go," I said to Mike, who was startled but stood up. I led him to the shuffleboard table. The last winners looked skeptically at the two obvious outsiders, a guy in baggy shorts and a T-shirt and his friend in a lifeguard jersey and sweatpants. After their scrutiny, they continued to look around us, but as there were no forthcoming opponents, we shook hands and collected our discs.

"What you wanna play for?" asked the man in overalls and a red-and-black checked flannel shirt and a black slouch hat (sometimes a cliché is just a cliché—I think Freud said that, or something close). It wasn't really a Jersey accent. More like something from farther south.

Mike looked puzzled. "Five bucks," I said.

"Let's see it," said the other. He wore an army green T-shirt and baggy-looking jeans that said Dickies in the back. I took a five-dollar bill from my pocket and slapped it on the rail of the table.

"Where's yours?" I asked. Two and a half pints in, I was feeling reckless.

"We've got it," Overalls said. I chose not to press the point, our being outsiders and all.

"You go first," said Dickies. We broke into teams at one end of the table.

I took a disc with a blue logo on it—we were blue, they were red, and I sent my disc down the plank. It just peeked over the edge of the table. A good shot. Overalls sailed a red disc down the board with an excessive force meant to knock mine off the end, but he missed by a whisker. Now it was Mike's turn. He had never played the game and self-consciously sent his disc so that it sat directly behind mine a few feet. He didn't mean to do it, but he had effectively blocked mine from Dickies. It looked like strategy.

Dickies slammed his disc into Mike's, and the two forked, leaving mine untouched. First points to us.

My turn again: I managed to slide my disc a few inches from the edge. Overalls sent his disc violently with an intention to smash mine to atoms, and he missed again by a fingernail. He let out a howl that would have made the Jersey Devil proud. Evers did a little better on this round and slid his to within a half-inch of the end, about five inches wide of mine. Two of our discs were in winning positions and Dickies couldn't knock them both off. His only option was to get his disc past Mike's. He warmed up his attempt by sliding his piece horizontally back and forth between his hands. His shot glided gracefully down the board past Mike's, but it couldn't put on the brakes in time, and it slid past the edge. More points for the outsiders.

The next points went to the Pine Barrens, though. Overalls got a hold of himself, and I attempted a conversation. "What are all the troopers doing here?" I asked.

"They're in an' out," came his terse response. Terse but civil. The game seemed to go back and forth between us. I didn't know the precise rules of scoring, but there were counters of blue and red beads. Overalls changed both our beads with the fidelity of an accountant, so I was able to keep track. After a number of plays, red beads and blue beads were equal. It was all beginner's luck, of course, since neither Mike nor I knew what the hell we were doing.

My turn came up again. Last round, Dickies said, alerting me to the importance of my next slide, throw, roll, shot, or whatever was the term. I didn't know why I thought the game was important, but I did. I tried to relax my excited muscles for a finessed whatever it was, and I pushed off my disc gently with a smooth follow-through. The chrome circle almost waddled down the table; it reminded me of a turtle sliding on an ice-covered pond, just poking its nose over the edge and pulling its head back before going over. It was a good throw, but going first is a vulnerable position with two players gunning for you. Overalls was excited and sailed one down at warp speed and missed me by a good three inches. *A bit too excitable for this game*, I thought. Rather than a howl, he put his head down on the rail and sighed. Mike's turn came, and he lobbed one that hung out on the side about three-quarters down the table. Dickies' shot avoided both Mike's disc and mine. My turtle won the game by a nose.

Overalls looked dejectedly at Dickies, a look that said *what do we do now*, as he took a few coins from his pocket and appeared to count them.

"Forget it," I said. "Beginners' luck. Come over to our table and have a beer."

Overalls' name was Roy and Dickies' was Bobby. Roy and Bobby joined us at our table. Eddie was off talking to Joseph and the state troopers. I ordered another pitcher, and Joseph brought it over along with two more Ball jars.

"They're lookin' for two orchid hunters gone missing," Roy said. Noticing my puzzled look, he continued. "You asked about the troopers. They're lookin' for two college students, boy an' a girl. They was looking for orchids last time anybody seen 'em. Failed to show up to their college group, yesterday it was. Troopers out looking for 'em. They questioned Bobby an' me. We collect sphagnum moss, people put it with flowers, they're interested in talking to us, because moss grows where orchids do." After that recitation, Roy drained his Ball jar. "OK if I get another one?" I was quick to fill his jar.

"So, you guys live close by?" I tried to ask the question casually.

"Yeah, up ta Leeds point." I recalled that the Jersey Devil was the thirteenth child of Mother Leeds. I made mental note but didn't ask any more about it.

"The last time the orchid hunters was seen, was around there. That's why the troopers was interested if we'd seen them."

"Had you? Seen them, that is," I asked.

"Saw two young people, boy and a girl carrying canvas bags early in the day, but not later on. They wrote it down but let us be."

"And they've not been seen since?" I asked and Roy nodded. The little mystery was coming along.

"So, you guys make a living collecting sphagnum moss?" I asked off-handedly while I refilled his jar.

"That, makin' charcoal, and huntin'. People gotta hunt to make it here."

"Whatcha hunt?" I asked.

"Deer, mostly, though it ain't deer season, but we take some anyway. Go spotlightin' sometimes. You know like the deer in the headlights thing, kinda freezes 'em at night. Got to. Land's hard here, not good for crops, only blueberries and cranberries in the bogs."

Roy took a sip of his beer and nodded over to Mike. "He a lifeguard?" he asked.

"We all are," I said, "up at Long Beach Island." I had overheard Bobby and Mike having a conversation about the finer points of charcoal-making. I'd noticed that Mike had gone to the bar and come back with a pitcher. The two of them seemed to be drinking a lot of beer.

"That's where you're from?"

"Yeah, all of us. Ever been there?"

"Heard of it, never been."

"You should come, it's got great beaches and the water's warm this time of year. I'll show you around."

"Can't swim. Every year couple of people pickin' cranberries fall into the bog and drown. Dangerous, pickin' cranberries. Nice talkin' to you, we should go back to our buddies." He stood up and nodded at Bobby, who then stood, too. "Thanks about the five bucks," he said.

"Anytime," I said. "Real nice meeting you, Roy." And I really meant it.

"What did you guys talk about?" I asked Mike.

"Charcoal."

"Anything else?"

"Charcoal," he said.

I filed up my jar and moved to the bar and sat next to Eddie. "The writer soaking up local color?" he asked.

"Yeah, good color." The state troopers had all left, and Eddie was at the bar alone. "You hear them talking about two college students who went missing while hunting orchids?"

"No, I wasn't listening to them. They don't tend to like it when people listen in. But ask Joseph. There's nothing much around here he doesn't know about."

Joseph came back after delivering a pitcher. "Introduce us," I said to Ed. Eddie obliged, and Joseph and I shook hands. I cut to the chase, saying, "I was talking to Roy about two orchid hunters that have gone missing. Do you happen to know anything about it?"

"I know the troopers are worried. Well, worried's not the word, but I know they're not optimistic about a good outcome. Still, they're out looking. People gone missing have a tendency not to show back up, least till they find the bodies." Just like two of my three flat tire guys, I mused silently.

"Do you know any of the particulars?" I asked.

"Just that they're two students from Camden Junior College who was here on a trip for their botany class. Told their teacher they was out for orchids and was last seen by the two guys you was playing shuffleboard with in the woods outside a Leeds Point. Failed to show up at their meetin' place, the teacher and his class waited a while. When they still didn't show up after a couple of hours, the teacher alerted the troopers and they started looking. Didn't find anything, though. The college is real worried. Troopers said their captain got a call from the president of the college, and there was a reporter sent down from the Camden paper. She was here late this afternoon asking questions."

While we were talking, a couple of Black guys came into the bar and nodded at Joseph, who bent down underneath the bar and came up handing them two small paper bags. Money was exchanged, and the two men left without a word.

"Do you know the students' names, ages, anything about them?" I continued with Joseph.

"Nope, that's all I know about it. You gonna have to get the Camden newspaper tomorrow if you want to find out anything more. That, or go out in the woods and look for 'em yourself."

Another Black man entered the bar and repeated the transaction of the first two. He left with the paper bag. "What's that all about?" I asked Joseph.

"They come in to buy pints of local gin. Don't drink it here but prefer to drink among theyselves. They're descendants of former runaway slaves and stayed here. Formed a number of small communities. Keep pretty much to themselves. Good neighbors, though."

I was interested in them, but before I could ask any more questions, Eddie said, "Time to buy some beer." Before we left, I snuck in a last question. "What's up with all the guns leaning against the wall?"

"Our only rule, no guns at the tables," Joseph said. "Safer that way."

Mike Evers, head down on the table, looked asleep. "Leave him. I'll get him a couple of cases, and we'll pick him up later," Ed said.

We followed Joseph to a walk-in cooler in the back. Eddie bought five cases for himself and two for Mike. I said I'd take three. That would leave me enough to buy a Camden newspaper in the morning and a Bromo seltzer at Flo's diner before work.

Joseph loaded the cases on a hand truck and took them out to Ed's Volkswagen. The little front trunk compartment was crammed, and one case had to go in the backseat. Still, Eddie had trouble closing it, but in the end, everything was made to fit. We went back and woke up Mike, who was unsteady on his feet, and installed him sideways in the backseat, his feet resting on the last case.

Joseph called Eddie over to him in the parking lot, and I could hear the conversation—a warning, really. "Whatever you do, don't stop your car along the roadway—even to pee. I'm not kidding," Joseph said. Eddie nodded and assured him we wouldn't. We left and were not two minutes out of town when Mike woke up to say he had to pee. "Can't stop till we reach the shore," Eddie said, trying to honor Joseph's instruction. Mike wailed and said he couldn't possibly wait, that he was about to go in his pants all over the backseat.

"He has had an extraordinary amount of beer," I said. I had taken my cue from Joseph and gone in the parking lot while Mike slept in the backseat.

Over the next few miles, Mike escalated the urgency of his request, including a threatening countdown to deluge in the backseat.

"I think it's getting serious, Eddie," I said. Eddie slowed down and looked to the side of the road, then turned down a nearly invisible dirt path driving into the pines. Mike was now groaning in pain. "What are you doing?" I asked.

"Joseph told me not to stop along the roadway," he said as he drove farther down the narrow lane. He stopped in a spot where the road widened. We both exited our seats, giving Mike full access to the out of doors. Mike got out with further groans and ran off into the woods. "Be careful," Eddie yelled. "I think there's a bog out there." To me, he said, "I can hear frogs." I could hear nothing over the deafening electric sound of cicadas. As we waited for Mike, I topped off my bladder. I was zipping up my shorts when there came an unnerving, shrill scream. I looked at Eddie. "Screech owl," he said.

A minute later, Mike returned, stumbling in slow motion, wild-eyed, out of the woods. "I heard him," he mumbled in low tones, "I saw him—bat wings. He was standing in the bog. Get out of here." He scrambled, still in slow motion, into the back of the VW. I was reminded of my Frankenstein dreams when I would be trying to run from the monster, my muscles working slowly, and I could never seem to outrun him. Eddie moved unhurriedly into the driver's seat and started the engine.

"Hurry!" Mike said.

Eddie looked casually at me, "He's drunk." To Mike, he said, "It was an owl, the beer, and your imagination— and maybe a stork or heron."

"Imagination. Hell, I saw it." I looked at Mike, and he was shaking. Whatever it was, it was real to him. He stopped shaking as we turned out of the woods onto the highway and gained some distance.

"You were the one that wanted to pee," Ed said. "Tell us again the story about your gullible cousin and the Jersey Devil." Mike was quiet the rest of the way to the Island.

27

It was a Great Blue Heron...Probably

The next morning, I walked to work a little early. For some reason, I'd found it hard to sleep, and I stopped at Flo's. Flo's was a classic diner, even then becoming a rare architectural feature made of chrome and glass, like an Airstream trailer. Flo was a middle-aged bottle blonde, full of goodwill and downhome wisdom to go along with her downhome menu. She shouted out my order to the cook, partially visible behind a barrier: pancake, two eggs over, hashbrowns, along with her frequently voiced couplet, "Oh, no! Another Bromo." Alerting everyone in the place that I had a hangover. She made me laugh. I had bought the Camden newspaper from a machine outside, and over coffee, I looked for an article on the missing orchid hunters. I found it on page four.

The reporter, Susan Saunders, wrote that two members of a botanical field trip from Camden Junior College had failed to return to the class after purportedly going hunting for an orchid, the pink lady's slipper, a species native to the pine barrens. The instructor of the class, a Dr. Bob Cobbe, had conducted a cursory search with the other students and waited two hours for their return before alerting state troopers. Troopers subsequently interviewed Roy O'Malley and Bobby Grimes, sphagnum moss collectors, who had seen the students carrying canvas bags around the Leeds Point area. (It made me feel good that I had obtained the same information from the same sources as Miss Saunders.) Police interviews turned up no further information.

A captain Crain (no first name) of the New Jersey State Troopers was contacted by Dr. Morris Becker, president of Camden Junior College, who was in turn, assured by Crain that the investigation was ongoing. Saunders interviewed a local state trooper named Gallagher (from this, I surmised that state troopers were all Irishmen who were reluctant to give out their first names.) Gallagher said the same thing that Joseph had said at the bar the previous night, that people often fell into bogs, and when this happened, bodies were hard to recover. It seemed to me a dog-ate-my-homework attempt at a get-out-of-jail-free-card. The two missing students were identified as Sarah Kennedy, age nineteen, and Matt Limekiln, twenty-two. Both were biology students. The names appeared at the end of the article, causing me to think that Susan Saunders was waiting for the names to be approved for release after her article was already written.

Other than the names of those involved, and the pink lady's slipper orchid, the article contained little new information. Saunders also interviewed a few classmates who participated in the field trip. The information most interesting to me was from fellow students Linda Track and Jeff Goldman, who both said that Kennedy and Limekiln were boyfriend and girlfriend. Track said, in her opinion, the search for the pink lady's slipper was just an excuse to go off alone together. This was the first I heard that the two students might have deviated from the field trip protocol. It was interesting.

I finished my breakfast, paid with quickly depleting funds, folded up the newspaper, and despite having dripped egg yolk on the article, took it with me. I walked down the remaining distance to what was now *my* beach to find Mike Evers arriving at the same time. I greeted him with good morning but said nothing about the beer trip, or his sighting of the Jersey Devil. Mike was quiet and perhaps a little embarrassed.

"I looked at a bird book this morning, what I saw last night might have been a great blue heron," he said sheepishly.

"Whatever," I said, meaning to convey *no big deal*. We dragged the stand into place and I put my rolled-up newspaper under it. After we put the flag poles in place and were sitting on the stand, he asked, "What's with the newspaper?"

"I ate breakfast at Flo's and bought the newspaper to check on the lost orchid hunters."

"You gonna write something about it?"

"I'm gonna follow it, see if something interesting breaks out, nothing much more." This was an outright lie. I was intensely interested it, and even in these early stages, I was concocting various scenarios that I could turn into a story. The thing about fiction is that it doesn't have to be factual, but it still needs facts. And I was intent on researching the story to flesh it out.

"If you write about it, you won't mention anything about me seeing the Jersey Devil, will you?" he asked haltingly.

"Absolutely not. There's nothing to say." He looked a little uncertain but seemed reassured by my words. This would also end up a lie, as I would use the image of a great blue heron standing in a bog. But I would tell myself it was Eddie who first brought up the heron. Still, my promise was a lie.

Throughout the day, we both went on a couple of perfunctory runs. Mike bandaged up an older man who spoke with what I thought was an Italian accent. He had sliced his thumb while opening a clam. Mike stanched the considerable blood flow and bandaged it with gauze from our oversized first aid kit. It was the first time I'd seen it used, though we lugged it from Ed's car everyday along with the buoy and the flagpoles. Mike took over the hauling duties in Eddie's absence.

The Italian man took his leave after heaping repeated and heartfelt thanks on Mike. In his absence, Mike derided the man's stupidity in his Jersey accent. "They can see the clamshell is sharp and rather than use a proper tool they use their hands. They're stupid!" he said, making the criticism general. The rant seemed to be cathartic, going a ways toward absolving him for what he felt were his own lapses of the previous night.

After this, he seemed to loosen up into the old sardonic Mike. He routinely referred to the girls and young women on the beach as *sea dogs, sea dawgs*. As the name was applied to all of them, attractive or not, I was undecided if it was delivered as a compliment or a derogatory comment. I decided not to ask, as it would only get in the way of my musings on fiction and orchid hunters.

I was interrupted in my reverie by the arrival of Chris Mackee, who quizzed Mike on the day's activities. Mike noted nothing out of the ordinary, didn't even mention the clamshell medical intervention. Mackee addressed me for the first time ever. "Pay attention to this guy," he said. "He knows what he's doing; he's a good one." He said this, I think, as a putdown to Eddie—a back-handed implication that Ed was other than *a good one*. I kept looking for a way to insult the guy, but he didn't give me much to work with. I answered that I paid attention to everyone. Our meeting with Mackee was almost civil. Still, he spun his wheels on the takeoff.

28

She Must Like Me

At the end of the day, I felt a slap on my shoulder and turned to see Roger. "You're back. I thought you were gone through the weekend," I said in surprise.

"Finished up early, not much going on. Heard you had a good outing with Jill."

"Yeah," I said. "Hips. I'm writing up the notes. I'll have them tomorrow. Would have had them today if I thought you'd be back."

"I liked your last notes, *Keep it Loose*, good take, good exposition. I showed your notes to my editor at *Surfing*. He liked them and gave his approval to work up an article and send him what we've got, when we've got it. Work on *Hips*, and we'll attempt a rough draft, or at least part of one, and send it to him." Roger went over to Mike, who had been listening to us, and greeted him warmly with a slap on his shoulder.

I looked up at the entry to the beach and saw Jill toting her board and dragging *my* cat along behind. I ran to assist her. "How was the Pine Barrens beer trip?" she asked. "Get anything to write about?" I began to tell her the story, and she stopped me. "Hold up. Mom's been asking for you the last couple of days. Tell us when we're at home." With that, Jill paddled out into the waves. I took my board over to where Roger and Mike still talked.

"Ready?" Roger asked. To Mike, he said, "Don't worry about the stand, we'll move it back when we finish." I said goodbye to Mike as he lugged the flagpoles and the no longer virgin first aid kit, saying I'd see him next Sunday if not before.

I paddled out with Roger, and we sat on the bobbing swells. "What's with the newspaper I saw under the stand?" I started to tell him of the missing orchid hunter and he stopped me. "Wait till we go to the house and tell me in front of Jane. It seems she's been missing you." I'd now been told this twice, so I had to guess it was a real thing.

"Show me some hips," he said. I tried to remember the lesson with Jill and re-create the feeling of getting my hips into the ride. I caught a wave, moved my feet toward the back of the board, and managed to turn parallel to the break. I maintained it for about half the ride in before I pitched off. I retrieved the board and paddled back to Roger, who waited. "Good improvement, a good ride. I'll have to leave you alone more often."

"I was hardly alone," I said. "It was Jill's idea."

"Well, it was a good one. I was surfing a month before I could cut a wave, nice going."

"It's all about baseball," I said. "I'll explain it in my notes." Roger took the next wave into shore with a perfect ride.

There was no more instruction, and I managed a few more good rides, a couple all the way to a finish. I could feel the improvement for the first time. It helped to think of living up to a published article in *Surfing* magazine. Roger waved me into the beach, his former girlfriend at his side. I caught a wave in with the intention riding it all the way in but pitched off halfway through. Oh well, it was still an improvement.

I said hi to Jane, who said, "Mom's waiting to see you." *She must like me,* I thought as we walked to her house. *That's three times.*

Inside, Jane handed me a jelly jar of cream sherry and bid me to tell about my last two days. I skipped my meeting with Pam and her cautions against Pineys and the Jersey Devil, but told them of my research on the Pine Barrens in anticipation of the trip. Jill didn't go upstairs to shower and change as usual but stayed down to listen. "Where's Richard?" I asked, and I was told that he had to return early as he doesn't like to drive in the dark. I wondered briefly if the Jersey Devil extended as far as Bethlehem, Pennsylvania. *After Mike, one can't be too careful.*

Everyone present seemed to be interested in my findings. And all had a take on the Jersey Devil. Jane had the most interesting comment. "When we were children, our parents threatened us if we stepped too far out of line they would call the Jersey Devil, who would take us away. We all believed in it." She finished with the word "creepy." Everyone, believers or not, ended their accounts with that word, creepy. Something to remember in my fiction.

I described my impressions driving through the town of Chatsworth, of the wooden planked bar, of Joseph the bartender, of the five state troopers and their three cars outside, of the shuffleboard game Mike and I had with Roy and Bobby. I told them of my subsequent conversation with Roy about the two missing college students out looking for a pink lady slipper orchid. During my telling, Jane filled my jelly jar twice, as she did hers. I told them of my conversation with Joseph that validated everything told to me by Roy.

It struck me that I hadn't realized until just then that Roy and Bobby were the last two people to have seen the two hunters before they went missing. If they were dead, the last two to see them alive. I felt a shiver down my spine. I told them of the Black guys who entered the bar to buy pint bottles of moonshine gin, how they left with brown paper bags but didn't stay to drink at the tables. Told them of Joseph's explanation that they were the descendants of runaway slaves, stuck pretty much to themselves and did not routinely mix with others. And of my interest in finding out more about them and perhaps writing something.

I described buying the cases of beer and Joseph's serious warning not to stop along the roadside, and of Mike's passionate pleas to stop the car and pee. Roger laughed uproariously and clapped from his regular corner. I told the story of how Eddie ultimately relented along a woodland road, and of Mike's insistence of sighting the Jersey Devil standing in a bog. Roger now had tears in his eyes, and I was feeling I had betrayed Mike and my promise not to write about it. Even though I was not writing it, I felt bad. I blamed it on the cream sherry. Jane filled my jar again, equaling my previous record. I continued with Ed's contention that Jersey Devil's cry was a screech owl and what Mike saw in the bog was a heron. I tried to mitigate my betrayal with Mike's consultation of a bird atlas and this morning's admission that what he saw was probably a great blue heron.

Under the influence of the cream sherry, I was verbose, and continued to tell them of Susan Saunders' article in the Camden newspaper, and how I was interested in the story and using it as a short story subject. Roger said he knew Susan, that I could use his name if I contacted her. "She did a story on me, and we got to be friends," he said.

Jane, the sister, said, "Oh, that's nice, a woman that it's safe to still use your name with." Roger ignored her.

"I don't know how I can get in touch with her," I said. "I work all day and only have Saturday off, and I don't have a telephone. My Aunt Clair has one, but she's never around to answer it, and Aunt Ibby doesn't have one."

Jane said I could use their phone, and she'd be around to take a message. I thanked her and said I'd check out the paper the next day.

"Give her a call tomorrow and tell her you're interested in the

SHE MUST LIKE ME

story and to keep you appraised," Roger said. Then, after a little thinking, he said, "Tell her you're nearby and you might be available to do a little legwork. Journalists are always looking for people to do legwork for them."

"I don't even have a way to get there. I don't think I'd be much use," I said.

"If anything turns up we could drive down together on Saturday. I'd like to see Susan again," Roger said.

"AHHH!" Jane expelled.

29

Squirrels vs Ducks

Roger, changing the subject, said, "Jimmy, it seems you have a number of potential irons in the fire. Missing orchid hunters, Black gin drinkers, not to mention a surfing article. You might want to limit your focus." I could see his point.

Jane jumped in with, "And remember the resolution of *Pablo's Cock*." It was something I'd not thought much about—at all, actually. "Multiple options at the same time aren't the problem for a fiction writer that they are for a journalist," she said. Roger conceded the point.

Jill, now restless, suggested we go for a walk, and I was glad to accept. "Take off your shoes, and we'll walk along the water," she said as we prepared to leave the house. It was our first walk as boyfriend and girlfriend, and we held hands, stopping periodically to kiss. It was nice. It was easy and surprisingly comfortable. We walked out onto the jetty and followed it into the ocean while the surf broke around the sides. I was all talked out, but Jill seemed content. We held each other at the end of the jetty, the surf breaking at our bare feet. It was a good image—romantic.

We threaded back up the slippery stones to the beach and settled down on the sand, the sound of the surf as the background to our words. "Are you really going to write about all those things?" she asked.

"I don't know. I'd like to. I plan to, but sometimes I'm not sure

I'm up to it," I said, expressing vulnerability, then getting hold of myself. "Yeah, I'm going to do it." Hubris to the rescue.

"Atta boy!" she said, smiling her ironic smile, tongue lapping up the boy. She was lying on her back, and I bent down and kissed the lisp. We spent time petting, exploring each other, tentatively at first, then with more confidence. It was pretty innocent stuff but exciting—a good first date.

We spent an hour groping, then returned to the house. There, I said, "I should say goodnight to your mother."

"She'll be OK," Jill said. "Plenty of time tomorrow."

I collected my shoes and left Jill at her front porch and walked the twenty minutes home. I took the paved road, thinking of both Roger's caution about having too many projects and Jane's view that a fiction writer should maintain a cache of future stories. What should be my approach—a squirrel stashing away nuts for a fallow winter, or become a ducks-in-a-row kind of guy? The distinction seemed clear. Never before having adopted a ducks kind of approach, I'd throw my lot in with the squirrels.

Though trivial, the rumination carried me home. I had promised Roger a writeup of my *hips* notes, so I went from thinking about writing to actually doing some. It felt good to bring it to physical action. I was worked up from my time on the beach with Jill and put that energy into my account of the trip to Chatsworth, the missing orchid hunters, and my promise to leave a message for Susan Saunders. I was intrigued with Roger's offer to travel with me to do some possible legwork and research in the Pine Barrens.

Then, keeping my promise, I unwound as I wrote out the hip notes on the old Underwood. The surfeit of whiteout scattered like a snowstorm in the light of my desk lamp and rested on the keys. I spent considerable time on the baseball analogy, relating it to the earlier simile of an anchor attached from my left foot extending through the underside of the surfboard, and adding stability. I emphasized the exhilaration of cutting parallel to the wave and the confidence it gave you.

I spent a little time expounding on the importance that similes and metaphors gave you when learning anything. It deviated from the functional account of learning to surf a bit into the philosophical. I wasn't sure how it would go over with Roger, but I liked it—we could always cut it later. I looked at a clock and was surprised that I had been at it for over two and a half hours.

I fell asleep thinking about the Jersey Devil and the missing orchid hunters. I was nagged by the thought that Roy and Bobby were the last to see the young couple. Again, I slept poorly and was up early. I walked to Flo's and bought the Camden newspaper, but I found nothing. I ordered a breakfast sans the Bromo seltzer. I paid the check and left the last of my coins for Flo as a tip. I now had no money until I was paid Friday. I literally couldn't buy a piece of bubblegum until then. I met Eddie at the beach and started my second week of employment. A lot seemed to have occurred during that first week.

As it turned out, I was a better surfer than I was a lifeguard. I had trouble deciding whether someone needed help or was just playing in the water. I would become more competent, but never in my estimation did I become a truly good guard. Still, as the days passed, I grew to be more proficient.

One time, however, I was truly embarrassed when Eddie took off his whistle and threw it, hitting my chest to alert me to a little girl who was having trouble in the surf. The incident bothered me for days, though Eddie tried to make me feel better, saying it happens, that all guards are alerted by their partners. I seriously contemplated quitting, but Eddie talked me out of it, saying, "It happens to all of us." I tried to believe him, but not once did I have occasion to alert him. Anyway, it never happened to me again, but still I had trouble deciding if someone was drowning.

30

Fish Food

As the days passed, I grew closer to the Deriksson family, spending a good part of my evenings with them after surfing. Jill and I would take walks on the beach that invariably ended in *making out*. When we returned, I would spend time with Jane, drinking cream sherry and talking about writers and writing, sometimes well into the night. She acknowledged my article with Roger but pushed me to account for my fiction writing even in its formation stage. One night, she probed me about my high school experience. I told her again about my trick of the variable-unit class that allowed me to graduate on time. And she said I should write it as a short story, and I said I'd try. I remembered that Richard had suggested the same thing.

I came up with a title: The *Art of Cool*. And in the end, I melded two stories into one. Jane and I would take considerable time discussing it. It was the first time anyone really took me seriously as a fiction writer, giving me their time and thought. Although Jane wasn't a writer, she was a reader and thinker, giving a lot of thought to her writers and their work. I imagined her a kind of Gertrude Stein. And a lot of cream sherry flowed past that story. I first wrote the autobiographical story of how I came to miss a month of school and not get caught. It centered on a character I called Tory Schweitzer, my high school friend Tony, who was the coolest kid there. The story focused on how he schools his awkward friend, the narrator (me), in the *Art of Cool*. Tony, or Tory, initiated the ploy by asking for a library pass from our first-period study hall. We would check in with the librarian, then discreetly walk out of the back and to his old station wagon parked nearby, drive to a pool hall, and hang out there until lunchtime, enter back through the library, eat lunch, and attend the last afternoon class. For me, it was English, the least odious of my courses. Since attendance was taken first period and after lunch, we never showed up on the absence list. We continued to fly under the school's radar, and our truancy was not discovered until my mother called the school, needing to speak to me. Our scheme blown, we were sequestered to spend our next two weeks of school in the office of the boys' dean, writing codes.

Codes were typed pages taken from various sources. Code 1 was one page long, used primarily for such crimes as not fully tucking in your shirttail or hair that was a bit too long (there was order in those days). Code 2 was two typewritten pages. As infractions became more serious, the codes got longer. Code 6, for example, was six pages long. Codes progressed to Code 11 (I guess they liked to end with prime number), which was eleven pages long. Tory's and my sentence was Codes 1 -11, three times. The material for the codes was taken primarily from literature, but the most amazing thing was that the content never repeated. There were endless versions of Code 3 or Code 10. I never found out who devised the punishment, though I asked several times, but it was a system created by someone with a brain, for the substance of the codes was brilliant.

Somehow in all my punitive school history, I had avoided contact with the code system, but now, put together, we took to each other like a bull elephant seal to his harem. I was now required to copy parts of Thoreau's *Walden*. A good part of it was the subject of different codes; I bet I copied a good third of the book. There was Twain, and not just *Tom Sawyer* and *Huckleberry Finn* (which I think is the best book in the world), but *Life on the Mississippi* and *A Tramp Abroad*. There was even part of a Kafka, short story, *A Hunger Artist* (who is responsible for this? I wondered). The Kafka story so absorbed me that I went out and bought a book of his short stories to finish it. I was introduced to the philosopher-psychologist Will James. Up till now, my high school had fed me fish food (got that from Harper Lee). I now was allowed real food, and it was wonderful!

My days rolled by. I sat at a little desk along the wall of the boy's dean's office, happily copying the code in front of me and anticipating the next one. Two weeks were almost over, and I was midway through my last series of codes. I was terrified that this was all about to end.

The system required that after completing two codes, I would have to account to the prefect, in the persona of the boys' dean, go in and explain the things I'd copied and tell what I'd learned from them. I had an idea that I thought might extend the time. The boy's dean had the graphic name of Mr. Meanen (I always wanted to use the name in a story), looked a bit like Humphrey Bogart, dressed like him, too, and thought of himself as clever, as he exposed the petty crimes of his student body. On one occasion when I had to account for my performance, I let it slip that I had not cheated by skipping any of the essay I was to have copied. Thumbing through the sheets of my longhand versions, he gave me a suspicious look. "We'll see," he said.

In fact, I had skipped two pages. I figured I'd make it easy the first time. It was Code 7 or 8, and of course he soon found it. Delighted to have caught me in an infraction, he smiled condescendingly. "You'll have to write this over again."

"The whole code?" I said in outrage. He thought for a minute.

"The whole series," he said. *God*! I thought. *This is too easy.* I left his office trying to look contrite and disgruntled. I repeated the ploy over the next week and a half, dragging my feet, until even Meanen caught on. But I had extended the two-week period to just under a month.

All of this led up to the encounter, described earlier in this story, where I was informed in a meeting convened by the vice principal and my counselor that due to my truancy I would not be able to graduate on time, coming up a single unit short.

My comment on the irony of a punitive action that extended my absence from classes for about a month didn't help my case, only transforming condescension into wrath. I backed off immediately and deployed alacrity. I let them know that the proposed punishment wasn't as odious as they thought. I alerted the dean through my magnanimity to the fact that although I would have to suffer through an extra semester of high school, he, too, would have to suffer me for a similar time. Thinking only punitively, he had not considered the effect on himself. When confronted with the faux cheerfulness of my response, and the cost to the boys' dean, the two men came up with the variable-unit strategy that allowed me to graduate.

31

Cleverness Redux

I wrote out the story in pieces, emphasizing Tory's instruction in the *art of cool* and Jane and I talked out each one. Over the next week, Jane, the daughter, was off on her American Airlines duties, staying in Chicago with husband Charles. Jill was involved in a summer camp for youth surfers that extended to workshops in the evenings. With Jane away, Roger stopped over less frequently. I was left pretty much on my own, but I continued to surf after work. Jan, the younger brother, ate, came and went, absorbed in his life with his friends. This left Jane and me alone for large portions of the evenings.

Over considerable cream sherry, we fashioned a tale that described the lead-up to the climax of the *variable unit*. Jane said she liked the character Tory Schweitzer and how he was a model for the narrator as he advanced toward *cool*. "It's a clever story, Jimmy, as was *Pablo's Cock*." I took this as a complement. "But," she continued, "clever is not always a good thing in fiction. Most stories don't wind up like Agatha Christie novels, tied up neatly with no loose ends—life is loose ends. When you try to blunt those loose ends, you weaken the story. Ambiguity is OK, but irony's better. Irony is kind of a mixture between tied-up-in-a-bow clever, and loose ends that makes the reader think." I remembered her criticism of the unresolved ending of *Pablo's Cock*; that the story relied a bit too much on clever.

Her words washed over me like a cold shower. I'd always thought of clever as a good thing. Now, beginning to understand the lesson that was being taught, I was uncertain.

I thought of the ending of *Pablo's Cock*, and Jane's criticism that I left it hanging. I actually shivered. Confronted again with my cowardice, I thought of Karen. I took a drink of cream sherry, it didn't help. Later, I would tell myself that the effect was so strong since I had always suspected it.

"What should I do?" I asked her. As if I were a seven-year-old asking her to explain organic chemistry.

She answered me with a question. "Where did the idea to fight the threat of failure to graduate with goodwill and a false alacrity come from? To turn the punishment back on the boy's dean. It's a clever strategy, but I believe there's an underlying irony that will make a competent story into a really good one." The Gertrude Stein of the Jersey Shore left me with a challenge.

It took me a day of exploring my past to come up with an answer. The trick turned out to be understanding the word *clever*. As I said, I'd always thought of clever as a good thing, a thing to shoot for in a story. But Jane used it as something less than complimentary, a trick even—shallow. Upon examination, clever seemed to me to be a hollow word—one without substance. It was not an inherent quality of itself. Clever was a word used to modify something else—something deeper—best used as an adjective, and not a noun. In the *Art of Cool*, the cleverness was about a trick, a clever trick, that caused Dean Meanen to reflect on the impact to himself of keeping *me* in school, and his ultimate decision that it wasn't worth it. The effect of the trick was that the narrator found his way out of a potentially catastrophic situation. My story was clever, but where did the trick come from? How did it get there? What was its substance?

I tried hard to find the inspiration. Did the *cool* used to keep hold of my panicked heart came from Tony, or Tory? Then I chanced across the Chief. The Chief was a Papago Indian, a pool shark and hustler who was the boyfriend of a young woman in our neighborhood, Lucy Romero.

My mother needed to have an operation, requiring a week's stay in the hospital, and hired Lucy to cook and generally keep me out of trouble in her absence. I took breakfast and dinner in the Romero home, and thus I came in contact with the Chief—and we just hit it off. I ditched school unbeknownst to Lucy and hung out with the Chief, who educated me in the art of the hustle. I went with him to various pool halls and other sites of his hustles, like card games in the backrooms of various bars.

At each place, the Chief instructed me in the finer points of the hustle. His best lesson came while we were sitting at the bar of the Aunty Ramos Pool Hall one Friday night. Lucy thought we were at the movies. One of the Chief's favorite hustles originated with the *Gillette Friday Nights Fights*, a telecast of boxing matches, ostensibly live. The chief knew that there was a short time delay between the actual fight and when it was aired in Tucson. He would call and find out the result and hustle people at the bar to make a bet on the fight. His first lesson was that you can't win every time, even if you knew the winner—especially if you knew the winner. So, he often bet on the loser and exhibited a good deal of emotion during the fight, but goodwill to the winner, lauding him for his acuity. The best fights, however, were when the underdog won in a close match. On these occasions, the Chief would let his mark choose to bet on the loser and reluctantly bet on the underdog, but not before he insisted on odds.

Throughout the match, the bet would be gently increased until the final result. In this, the Chief was also gracious, admitting that he had been lucky and had just got excited. The match I had watched, he had lost. This was before he enlightened me and I was surprised, since he had known the winner beforehand. "If you win every time, no one will bet with you," he explained. "The hustle is a long game. It's like earning a salary. You make your money over time."

Then came the golden rule of the hustle, as he called it. "Both winner and loser must get something positive out it. If you win the bet, you get the money, but the loser must come away thinking that he played the game better, and you just won by luck."

Both winner and loser must gain something, and that something is in the clever, which in the end makes clever superfluous. Substitute the word art. That's what the story was missing! The art of cool was the art in clever. I'm not sure that the Chief's wisdom was the source of my inspiration with Meanen and the *variable unit*, though the Chief did predate Tory, but it worked in the story. Both, Meanen and I got something out of the interaction, and we both came out winners. And this was fiction, after all. It wasn't a just a clever trick, it was spawned by wisdom, by a philosophy.

It took little to inject the Chief and his lessons into the story, what with pool halls and all. And as time went by, I even convinced myself that this was how it actually happened—fiction is like that.

I wrote out the story with the lessons of the Chief and showed it to Jane. We were alone that evening. She smiled a deep smile, said she liked it, refilled my cream sherry jar and kissed me after I read it to her. It was a most important lesson for the young writer. It was a lesson about the potential hollowness of words and how to fill them up with irony.

32

Cardboard, a Linebacker,
and Holes in the Sand

I t took several weeks for the *Art of Cool* to write itself to the end. Meanwhile, back to my second week on the beach. On Tuesday, I called up Susan Saunders before surfing and was surprised to reach her. It was easier than I'd expected, as Roger had already alerted her, and she was expecting my call. She said that there was nothing new from the state troopers, and the orchard hunters were still missing. Said that she'd like to meet Roger and me at Leeds Point on Saturday if that was all right.

"I want to interview the two that had seen the students last, and they both live around Leeds Point." I knew from my research that Leeds Point was the birthplace of the Jersey Devil. Also called the Leeds Devil.

Susan continued, "I'm told you've already established a relationship with them that could be helpful." She also said that she would let me know if anything emerged in the meantime. We hung up, agreeing to meet on Saturday at a restaurant called the Oyster Creek Inn in the heart of the town at ten o'clock. I figured this would be all right with Roger, since he'd probably set up the meeting to begin with.

After I hung up with Susan, I took the cat to the beach and surfed by myself for an hour and a half, then returned to Jane's, where we drank cream sherry and continued to thrash out the *Art of Cool*. She said Roger had called and had some news about the surfing article and he'd tell me at the beach the next day. At the end of our session, Jill returned from her workshop, and we took a walk on the beach.

I was still suffering depression from the *whistle-girl* incident the next day at the beach, but something happened that afternoon that made me, at least briefly, forget about it. Chris Mackee made his perfunctory visit about four o'clock. Ed was out making his rounds of the beach, and Chris was forced to talk to me. He asked me how things were going, if I'd had any runs. I said a couple, nothing out of the ordinary. Then he asked me if Eddie had been showing up on time. "I've been showing up on time," I said, "and Eddie's always here before me, so I would assume he's here on time." Mackee took this as a smart-ass response to his probe. But by then, Eddie was back from his patrol. "What's up?" Eddie asked. "The flags at the right distance?"

Mackee ignored his question. "Just want to inform you that there will be a drill tomorrow at the start of your shift."

"Just like every Thursday?"

"Yeah, but this time it'll be under supervision."

"We'll be sure to give you a lesson. Watch closely," said my hero.

Again, Chris Mackee left without a word, spinning all four of his tires.

This time, as he was moving over the narrow strip of beach at the end of the jetty, we heard an angry yelling. We both turned to see Mackee's Scout stopped at the jetty and a large man pulling Chris out of the jeep. "You almost hit my kid, you son of a bitch." We, of course, were hoping the man would hit Mackee as he danced on one leg as he tried to maintain his balance. Rather than a hit, the large man shook the diminutive Chris Mackee as the little boy looked up smiling (maybe I made the smile up), but the man's anger was real. "You must be crazy to drive that fast in an area where people are walking. I'm going to report you to the township." He gave Chris another shake and pushed him back toward his Scout. Chris mumbled something that seemed wisely not provocative but drove away at a similar speed as the man shouted after him.

Eddie clapped and said, "We should really do something about that guy."

"Like what?" I asked.

"We have a campfire tonight. You should come. A lot of lifeguards will be there, and we can discuss it. I'm bringing a case of the beer we bought at Chatsworth. It's at the beach near my house, 33rd Street.

"Bring one of mine," I said.

Eddie smiled. "Right on."

The large man who confronted the wayward Scout driver and his young son were now in the water in front of us. I can guarantee that no one on the beach was ever supervised more closely, I can tell you that. At the end of the day, Eddie and I moved back the stand and took the buoy, the first aid kit, and the flagpoles to his car. We agreed to meet at the campfire at dark. I went to Jane's to retrieve *my* cat, which I now referred to as Tabby, and set out for another solo surfing session. Midway through, I saw Roger paddling out to me.

"Sorry, I planned to be here earlier. Good to see you doing it on your own, though."

"Jane said you had some news about our article?"

"Yeah, I'll tell you later. Let's surf," he said as he caught the next wave, and I was right behind, cutting the wave and managing to stay atop my board to the shore. Roger was already paddling back, having learned to exit his ride and catch his board under his arm before it washed to the shore. Not having learned that technique, or even tried it really, I needed time to retrieve Tabby and paddle back out. I sat on my board next to him and waited for his next move.

"It's good news, but I want to tell you in front of Jane." *Everyone seems to function as a current pushing me toward Jane*, I thought. Roger caught an incoming wave, and I was left to wonder why. I began to worry that I was becoming an object of a pissing contest between Jane and Roger concerning whose protégé I was. *Is protégé a monogamous relationship?* The thought was lost in the next wave, a particularly big one. Still, I managed to ride it most of the way in. Roger was waiting for me

"You're really coming along, Jimmy," he said. "Let's catch a few more, then go to the house."

Under the compliment, my surfing suffered. My next ride was a wipeout pretty early on, while the next one was little better. Roger lasted about three-quarters of an hour. I had some better rides but didn't achieve my previous proficiency.

At Jane's, after drinks were made and cream sherry jars were filled. Roger said, "I liked your hip notes, baseball, and the importance of metaphor. I read it to my editor at *Surfing*. He liked it too, and said the next edition of the magazine was slanted toward the younger surfer, said they had to table an article originally slated for the edition and our article would be perfect for it. Usually, it takes months for an article to appear. He's saving space for twenty-five hundred words and room for a photo. So we need to get him a first draft. Like yesterday."

Jane expressed pleasure with her words but didn't show it in her eyes. I, on the other hand, was over the moon.

Roger took out a few pages from a folder under his chair and handed them to me. "I've done a rough draft of what we've got from your notes and gave it some context. Read it and see what you think, make corrections and observations, get it back to me as quick as you can, we'll work up the next one and get it to *Surfing*. I think we've got about a week to send it to them and integrate their recommendations."

"Do you think I'm ready? I mean, as a surfer, to write this article?"

"After today's mixed bag of rides? Yes, I think you're authentic." he said. I was over the moon.

At this point, Jill walked in. "What's goin' on?" In her Jersey accent it was more like, "Wa's gowin owun?"

Jane answered, "Jimmy's about to be a published author, awuthor," and she gave Jill a synopsis of our conversation. Jill squealed, then came over and kissed me on the cheek. I was embarrassed, but it felt good, too.

I told them about the Chris Mackee drama with the father and son, and about this night's upcoming bonfire on the beach where we'd discuss what to do about Mackee.

"I want to go," Jill said.

"So do I. I've hated that little bitch since I first met him," Roger said. It was almost dark when the three of us left for the 33rd Street beach.

Though not quite dark, a number of people sat around a large fire. Eddie saw us and waved us down. The only other person I knew was Mike Evers, but I recognized faces from the first meeting at the township building—both men and women. Some of the assembled came over and greeted Roger and Jill, and we took our place around the fire. I sat between the two, Jill sat close to me, I thought to let people know that I belonged. Many stared at me, and the most benign expressions asked, "Who the hell is this guy?" Eddie seemed to notice and said, "The guy next to Jill is Jimmy. He's my fellow guard at the 29th." The stares mostly loosened up, turning to smiles and nodding heads, and I nodded back. A muscular young man reached over Roger to shake my hand and introduced himself as Bob Worm. People continued to arrive until we were two concentric half-circles around the fire.

Eddie remained standing, and Bob Worm got up and went to the cases of beer and began to dismantle them, throwing beer cans (no glass containers on the beach) to everyone in the group. Eddie waited until we all had our beers, then began. "Most of you already know about the incident this afternoon with Chris Mackee. For those of you who don't…" Eddie provided the group with a description of the action. "That's what Jimmy and I observed," he added, nodding over to me "Anything to add?" he asked me. People's faces turned to me for the second time, and I just shook my head.

"Articulate," Jill said under her breath with her ironic smile and a lap of her tongue. She squeezed my hand. The strength of the flames thankfully hid my blush—I hoped.

Eddie continued. "Mike Evers has some additional information. Mike…"

Mike stood. "I was in the township after work, getting new assignments since a number of guards have taken sick lately," began the itinerant guard. "So I was down in Lifter's office in front of his secretary. There was a man in his office, and even though the door was shut, I could hear them. The man was yelling about Mackee almost hitting his son with his Jeep, that he was driving way too fast and was a hazard to everyone on the beach. He said that he should be fired immediately or he was going to do something. Lifter tried to calm him down, but the man wouldn't calm and went on yelling. I looked at the secretary, whose eyes were as big as clam shells. 'He's a linebacker for the New York Giants,' she said, 'I heard him say so.'"

"I told you he was big," I whispered to Jill.

Evers continued. "After more yelling, the man came out of Lifter's office and slams the door. Slams it hard. I left. Figured I wouldn't bother Lifter until morning."

Eddie took over. "Let's throw it open to discussion," he said.

A short, muscular guard by the name of Bataglia stood up and said, "Lots of people complained before, nothin' ever happened."

A girl sitting in the first row said, "Not a Giants linebacker, though." The group laughed. The girl's name was Amy Trinket, and I would come to know her.

"I think it's gone beyond complaints. We need some action," Bataglia continued. This suggestion was greeted with cheers, yeahs, and waves of nodding heads.

"But what?" said someone behind me in the second circle.

A female guard still in her uniform stood and said, "Lets strike 'em, till they fire the guy." This raised some applause, and a discussion followed. In the end, it was deemed simultaneously both too radical and too passive.

Another idea was that we could just stop listening to him, ignore him, and not do anything he says until he just went away.

I responded that this was somewhat of an optimistic strategy. "Eddie's already doing it, he just ignores him and drives away."

Bataglia spoke up again. "What we should do. We should dig some deep holes in the sand in the narrow area behind the jetty. He'd have to slow down then."

Someone ventured, "He'd see them and just avoid them."

"Not if we put cardboard over them and cover them with sand," the quick-thinking Bataglia said.

Everybody liked the idea, until someone said, "Won't the people going to the beach get caught in the trap?"

Discussion halted for a minute while we thought this over, until Eddie responded. "Mackee's due to do a supervised observation of Jimmy and me early tomorrow morning. If we do it tonight, Mackee will be there first thing. Once he drives through the holes we make, it will be apparent to the beachgoers what the situation is." Roger stood and applauded, and everyone else followed. It was decided that we would form two crews: one to shovel out the holes, and one to gather the cardboard and meet on the 29th Street beach.

Eddie and I were on the cardboard detail, Roger and Bataglia would form the shovel squad. Jill said she wanted to go with us. Roger handed Eddie the keys to his Volkswagen, saying their cars are the same size but his convertible would make it easier to transport large pieces of cardboard. After a few more beers, the two crews left the rest at the fire. Eddie opened up another case of beer, looked over to me, winked, and said, "Yours."

We drove behind a furniture store called Needles and found plenty large boxes big enough to ship refrigerators or couches. We dissembled them into panels and stuffed them into the backseat with Jill, thinking twelve panels should be enough. We met the shovel crew at 29th. The crew, now made up of about eight people, had dug four deep holes in two rows in the narrow strip between the sand fence and the jetty. Our cardboard panels proved large and strong enough to hide holes when covered by sand. We looked at our work and marveled with anticipation. A few voiced disappointments that they wouldn't be there to witness the result of their handiwork. Bataglia, the author of the intervention, was the loudest. Eddie said, "Don't worry, Jimmy's a writer, and he'll write out an account for you." As it turned out, I would not put anything in writing, but I would get to know Gino Bataglia and like him a lot.

Before we left, Roger took out some short strips of yellow tape, the kind used in police barricades, and tacked them into the sand with some sticks taken from the surrounding foliage. "Chris won't see it, but early-morning walkers might," he said. We all took one last look. With nothing left to do, we waited for the morning.

33

Four Holes, Four Wheels

The next morning, Ed and I were early on the beach. Our motto was *Thrash Like MFs*, and put on a show for Mackee. Show him what it meant to be a lifeguard.

Mackee, right on time, stood legs apart, hands on hips, a stance meant to show just who was boss. Ed rescued first, and I swam out about thirty-five yards, a good ten yards farther than usual. Eddie swam out, rope over his shoulder, towing the buoy behind. The first thing I did was to go underwater, forcing Ed to go down and get me. I came up thrashing, true to our prepared motto. I refused to be transferred to the buoy and be towed in, making it necessary for Ed to put me in a hard-fought chest carry. I kept thrashing back and forth, slipping off his hip. In the end, I was hauled onto the sand and deposited like a wet paper bag.

Not stopping to rest, Eddie swam out probably forty yards, and that was just the beginning. When I approached him, he began by throwing punches that I blocked and parried. Moving away from me, he made it hard to grab his wrist, turn him around, and put him in a chest carry, all the while throwing punches at me and twisting away. I took a slight blow to the nose, and Ed backed off a little, allowing me to approach and put him in the carry. He bucked up and down on my hip like a piston all the way to shore. When we got to the shore, we both stood at rigid attention, also according to plan, and looked at our astonished supervisor, who stood with his mouth open. It was a few seconds before he said, "A bit rigorous, don't you think, Lambert?"

"Just showing you what good lifeguards do." From his position of attention, Eddie could have added "sir" but didn't, but the intention was complete. Mackee ignored the sarcasm and turned to me with some sarcasm of his own.

"You got a bloody nose there," he said casually.

Resisting the urge to confirm this with a swipe of my hand, I said, "All part of the show," then I added "Sir!" as an exclamation point on our statement." Eddie snickered, and Mackee pretended not to hear. Wordlessly, he turned his back to us and walked toward his mount.

"We hear you've been told to slow down after yesterday's incident," Ed said, in a parting shot. It was a guess, but it turned out to be a good one. Mackee stiffened his back but continued to his Scout, roaring off with four wheels spinning clouds of sand. What happened next became legend—an oral history of the Island, since nobody wrote it down.

We looked on in rapture as Chris Mackee's wheels, spitting rooster tails of sand, homed in on the narrow strip of beach limited by the stone jetty. Our cardboard-and-sand-disguised phalanx was configured like four compartments in an egg carton, each hole about a yard in diameter. Mackee hit the first row going thirty to forty miles per hour. Both wheels must have hit the holes, as his hood dug into the sand and the back end of the car left the beach. He could be seen hitting his head on the roof. The somewhat underpowered but gallant Scout remained running and forged on into the second row of the object lesson. Mackee at this point was out of his seat, holding to the steering wheel like a fish hooked on a line. The hood of the car buried itself in the sand again, and this time the engine died, leaving the stalled Scout with a wheel in each of the four holes. The driver's head rested inertly on the steering wheel, and the horn was blowing.

A small crowd now surrounded the disabled car and driver. Ed and I ran and approached the driver's window. Mackee raised his head, shook it, and it seemed to clear enough for him to engage the ignition, his wheels spun independently, and the horn continued to sound. The wheels moved only a few inches forward before they slipped back into the holes, but Mackee was enough of a driver to throw it into reverse, gaining a little purchase on the back of the depressions before it slipped back down and he could move the vehicle a little farther forward. He continued the process, rocking out incrementally a little each time, until the car was sitting on firm sand.

He gave us a look that could have wilted a hydrangea, spun his wheels, and drove down the beach, the sound of his horn receding in the distance.

Ed looked at me and said, "You're not the only one with a bloody nose—and yours is still straight." He slapped me on the arm, and we returned to the stand to make sure nobody had drowned in the chaos.

34

Up and Down the Lifeguard Wire

I t didn't take long for the event to be broadcast along the island, up the shore and down the bay, then back around. Our telegraph line was activated by Mike Evers, who stopped by the stand shortly after it occurred. He said he had gone into the township to get his assignment, and the guard he was told to replace was on the job. So, walking back to get another, he thought he'd stopped by to see if there'd been any action. We filled his ear, and Mike broadcast it up and down the island on the lifeguard wire. By the time the account traveled back to us, we could hardly recognize the tale, which had been given color in each retelling along the lifeguard line. We just had to wait until we had more facts, and they were a while in coming.

When we were just about to knock off, a Scout cautiously pulled behind the stand. Mackee was not driving. It was another supervisor named Dan. Dan said hi to Eddie, and he introduced himself to me, something Mackee never had done. Dan wore a pith helmet, had a red mustache, and a large nose covered in zinc oxide that glowed white in the lowering sun.

"Just here to tell you that Lifter's called a meeting at the township. Nine o'clock tomorrow. Everybody's to attend," he said without attitude. Eddie probed what it was about, and Dan said that was all he could say.

"Is it about Mackee?" asked Eddie.

"I was told not to say anything about it," Dan said with an embarrassed smile, then he continued making his rounds. He stopped, got out, and walked around the still-open holes. We had removed the carboard and put it in the fifty-five-gallon cans removed by the higher-caste garbage men. The holes were a lot lower as beach goers had been walking through them all day. With the next day's traffic, they'd be gone. We'd just had to wait it out for the next day.

35

End of a Good Day with Nothing to Add

I said goodbye to Eddie, we fist-bumped, and I walked to the Deriksson house. I was glad to see Jill and Roger there. They'd already heard about the incident, and I gave them an unembellished report, which was a little tamer than the ones they had received.

Jane, the mother, said she'd never liked Chris Mackee when he was a lifeguard. "Officious young man," she said. Jill said she observed the incident when she heard the horn. "So, I went to the beach and saw a good part of it." I told them of the meeting planned for the next morning, then we all went surfing.

I left early, as I had planned dinner with Aunt Isobel, who had been tolerant of my erratic schedule. Before I left, Roger and I planned to meet up on Saturday for our trip to Leeds Point to see Susan Saunders. He gave me his tentative rough draft of our article, and I said I'd get it back to him the next day.

Dinner with Ibby was lovely. She had cooked a casserole, and I drank martinis before, and red wine with dinner. Aunt Clair stopped over, saying with my late-night and early-morning schedule she hadn't seen me. She had a martini but declined dinner. Conversation, of course, was about Paris and the Rivera, and I loved the old stories.

A little bit *in my cups,* a phrase of my aunts, I reviewed Roger's take on the whole surfing thing, which was pretty good. He wrote what it was like to be a mentor to a new surfer. It was really a lesson to surfing instructors, saying what you didn't tell your pupil was as important as what you did. "You have to give them opportunities to feel their way through and let them discover things on their own. Comment on what they're doing right and tell them how to make it better rather than tell them to do it differently." Which, I realized, was exactly what Roger had done with me.

He integrated almost all of my notes, writing it in the first person, as I had in my notes. Where I fell out of the first person, he put me back into it. He even cited Jill as the inspiration for the baseball analogy in the *hips* section. I wrote at the bottom of the last page in blue ink:

I tried to add something but I couldn't. Bravo.
I went to bed.

36

Lifter's Meeting

I woke up full of anticipation at six and walked to *my* beach early. I gave Flo's Diner a winsome glance, since I wouldn't have breakfast money until I was paid later in the day. I traveled slowly, then sat on *my* beach and watched the early morning brighten over the waves. I experienced a feeling of calm that was as close as I'd ever come to meditating—though I suspected the shit was about to hit the fan. The offending holes were just ripples now, I observed as I strolled past them to the township building. It was a good hour before the meeting, and I sat on one of the benches that surrounded the deck, longing for a to-go cup of Flo's coffee, and watched the various township employees enter the building. I knew no one but Art Lifter, and he made no eye contact.

Other people started to arrive, some now-familiar faces. I smiled at Amy Trinket, she smiled back, though surreptitious smiles were our only communication. I made eye contact with several of the nighttime revolutionaries, but everyone seemed to keep to themselves. Several supervisors had arrived and settled together around the main door of the building. I knew none of their names, with the exception of Dan, but could tell they were supervisors from their jerseys that displayed *Supervisor*. (Astute, eh?) This group seemed nervous and stuck together, moving like a herd of cattle before a slaughterhouse gate. Mackee was not among them. The porch filled up until there was little space between any of us. Roger worked his way through the crowd and sat beside Eddie and me. He held a reporter's notebook with a poised pen, making it clear he was there in an official capacity representing the *Islander* news rag.

When it appeared that the deck would burst its surrounding railings, Art Lifter exited the door. It seemed impossible, but the crowd moved away, creating a little space around him. It was a moment before he spoke, as he looked around at all those assembled.

"Yesterday we had an incident that has caused me shame, brought shame to our island community. Chris Mackee was injured in an act of sabotage and spent the night in the hospital. The people who engaged in this incident *will be* caught and punished."

Punished? We probably saved the health of countless beachgoers, I thought. Probably fifty of the hundred people assembled could have ratted most of us out, but no one said a word.

I'd never thought of Mike Evers as a particularly courageous guy, but his next words caused me to reconsider. "We heard Mackee had a run-in with a New York Giants linebacker for almost hitting his kid while driving on the beach. Do you think the Giants might be behind the incident?" We were all trying to look contrite, but a few snickers escaped our collective lips.

If Lifter could have breathed fire, Evers would have been ash. The words came as if Lifter were chewing them. He then spit them out. "I met with Mr. Taylor, about the *alleged* incident, and we disposed of it at my office. There was nothing further." Lifter stared at Mike. Roger, doing his best to mitigate the danger to his friend, spoke up. He stood on the bench so that he looked directly at Lifter over the crowd.

"Roger Axxst, representing the *Islander*. This is the first time I've heard of this. What was the incident, and the man's name is Taylor? Is he, in fact, a New York Giants linebacker?"

Lifter was quiet for an awkward few moments while he temporized. "I'll meet you after the meeting, Roger. And as I said, the incident's been resolved."

The door behind Lifter opened and a short, stout township policeman took his place beside the head of lifeguards. "This is George Mackee," Lifter said. "Most of you know him. He'll be in charge of the assault investigation. George…"

"Assault!" I whispered to Eddie and Roger.

Eddie leaned over to me and whispered, "Mackee's brother."

"Thank you, Art." George Mackee then provided an account of the event, which resulted in a broken nose, a concussion, and a night of observation at a Manahawkin hospital. The broken nose and concussion were news to me. I looked at Eddie, who looked back but remained stone-faced. I took my cues from him and put the brakes on any signs of emotion.

After George Mackee's account of the *crime*, Roger stood again and directed a question, this time to Mackee. "George, doesn't the fact that you're Chris' brother represent a conflict of interest?"

"I'm just conducting the investigation, and I'll report the findings to my superiors. They'll make the final determination."

"Still…" Roger said to himself but loud enough for the crowd to hear. He followed this with, "Is assault the proper charge? Someone dug and covered the holes, but didn't Chris drive too fast over them? In the end, isn't he responsible for his injuries? And wasn't it the fact he was driving too fast that formed both the basis of the complaint by Taylor and the injuries to Chris?" Lifter looked at the reporter as his next candidate for a pillar of fire, turned a bit red, but remained silent. Mackee picked up the baton in the awkward silence.

"Assault doesn't have to be a direct act, but an intent, by arranging a situation to cause harm," he answered, clearly within an area of his expertise.

The meeting did not go as Lifter had anticipated, but he held in his fury and closed the meeting with, "We will be interviewing many of you; if any of you have some information about this, I expect you will come forward to Officer Mackee or to me. Get to your beaches."

The group disbanded and moved slowly off the porch. Roger moved to interview Lifter, and Eddie and I attempted to leave, following the others. As we moved past Lifter and Officer Mackee, Lifter said. "Eddie, we want to speak with you and your partner." *Maybe it's good not to have a name,* I thought. To Roger, he said, "I'll have to meet with you later." It was a terse statement meant to dismiss him.

"When?" Roger pushed.

Lifter, irritated, said, "Try me tomorrow."

"OK, but my first article goes in to the *Islander* today. But I can run the article by you this afternoon."

"Come by at four," Lifter said, still irritated. Roger said he'd be there.

We followed Lifter and George Mackee down to Lifter's office. It was a little crowded with the four of us, and Eddie and I took two folding chairs set against the wall. "The assault happened on your beach," Mackee said. It wasn't a question, so Eddie and I said nothing. Time passed. "Well?" Mackee asked.

"Well what?" Eddie took the lead. I felt like I was back in Dean Meanen's office.

"Variable-unit class," I whispered to myself," but Lifter heard.

"Lambert, if your partner has something to say, tell him to speak up." I suppressed the urge to tell him my name was Jimmy, feeling it might be best to remain anonymous.

"Jimmy and I will speak up, but we have to be asked a question. 'Well' just doesn't cut it." He looked directly at Mackee. It seemed that Eddie's antipathy toward Chris Mackee extended to other members of his family.

My de facto anonymity blown, I spoke up. "I think that Officer Mackee's implied question was: Why did the incident occur on our beach?" I didn't look at Mackee but continued. "I don't know why, but I think the location may have been selected since it was where the incident with the linebacker, his son, and Chris occurred. Eddie and I were privy to each of the events. That's all I know. Ed can speak for himself." I felt I had kept my account just a hair's breadth below the level of smartass.

"I would agree with Jimmy's analysis of why the occurrence of both incidents happened at our beach, because the two incidents are connected. Also, if we had anything to do with an *assault*, as you call it, we probably wouldn't have staged so close to home."

"You don't like Chris, do you, Eddie?" Mackee asked.

"I don't like the way Chris endangers beachgoers through his reckless driving, If he had been driving more carefully, he wouldn't have had the altercation with Mr. Taylor over the safety of his son or received the severity of his injuries driving into the holes." To Lifter, Eddie said, "I've complained about Mackee's driving to you before."

Mackee glared at Ed but didn't comment on the substance of what he said. Rather, he said, "Just before the incident when Chris was injured, you and your partner underwent a supervised observation of rescue procedures by Chris. Can you describe the review?"

Eddie responded. "Yes, we were made aware of the observation by Chris the day before. To be honest, Chris is often overly critical. Jimmy and I decided to put on a demonstration of just what good lifeguards we were. So, our rescue exercise was rigorous. Rather than acknowledging our rigor, he called our performance aggressive. We were just too good, and Chris was offended, and he drove off at his usual high rate of speed."

"You gave your partner a bloody nose in the process, did you not?" Mackee asked.

"It's obvious you've begun your investigation with an interview of your brother. I think Roger's question about a conflict of interest might be right on." Mackee stiffened, making an effort to remain in his seat.

Lifter slammed his open hand on his desk and shouted. "Enough of this pissing contest. Are you both saying you had nothing to do with the incident when Chris was injured?" We both shook our heads and mumbled our innocence, and we were dismissed.

As Eddie and I walked out the front door of the township building, he said. "George Mackee is a lousy officer. Runs in family."

37

An Island Tradition

Despite its tumultuous start, our day at the beach was routine. At four o'clock Dan came by with our first paychecks. At four-thirty, Jill came by the stand holding her surfboard and dragging *my* cat. We acquainted her with the morning meeting and our interrogation. She said that Roger was meeting with Lifter now and would meet us here when he finished.

Just after five, Jill and I were in the water. We caught a few before Roger joined us. Roger and I sat bobbing on the swells, letting potential waves roll by as I told him about Ed's and my time in Lifter's office.

"Did you submit your article after you talked to Lifter?" I asked.

"No, I have another day, I just told Lifter that because I wanted to talk to him today. Besides, we have an early date with Susan Saunders."

"I can't believe Mackee's brother is in charge of the investigation," I said. I then caught the next wave, and rode it into shore. Roger was right behind. We paddled out and sat bobbing on the swells and Roger informed me of something I didn't know.

"Mackee's no longer in charge of the investigation. You and Eddie started it, and Lifter's observation of George in various interviews confirmed that Mackee didn't have the necessary objectivity to lead it. Also, Lifter felt he antagonized those he interviewed. Got that from Shirley, Lifter's secretary. Lifter called the chief and had him replaced. I haven't got word who replaced him. I'll have to confirm it with the chief of the township police before I use it, so I don't expose Shirley. Lifter's a good guy, he's just had the misfortune to be Chris Mackee's godfather." More new info. "Lifter's worried about the sentiment on the Island that Chris got what he deserved. I think we're all right." As he finished, Roger caught a wave.

I put in a fairly respectful surfing session, then we departed for Jill's house. I asked Roger where I might cash my first paycheck before we left for our meeting the next day with the reporter. No problem, he told me. "The local grocery store will cash it. They put on extra cash when township employees get paid. I'll take you down there after we put our surfboards away."

We went inside the house, greeted Jane, and said we were taking a brief trip to the grocery. "I want to go," said Jill, and the three of us left in Roger's Volkswagen.

At the grocery store Roger informed me of a local tradition. "When I was a lifeguard, on payday we would celebrate with a three-pound can of crabmeat and a bottle of red wine, then take our girlfriends for an evening on the beach."

I looked quizzically at Jill, who, mouth open, touched the tip of her tongue on her upper lip and nodded. "Take us to your crabmeat," I said.

I selected an Almaden Mountain red burgundy, Aunt Isobel's go-to, and handed it to Roger with five dollars from my newly cashed paycheck. I grabbed a cheap corkscrew and a pack of two plastic wine glasses for twenty-five cents, and we returned to Jill's.

38

Watershed

Jane, the daughter, was still in Chicago, and little brother Jan was out somewhere with his friends, so it was just the four of us. After drinks were poured, Jane said, "The whole island is buzzing about the Chris Mackee incident." Knowing the whole story, she continued. "You guys need to take care."

"Tell me something I don't know," I quipped.

Jane gave me a stern look, eye contact not wavering. "It's no joke, Jimmy, as absurd as this seems, it's serious." She turned her gaze on Roger. "And you. You're not only a participant but a journalist. I have no idea what ethical lines you may be crossing." She took a long swallow from her cream sherry jar.

Roger, who had donned Jan's orange plastic military helmet, looked ridiculously handsome, two days of dark shadow gracing his face. He smiled. "Jane, the island is mostly happy with what happened to Mackee, the investigation will peter out, we'll be all right. Lifter's already had George Mackee taken off the investigation."

"Lifter's a fair man, but he has a history with the Mackees that goes back a long way," Jane said. "The township is taking the investigation seriously, and there will be hell to pay if they come up with anything. All I'm saying is for all of you to keep your heads down until this all blows over. Do your best to keep arm's length from anything to do with it. That goes for you, too, Jill." A single tear rolled down Jane's cheek.

Roger left his chair and took Jane's hand in both of his, and Jill rose to take her mother's other hand. Under the show of sympathy, Jane broke down. I hadn't moved from my seat, but I was drawn to Jane with a power like magnetism, or gravity—attraction at a distance. I was surrounded in a cocoon by the beauty of this woman. This affection would mark a watershed in my young life and affect everything that has come after.

Jane quickly asserted control of herself, wiped the tears off her face, and refreshed our drinks. To Roger she said, "How far have you come on your article?"

Roger outlined his article: the incident of Mackee's injury, the precursor of the altercation with the linebacker Taylor, the assignment of George Mackee, the question of conflict of interest, and Mackee's ultimate removal as lead investigator. "The article's mostly written. I'm only waiting to talk to Taylor. He's staying with the Fairfields, and I've left word for him to give me a call. If he doesn't before Jimmy and I leave for Leeds Point tomorrow, I'll submit it before we leave. I've written it as an account from Eddie Lambert and Jimmy, who observed the interaction, and Mike Evers, who heard the conversation in Lifter's office between Lifter and Taylor."

"Let's make dinner," Jane said.

"Just for the two of us," Roger said. He explained about the red wine and crabmeat. Jill and I left for the beach.

The setting sun bathed the sky over the waves in a thin orange light. The tide was going out, and we seated ourselves on the dry sand closest to the waves. It was a romantic setting indeed. After some fumbling around, I managed to remove the cork, though it came out in three pieces. No worries. The cork had completed its job. Jill fared more skillfully in opening the crabmeat and freeing the plastic wineglasses. We sat on a large beach towel, sipped red wine, and munched chunks of crabmeat. (Genteel, eh?)

"Your mother was emotional about our involvement in the Mackee affair," I said, opening the topic.

"Yeah, she gets that way sometimes when she feels passionate about something. Often, she has tears in her eyes when she relates something she's read that's touched her."

"Do you think we should be worried?"

"I've learned to take her cautions seriously, if that's what you mean. I think we should just go about our business and leave the investigation alone. The sky is lovely, don't you think?" she said in an example of her advice.

I followed her lead.

"Yes," I agreed. I leaned over and kissed her. But I was thinking of Jane.

The sun went down, the crabmeat was gone, the wine half drunk. We lay back on the beach towel and began to explore. I noticed immediately that Jill wasn't wearing a bra. She had changed into a wool sweater before we left. *This is the first time*, I thought. I made no comment but wondered if this was a kind of rite of passage. The sound of the waves had taken the place of conversation, and our tongues were engaged in a different communication.

The waves and tongues continued their rhythm. I became aware of the tactile difference between the wool of her sweater on the upper part of my hand and the smooth suppleness of her breasts in my palm, like the horizon that divides the sky from the sea.

Jill reached under my trunks and fondled my penis, which had taken on the characteristics of a fallen tree in the petrified forest. Her wet hand continued to stroke as my organ deflated, and I moaned.

Or was that the sound of the wind? She withdrew her hands and licked her fingertips. The flaccid tree petrified again.

On my walk home, I was disconcerted to recall that during our time of ecstasy I had mentally replaced Jill's name with *Jane's daughter*.

39

A Pretty Mature Approach

P er our agreement, Roger picked me up in front of my aunt's complex at nine. Taylor, the linebacker, had called him while Jill and I were on the beach, and Roger had confirmed Mackee's replacement with the chief. He had delivered the finished article to the *Islander* just before he picked me up. "Taylor's account agreed with yours and Ed's, and with Mike's at Lifter's office. He did say that they never agreed on a resolution." Roger said that the article would be in the twice-weekly publication that afternoon. We drove off the island to the town of Manahawkin on the mainland at the other end of causeway, and I was glad to be thinking of things other than Chris Mackee or the petrified forest, even if they were of the Jersey Devil and lost orchid lovers.

We stopped at a little coffee shop on the way. We were early, and the drive was only a little over half an hour. Roger began talking about the article for *Surfing,* which he said was a done deal, that the editor had recommended just a few copy edits, and he had given our approval to change them. I asked him to explain copy edits. "Just commas, punctuation, capitalization, paragraphing, little shit like that." He dismissed them cavalierly.

"Well, I do have a comma problem," I said.

"Who said that?"

"You did. I did."

"No problem. That's why they have copy editors. I wouldn't worry, your writing's fine."

With that vote of confidence, I decided to take a chance. I waited for the waitress to refill our cups. "What happened between you and Jane, the daughter, that is? I think she's the most beautiful woman I've ever seen."

"You think so?" he asked seriously.

"Yeahaa..."

"I do, too. I've thought about it a lot in the past, in the present, too, and I've come up with a number of explanations. The first, and easiest, is that I'm a fuck-up. I'm not responsible enough to be a good partner. Not responsible enough to lead a conventional, responsible life. I'm an arrested adolescent, and Jane's a mature woman. There's a good deal of truth in this view. But I feel it's a little more complex than that. I'm a twenty-five-year-old adult that is engaged in activities that are not entirely adult, or at least in the way I pursue them. I surf not as a diversion but as a lifestyle. I engage in journalism not as a profession but as a diversion, a source of money to continue my lifestyle. These may be viewed as irresponsible—not taking them seriously. And not the stuff from which good husbands are made. The fly in the ointment is the definition of responsibility. But what I've done *is taken* responsibility—consciously—for the decisions I've made. The fact that some people define these decisions as fuck-ups or immaturity doesn't make them less conscious."

Roger shifted gears. "Have you ever read Huckleberry Finn?"

"*Huckleberry Finn* is why I'm a writer," I said, elevating my status.

"Do you recall when Jim and Huck escape to an island and engage in a conversation about signs and what they mean. Huck notes that most signs seem to be about bad things, and he asks Jim if there weren't any good ones. 'Few,' says Jim. 'What you want to do keep them off?' He thinks it over, then says, 'Like if you got hairy arms and a hairy breast it means you're going to be rich.' Huck then asks Jim if he has hairy arms and a hairy breast, and Jim acknowledges that he does. 'Well?' Huck asks, 'are you rich?' Jim's answers that he's been rich before and will be rich again. Then relates how he once had ten dollars and invested in a cow—but the cow died. The runaway slave then pauses and observes, 'Come to think of it, I'm rich now. I owns myself, and I's worth 800 dollars.'"

Roger took on a faraway look.

"That's the final answer, Jimmy: I owns myself, and that worth is so precious that it leads to sacrificing the most beautiful woman in the world. Not because I made a choice, but because that was the choice."

I thought I might have ruined an otherwise gorgeous day. To cut the seriousness that had descended upon us like an ominous shadow, I said, "I wonder how much Jim would be worth today."

Roger's previous dark mood was shed like a wet dog shaking himself, and he exploded in laughter. "That's your next short story, Jimmy. *What would Jim be worth today.* Brilliant." His disposition darkened again slightly. "In the end, Jane engineered a compromise. She married Charles, who's a stable, gentle, and loving man, he provides her with stability, safety, and security. She continues to see me, and I provide color and diversion. Pretty mature approach, don't you think?"

After our third cup of coffee, we peed, then continued to the Oyster Creek Inn, Susan Saunders, and the Jersey Devil.

40

A Scream From the Outhouse

Our route diverged from Highway 72 and the road to Chatsworth, winding through the Barrens. "This seems to be a long way away from Chatsworth," I said.

"It is by the main roads but not as the crow flies. There's lots of backroads through the Barrens."

"You probably really don't want to stop to pee on one of those."

"What?"

"Nothing." I hadn't realized I'd said it out loud.

We drove along a large creek, or small river, until Roger pulled into a parking lot in front of a picturesque rambling wooden structure built on the water. It looked closed, but a few cars were out front.

We found an open door in the back, then wound our way through empty rooms until we reached a bar overlooking the water. We were greeted by a hostess who stood behind a lectern-like thing whose pedestal was a carved wooden figure of the Jersey Devil. We were in the right place.

It was still early, and Roger took a seat at the bar and ordered a beer. I did likewise but was unable to produce an ID at the bartender's insistence, so I ordered a Coke. Roger engaged the tender in a conversation about Leeds Point and Mother Leeds. He was told that the original Leeds house was just down the road but was now only a foundation. Roger continued to mine the bartender for demographic information about Leeds Point, and I got a lesson in how to conduct an interview to gather information. Roger may have been a journalist as a diversion, but he was a real professional.

Roger was getting material about the vocational activities of residents of Leeds Point as Susan Saunders slid onto the stool next to him. He turned from John, the bartender, hugged Susan and introduced me. A history between the two was clear by their embrace. Susan was tall and slim, just an inch or two beneath Roger. She was dressed in jeans and a denim work shirt tied at her waist. Her hair was auburn that edged toward red when the sun hit it; her smile was a bit crooked and infectious.

A solo figure entered the bar, and I recognized Roy O'Malley. He walked tentatively over to Susan and waited to be noticed. She greeted him with a smile. While he shook hands with Susan, he noticed me, smiled, and shuffled over.

"Good to see you again," I said.

"Good to see you, too," he said. Glad, I thought, to see someone he considered a peer, as he took the stool beside me and ordered a beer. The bartender didn't ask him for an ID.

"Where's Bobby?" Susan asked.

"Didn't want to come, said he had some things to do but didn't say what."

Susan waited patiently for Roy to finish his beer while Roger continued his probing of John and conversed simultaneously with Susan.

Susan had interviewed Roy and Bobby at the Chatsworth beer barn but wanted to investigate the location where the two students had last been seen. "Can you take us to where you and Bobby saw the two students?" Susan asked Roy.

Before Roy could answer, Roger intruded. "The foundation of the

Mother Leeds house is nearby. Can you show us that?" He looked over to Susan, who nodded.

"Sure," said Roy, "it's walking distance." Susan paid our tab, and we exited the restaurant and walked down the dirt road that had brought us there. After about a quarter of a mile, we veered off the road to the left and entered a tangled wood. There was no formal path, and we weaved our way through the vegetation reaching out to hinder our progress. The canopy blocked out the direct sun, contributing to the ominous nature of our trek. Our guide, however, seemed to know his way, and we followed. It was probably no more than 200 yards, though it felt a lot longer, before we arrived at a rectangular alignment of foundation stones and low interior walls that marked the outlines of a modest dwelling. In its center was the intact, albeit skeletal, remains of a fireplace constructed of volcanic stones.

Roy pointed to it and said, "That's where the Jersey Devil flew up the chimney." *Flew up the flue,* I thought, as I rubbed the recent scratches on my arms. I noticed that Roy stated it as a historical fact, with no qualification.

Susan quizzed Roy on the history of Mother Leeds and the birth of her thirteenth child, while Roger and I explored the ruin. Despite some broken glass, the site had been picked clean of artifacts. However, I found a piece of a broken plate or saucer, and I wondered if Mother Leeds ever served it with tea or dinner. The fragment was roughly an inch and a half equilateral triangle decorated in yellow and blue. I slipped it into my pocket, adding my part to the almost complete pillage of the ruin. I looked around to see if anyone noticed my theft.

I commented about the absence of any nearby dwellings. Roy answered that when the house was built it was mostly farms, so there was a good amount of land between houses. I nodded at the logic, then closed my eyes and tried to feel what it would have been like in Mother Leeds' time. For some reason, I thought instead about Karen. This seemed to me to be out of context, and I quickly went on to other thoughts.

Throughout, Susan and Roger took notes, as I was stealing pottery. I felt like a rube. We wove our way back through the hostile vegetation and emerged at the dirt road with only a few additional scratches. We had come in Roger's VW, Roy had come on foot, and Susan had borrowed a Jeep from the paper that advertised *Camden Ledger News* on its flanks. So much for anonymity on Pine Barrens backroads.

We all got into the Jeep, Susan behind the wheel, Roy shotgun, Roger and me in the back. All assembled, Susan asked Roy, "Can you take us to the place where you and Bobby saw the two college students?"

Roy guided us through a maze of dirt tracks. Rather than giving Susan directions, he placed his right hand under the review mirror and pointed silently to the path we should follow. At first, I was disconcerted by the procedure, but as I looked out of the windshield, I saw how the tracks branched out into a veritable delta of side roads. Rather than saying, "Take the second from the middle—two from the right," pointing seemed a necessary adaptation to traveling the backroads of the woods between Leeds Point and the Chatsworth beer barn. Either Susan had done this before or she was an incredibly quick study, and we moved on flawlessly.

The paths were so narrow that the aggressive vegetation reached out to claw the sides of our car. "It's a new vehicle," Susan said, "it can use a few scratches to give it authenticity." She expelled a chuckle. "Though the administrator of the motor pool is much harder on the woman reporters than he is for the guys. There'll be hell to pay for that authenticity, I imagine, but fuck him." I was beginning to like Susan Saunders.

We slipped by sundry dwellings to which Roy gave a running account of those inhabiting each, by name and livelihood. "Them's the Williams, they get by gathering moss and making charcoal," he said as we passed one. "Them's the Kerrigans, they're mostly cranberry boggers," he said as we passed another. "There's more houses around here—not as much land around them as there was around the Leeds house."

"Why is that?" asked Susan.

"Leeds home was a farm back when people thought you could farm here. Nowadays, we've learned the land's poor for crops. That is, other than cranberry bogs and blueberry patches, but those aren't really farms anyway. It's why everybody has to hunt to make it through."

"Who owns the land where the Leeds ruin sits?" asked Susan.

"Don't know, really, think it's the county. I know that when people have tried to build near to it they weren't allowed."

Throughout, Roy's index finger compass never faltered. Susan responded accurately until we pulled into a clearing with four or five houses. The number was uncertain as it was difficult to distinguish the actual dwellings from the privies between them. "This is where I live," Roy said, pointing out one of the wooden structures. Pointing to another, he said, "That's Bobby's."

Roy's narrative was halted by a loud scream that seemed to be coming from a freestanding outhouse on the edge of the clearing. We all turned toward to the noise.

"That's crazy Thomas, he's our local hermit. Lives in the woods. We built him that outhouse so he'd leave ours alone. He's harmless, mostly lives off the land—pretty much like all of us, come to think of it," Roy said. Crazy Thomas exited the outhouse, gave us a look, but turned into the pine forest.

"Where's the last place you saw the students?" Susan asked.

"There's a big cranberry bog just down there about a half a mile." Roy pointed down the track that circled the compound. "Saw 'em at the end of the bog."

"Can you take us there?" Susan asked.

"Sure." Roy's finger compass engaged, and Susan followed a short way until we turned off the track. After a few hundred yards we stopped in front of a tangled section of low bushes I assumed to be cranberries in their native state. "From here, we'll need to go on foot," Roy said. "Careful. It's wet and muddy here."

We followed Roy single-file along a narrow path, Susan behind Roy, me behind her, Roger to the rear. Roger had remained quiet throughout our trip, content to take notes. Roy gave us a lecture on cranberries and their attendant bog.

"Mostly cranberry bogs begin as kettle holes," he began with his knowledgeable account. "Water left over from glaciers that filled depressions forming ponds, little lakes, or swamps. The plants themselves grow on a level of moss that makes the water acid. The acid in the soil is what makes farming round here so bad, but the cranberries seem to like it."

We looked out at the expanse of low-slung, vine-like plants, none of which were over two feet high. The branches grew in a close tangle, so it was difficult to identify where one plant ended and a new one began. The landscape was formed by a spreading mat of waxy leaves and white flowers.

"Where are the cranberries?" I asked.

"In the flowers," Roy said, poetically. "The harvest's in the fall."

"How deep are the bogs?" Susan asked a more adroit question.

"Many are waist-deep, but some can be a lot deeper. Our bog was measured at forty feet. Makes harvesting difficult."

"How do you harvest, then?" Susan followed.

"Many just harvest in the shallower parts. Others use rafts or make floating scaffolds to gather in the deeper parts. It's dangerous. If you fall in, you can be trapped under the layer of moss and drown." He added: "The acid in the water stops bodies from decaying, so when we pull 'em out, they look just the same, no matter how long it takes us to find them." Roger, still quiet, scribbled furiously.

I shivered up my spine, imagining the bodies of the students mummifying in the acidic soup underneath a mat of sphagnum moss.

We walked another ten minutes in silence. Roy stopped. "This is the place where Bobby and I seen 'em," he said. "They came over to us and asked where they could find some orchids. Bobby didn't know from orchids till I told him pink lady slippers, and he pointed out into the pines. I asked who they were and what they were doing here. They told us that they were college students, then they went off in the direction where Bobby had pointed."

"They were holding hands," he added. "I asked Bobby how he knew there were pink lady slippers in that direction. He said he didn't, but it would a been rude not to give them an answer. So we went on our way."

"What were you doing out here?" Susan asked.

"We told the troopers we were out gathering moss, but we was mostly huntin'. Heard there was deer west of the bog, but we didn't see any."

I didn't have any more pearls like *where are the cranberries*, Susan seemed out of questions as well, Roger continued to take notes. Finally, Susan asked Roy to guide us in the direction that Bobby pointed out. "See if we can locate any pink lady slippers," she added somewhat apologetically. Roy said, "Sure." And we left the bog and entered the pine forest down a dirt tack.

"What does the pink lady slipper look like?" Susan asked.

"It's a plant that's about six inches to a foot, has a flower that's different shades of red, pink to white, and has two large leaves. It's often found around bogs since it likes acidic soil," reported our Pine Barrens encyclopedia.

We traveled what must a been a quarter-mile or so, scrutinizing the forest floor for the elusive flower and coming up empty, until Susan drew our attention to an amorphous structure constructed of cardboard, plywood, and pine branches. "What's that?" she asked.

"Crazy Thomas' most recent house. Try not to get his attention," Roy said. It was a moot statement, as Crazy Thomas came out of the structure, approached us and asked the compound question: "Who are you, and what do you want?"

Roy stepped out in front of us, holding us to his back with his outstretched arms, and said, "Afternoon, Thomas. You know me, I'm Roy. We're just out looking for lady slippers.

"Why?" asked a skeptical Crazy Thomas. The interaction was ludicrous.

"Let me talk to him," said Susan, stepping forward. Roy shushed her, keeping her behind him.

From behind Roy's outstretched arms, Susan spoke up. "Mr. Thomas, my name is Susan Saunders and I'm a reporter doing a follow-up story to the disappearance of two college students who went missing near here several days ago while looking for lady slipper orchids. Roy is helping us to find information that explains their disappearance."

Crazy Thomas listened through her mouthful. "Who are the others?" asked the still suspicious Thomas.

"Roger and Jimmy are also journalists helping with the story. Did you happen to see the students, a young man and young woman?" Susan continued.

"I saw 'em," Thomas said. "Walked by here, just like you did. Asked me about the flowers. I said lady slippers didn't grow round here, land's not acidic enough. Sent them off towards Derry." Crazy Thomas was sounding somewhat reasonable. *It seemed to me everyone here was well informed about their acids.*

"What's Derry?" Susan asked. Roy had retreated behind Susan, who was now face to face with Crazy Thomas.

"It's the next town over that way." He pointed obliquely from our previous direction.

"Thank you, Mr. Thomas, you've been very helpful." With that, Susan turned and moved back down the way we came. We all followed behind her until we were out of sight of Thomas' cardboard cabin, and she stopped. We all came together, "It's obvious that if the couple is not dead they headed for the town of Derry," she said. "Can you guide us there in the Jeep?" Roy nodded.

By mentioning the possibility of death, Susan brought forward the thought that was in the back of all our minds. I first imagined a scenario where the hapless couple was killed by Roy and Bobby and dumped in the acidic bog. Though short on motive, I thought of how hard it would be to drag a forty-foot-deep cranberry bog, with every bit of surface covered by the woven tangle of dwarf plants. I searched vainly for an ending to the story. Then there was Crazy Thomas, discovered as the new last person to see the couple alive. I fixated on the primitive dwelling cobbled together by bits of cardboard, plywood, and native vegetation as an image equally compelling as a cranberry bog—I wished I had thought to bring a notebook. *I'm not yet a real writer*, I chided myself. My reverie was broken as our group, now headed by Roy, moved back toward the Jeep and an impending trip to Derry. Amid my crime musings, I struggled to keep up.

Back at the car, Susan looked for Derry on the map. "It's not here," she said.

"It's small, but I can find it," Roy assured us. And off we went under the guidance of the infallible index finger navigating the delta of dirt roads. I was beginning to get carsick from all the sudden turns when we pulled into a clearing in the pines where sat a little village made up of about two dozen wooden structures, many with what looked like thatched roofs. It was a picturesque hamlet, as if we'd just entered a fairytale. We exited the Jeep, and I was glad to stand on stable ground and let my stomach settle.

No one was around, and Susan searched out what looked to be a grocery. She asked the proprietor if she'd seen the students come through here a number of days back. The proprietor shook her head. Roger asked if there was a bar in town. It was the first words he'd ventured in over an hour. We were told that the only bar in town was at the gun club. Across the square and down an alley we found a large, low-slung wooden building with *Derry Gun Club* hand-painted over the front door. Inside it was reminiscent of the Chatsworth beer barn, down to the shuffleboard table. I looked over at Roy, who smiled back.

Susan interrogated the bartender, who said, "Yeah, they were here and asked if there was someone who they could hire to take them to Bridgeton. I called Rudy, who drove them there for fifty bucks." This removed Crazy Thomas as the short-lived last person to have seen the students alive. I felt a twinge of guilt for my suspicions of Roy and Bobby and Crazy Thomas, but I thought in short stories they each still held promise.

Susan asked where we could find Rudy, and Kelly, the bartender, pointed to a table near the shuffleboard pitch. While Susan talked to Rudy, Roger ordered us all a beer. As in Chatsworth, there seemed to be no ID requirements, and Kelly set down four beers. Susan returned and picked up the orphan.

"So, we're off to Bridgeton?" Roger asked.

"Not quite yet. I still have some more legwork to do," Susan said.

"Rudy said he delivered them to Bridgeton at a hotel named Whispering Pines, said they held hands the whole way, regularly kissing and petting. Didn't even quibble over the price. I can't close it out until I do some additional checking. I'll begin over the phone with the Whispering Pines Hotel, then travel there."

"No murder—damn," I said. Undaunted, however, I filed away *Whispering Pines* as a potential title for one of my short stories.

Susan took a sip of her beer, and said, "We've done enough for one day." She smiled at me. "Besides, look on the bright side, they may have been killed by Kelly or Rudy."

41

Driving With Mother Leeds

On our way back, I sat behind Susan. The kitty-corner position allowed for unobstructed conversation with Roy, who sat shotgun. We talked about the day's events, and Roy said he was glad not to be one of the last people to see the two students alive. He seemed to be genuinely relieved, and for the first time, I could see a residual stress in his young face. He said that he and Bobby had been called by Captain Crain of the state troopers to meet with him next week. And maybe with what we'd found the captain would call off that meeting. Susan listened closely to our conversation.

Roy delivered us through the tangled maze to the Oyster Creek Inn. Susan apologized for not being able to leave him at his house. Before he left on his trek back home, I told him to try to arrange a trip to Long Beach Island for his first view of the ocean and gave him Jane's phone number. I said I could put him up. I didn't think Aunt Clair would mind. Susan thanked him for his expertise and said they'd get back together in a few days.

Roger took the passenger seat, and as we drove into the parking lot he asked Susan, "Did you pay him anything?"

"Not before I've published the story. Don't think it's ethical to pay for an interview. After the story's written, I'll get with him around his guide services," she answered. I got another journalistic lesson. Writing fiction seemed easier.

Back at the Oyster Creek Bar, Roger asked me if I could drive his VW back so that he could go with Susan. "I do need to get this out for the Sunday paper and could use Roger's help," Susan said with a radiant smile. It was a setup but a benign one. I assured them I could make it back with the car.

"Just park it around Jane's and put the key under the driver's floor mat," Roger said as he handed me the key. Susan and Roger went into the bar, and not needing a Coke, I left. On my hour's trip back to the island, I had ample time to review the day. During our sojourn on the track of the missing couple, I'd not given thought to the Mother Leeds ruin.

Now the image of the extant fireplace wouldn't leave me, and I assembled visions of the birth of the thirteenth child, who would become the Jersey Devil. I pulled out the triangular blue and yellow ceramic shard I had surreptitiously slipped into my pocket and looked at it as I drove. "*You were there at the time of the birth as a plate or a saucer, and witnessed it all,*" I said to it, out loud. Despite myself, I shivered. I conjured an image of the large room in which I had discovered the bit of colorful pottery. As the walls rose from the foundation, white curtains framed the windows (what time of the year was it?), a narrow brass bed faced the fireplace (was it burning?). Probably not, since the child would soon fly up the chimney. Mother Leeds was in the bed dressed in a white nightgown and white cap, her legs bent at the knees (a cliché for sure). She was looking down at the floor off to the side of the bed where a fetal-like being grew to adult-sized proportions. The form was that of the wooden pedestal that supported the podium of the hostess back at the Oyster Creek Bar. In a puff of smoke, the newly birthed creature rushed up the chimney, followed by an unsettling scream.

The scream, however, morphed into a sustained honk of a horn from the car a short distance behind me. I realized that in my musings I had only been going only thirty miles an hour on the two-lane highway.

I immediately sped-up to sixty-five, waving an apology to my irritated follower, as the vision of Mother Leeds and her birthing room dissolved. I was approaching the town of Manahawkin, which marked the entry to the causeway that would take me to the island. It was still light, the summer sun just beginning to sink below the horizon, the clouds showed pink and orange, the wind beginning to slow with the sun's disappearance. As I parked across the street from Jane's screened-in porch, I was struck by an image of Karen, her arms flapping happily as she chased her dog, Beverly, across the sand in front of the ocean waves. I was disconcerted by the juxtaposition of the two vivid images of Mother Leeds and Karen inhabiting my mind so close together.

I had little time to ruminate on the disparity. I turned off the engine as Jane, the daughter, exited the porch and came across the street to greet me. "Where's Roger?" she asked.

The orange and pink clouds had darkened. I sought to change the subject. "It looks like it might rain. I need to put up the car's top."

"It's a bit of a trick," she said. "Here, I'll help you." After a good ten minutes, we secured the intractable roof. "Where's Roger?" she asked again. There was no avoiding the question, and I was forced into an answer.

"We were out running down a story for the *Camden Ledger* newspaper, about two college students gone missing in the Pine Barrens. Roger and I met the journalist at Leeds Point. Roger left with the journalist to help write the story, and I drove the VW home." I chose my words carefully, avoiding pronouns.

"Is that journalist Susan Saunders?"

"Yes, that's her name." Jane could see I was uncomfortable. Aware of my awkwardness, she smiled, taking pity on me, and asked, "You coming inside?"

"Is Jill there?"

"Still surfing, but Mom's there. She'd like to see you."

42

The Difference Between Have and Make

We entered the house. Jane came down the stairs drying her hair. "Been at the beach all day—just showered. Jimmy, how was your day as a reporter? Want a sherry?"

I said I did indeed. "I wasn't really there as a reporter, more as a tag-a-long, but I did get some material for stories."

She handed me a jelly jar of cream sherry. "Tell me about it."

I settled into the couch, and the cream sherry relaxed me from what I realized was a significant day. I first told her about our exploration of the Leeds ruin and the birthplace of the Jersey Devil. I didn't mention my vision of Mother Leeds and the birth of the Jersey Devil on my trip home; I remained unnerved by what I felt was the intrusion of the Karen image I still didn't understand. I took out the triangle of yellow and blue pottery I'd found at the Leeds homestead, and tried to hand it to her. She shook her head vigorously and backed away, refusing my offering. I was confronted with the still-operational power of Jersey Devil.

I put the colorful shard back into my pocket and said, "The mystery is basically solved." I took Jane through the progression as we followed the missing students on their trek from the cranberry bog to the Whispering Pines Hotel. "Susan feels she still needs to close out the story over the phone and with a trip to Bridgeton." But the mystery was solved. I didn't mention the possible murder by the bartender and Rudy or how impressed I was by Susan coming up with the scenario.

"What impact did any of this have for your fiction?" Jane asked.

I told her about the strength of the image of the cranberry bog, and the potential villains of Roy and Bobby, and a short story that might be created from it. About Crazy Thomas, his scream from the outhouse, and the powerful image of the jury-rigged cardboard, plywood, and tree branch habitation. All of it formed the foundation of possible short stories concerning the missing couple. Although my account sounded confusing even to me, Jane seemed to understand. Jane, the daughter, had gone upstairs, leaving us alone.

"How does the Jersey Devil play into your story?" she asked. It was an awkward question.

"I don't know," I said. "I'm not sure it belongs with the two botany students. Perhaps it's its own story."

Jane took my empty jelly jar, refilled it, and handed it to me. She sat beside me on the couch, while placing her hand on my thigh. She looked at me, and my body reacted. *Was it noticeable?* Could she feel my metabolism reorganizing itself?

"As a younger woman I always wanted to be a writer," she confided. "Richard came along and then the children; as my dream faded into the background of wife and mother, I became a reader. While I didn't have the time to write..." Here, she stopped herself, then said, "While I didn't *make* the time to write—Jimmy, you can always make time where it's important—I used my time to read the work of others. To read closely, to read critically the work of others, paying close attention to writing and to plot and its structure.

These were really two lessons I was getting as a writer: The first was the difference between the words *have time* and *make time*, and the second was the act to make time rather than to wait to have time. Despite my runaway metabolism, I took note.

Jane continued, her hand patting my thigh in cadence to her words. "As a reader, I can't over-emphasize the importance of images in organizing the narrative around plot and writing style. Images are, in fact, the fulcrum for the ideas that give life to the story. That this is your starting point as a young writer is impressive."

I looked into the middle-aged face of this woman. Her skin was not the cream complexion of her daughters. Her hair was shot through with streaks of silver. There are little wrinkles around her eyes, the artifacts of years of sun on beaches of the Jersey shore. I had to work hard not to bend over the four inches between us and kiss her.

A good thing my prudence held, as Jill came through the door. Jane stood up and moved to the center of the room. "I'll be interested to see what comes from your images."

"What images?" Jill asked. Not waiting for an answer, she went on. "Where's Roger? His car's outside. Where's Jane?"

I gave a slightly self-conscious account of Roger's location. "I feel I'm betraying him," I said.

"Oh, don't worry about Jane and Roger," Jane said from the kitchen. "They made their beds a long time ago. Their relationship is like the aftertaste of a good wine gone beyond its prime."

43

When a Choice Is Not a Choice

I spent a fitful night of unsettling dreams. I few years earlier, I had read a poem. I think it was by W.S. Merwin, although it could've been by the poet Jon Anderson, or really someone else. My apology to the author, whoever it was. It was about hitting a deer on a mountain road. As the poet dragged the deer off the road, he noticed movement in her belly. The dead deer was pregnant with a live fetus, and the poet was confronted with an impossible choice—a choice that really wasn't a choice. For me, the poem was about the agony of choices that weren't, in the end, choices. I felt it was analogous to the situation of Jane and me. That night, one of my dream vignettes was dragging a pregnant deer off a dark mountain road. I woke up trying to remember the title and author of the poem so I could see how he had handled it. But all I was left with was a choice that wasn't one.

Anyway, I struggled into the morning light, got up, and worked my way to Flo's. I bought the Sunday *Camden Ledger* and took it to the counter. I had money from my Saturday paycheck so I could afford breakfast. I found the article on page three. The byline was shared between Susan Saunders and Roger Axxst, and the story described the peripatetic sojourn of the two students in their travels from the cranberry bog, where they encountered Roy and Bobby, their movement toward the pink lady's slipper orchid, as indicated by Bobby, through their meeting with a Pine Barrens hermit named Thomas, who directed them to Derry. There, at the Derry Gun Club, bartender Kelly said he arranged transport with a local named Rudy to the town of Bridgeton. Susan had professionally included the last names of all those involved other than the eccentric Thomas. The article included examples of dalliance between the two, reported by Rudy, and ended with the couple's purported delivery to the Whispering Pines Hotel.

I was impressed by the writing, and to my mind the way the article was presented as a still unresolved mystery that just went so far. I felt it left the reader awaiting a final resolution. Perhaps, it was just a projection of the fiction writer in me. I was sure a final resolution would be forthcoming Monday, and I imagined Susan and Roger traveling to Bridgeton. Good job all around, Susan. The article also graciously identified me by name as a contributing researcher. I wasn't sure what research I had provided, but it was nice to be mentioned. I finished my pancakes and eggs and paid up. I still had a little time before work, so I walked back to the apartment and cut out the article and added it to my portfolio.

On Roger's suggestion, I had bought a leather folder that held *Pablo's Cock*, which was still waiting for a definitive ending. It also held the still-to-be-finished *Art of Cool*, which I continued to work on with Jane, and the final draft of the surfing article Roger had sent to *Surfing* magazine. Also on Roger's suggestion, I had taken the unresolved short stories to a store with the new Xerox machine and made a couple of copies. It also contained handwritten attempts of my story about Karen. I set these aside on my little desk, thinking they might have something to do with the Jersey Devil story. But of what, I had no idea. (I recalled a line from a blues song sung by John Hammond that said, A*in't no devil, just God when he's drunk*. I didn't remember which song. And I didn't know what that had to do with the Jersey Devil story either.)

I walked to my beach. Eddie was on his day off, and I was greeted by the thick Jersey accent of Mike Evers. He asked me what was new.

I provided a thumbnail of our trip to Leeds Point and a synopsis of the morning's article, modestly omitting myself as a contributing researcher. He seemed impressed—mostly, I think, that Roger took me along.

Not letting me rest on what he perceived as my laurels, he moved smoothly into the local gossip about Chris Mackee, which he had kept on top of. Chris had been released from the hospital and had returned to the island but had not returned to work, suffering intense, recurring headaches. The interrogations, rather than drifting away, had intensified.

"So far, everyone's sticking together, despite Lifter's threat that anyone withholding information would be fired. Personally, I think Chris is faking it to get sympathy and keep the investigation going. He's told anyone who'll listen that you and Eddie are responsible. Hal Gunther's taken over the investigation from Mackee's brother. Hal's as good as policemen get. He's been interviewing everybody on the island. You and Eddie can expect to hear from him soon."

The day was warm, with a few clouds traveling across the sky. A gentle breeze cut the heat of the sun. I whistled a couple of kids off the sandbar. We'd been told to keep swimmers off the sandbar that provided a place to stand forty yards offshore. The beach veterans resented the policy, as they liked to swim out to it and stand around in the ocean. Eddie and I enforced it periodically, just enough to deflect the criticism that we weren't doing our jobs. With Mackee out, there was little chance of trouble. I felt a twinge of guilt about calling the two youngsters off the bar. Life was certainly easier without the specter of Chris Mackee.

With cranberry bogs, crazy piney hermits, Mother Leeds, and the Jersey Devil, I'd mostly forgotten about Chris Mackee. It seemed I still had to keep my head down. In fact, I reveled in the role of outlaw and was content to wait it out.

Evers seemed disappointed in my reaction, or lack of one. "Just look at that Sea Dawg," he said, as Shelly Goldberg sidled toward the lifeguard stand.

44

More Bubbles and Hansel & Gretel

The first time I'd met Shelly, I marked the event with my hormones bubbling in my blood like club soda in a vodka drink. This time was different. What with my relationship with Jill and my disconcerting evening with Jane, I was already confused. I thought of the deer at the side of the road, but it made no difference to my body, which bubbled at her approach.

If Mike Evers was impressed by my relationship with Roger, he now sat looking on open-mouthed as Shelly came over to the stand. "I've been thinking of you," she said, using my name. If someone had needed saving, they would have drowned, as Shelly Goldberg held the total attention of both lifeguards.

I swallowed hard. "It's good to see you, Shelly," I said, hoping someone would yell for help. Of course, nobody did. "You're back on the island," I went on, stating the obvious. Shelly ignored the lame statement. "How've you been?" I asked—another pearl. *It wasn't for nothing I'd had so few girlfriends in high school, none really,* I thought.

"Good. I'll be here the whole week," she said.

"Great," I said, as my body roiled. *Somebody yell for help.* "That's great, let's get together," I said despite myself.

"That's my plan. I brought you lunch. I'll bring it by." With that, she sashayed back to her towel, releasing me—me maybe—but not my body. I realized that Shelly was not unaware of how she affected the opposite sex, so I didn't much chide myself for my awkward performance.

Evers waited until Shelly was beyond earshot before he said, "Boy, was that lame! I would have asked her out immediately. *It's good to see you? How've you been?* Really lame."

"Yeah, it's complicated." I spotted a young boy who was having trouble getting back into shore. I ran out, grabbed his outstretched arm, and pulled him onto the sand. He was polite and said thank you as he joined his mother on the beach.

"No big deal," I answered him. *Where were you when I needed you?* I thought as I returned to the stand.

"It doesn't seem complicated to me," Evers said in thick Jersey, seeking to resume our exchange. I remained silent. The morning rolled by. At noon, Shelly returned with lunch, and it was a good one, too. Two lox and bagel sandwiches with cream cheese, lettuce, tomato, potato chips, an apple, a Coke, and a bottle of Gatorade—the best lunch to date. I gave Mike one of the sandwiches, the bag of potato chips, and the Coke. I kept the Gatorade and apple for myself.

I could feel my body beginning to percolate, and it didn't help that Shelly sat open-legged on the buoy in front of the stand. "You still surfing in the afternoon?" she asked.

Good as it was, the sandwich went down in lumps, and I was glad for the Gatorade. "Um hum," I grunted.

"Going to surf today?"

"Yes," I said, one syllable seemed all I could manage. *Get a grip*, I told myself.

"Good, I'll try to be there."

"That would be nice." I could hear Evers repeating my inane responses after Shelly left. While she remained on the buoy, I was thankful for the baggy lifeguard shorts.

Sometime in the afternoon, Shelly moved back to her friends.

At five o'clock, I was glad to see that she had abandoned the beach. Roger's VW hadn't moved, indicating he was probably still with Susan. Jill hadn't come to the beach, removing any onus to abandon surfing. I walked home. I needed time to think.

Thinking came hard, writing was easier, and I took a shot at *The Cranberry Bog story* mostly to wind down. It was ineffective at ridding my body of the bubbles in my blood, as my body's priorities continued on their own. I told the story of two high school students who became separated from their botany field trip. I thought the demotion to high school added vulnerability to the two. The plot line was parallel to our trek with Roy and Susan to Derry. The story deviated into fiction with Crazy Thomas' outhouse scream and his raggedy appearance that unnerves the children, propelling them down the road to the cranberry bog and to the edge of paranoia. The children meet Thomas at the bog, and though his manner is cordial, they can't override their biases, and paranoia takes over. The boy hits the hermit on his head from behind with a rock, killing him instantly. The story was unmistakably reminiscent of *Hansel & Gretel*, with the bog substituting for the oven. I finished the unworthy effort as the sun leaked through my windows. I had written all night.

My initial evaluation of the story was not positive, as I turned to what the story was about. In the increasing light of the morning, I felt the story primarily dealt with the bias about how people view those who are different. How bias engendered fear, and fear determined actions. The way Thomas looked, his ritual scream after a bowel movement, further unnerved the two students, pushing them over the emotional edge and resulting in an unfortunate series of events.

With this analysis, I felt a little better about the story. I had written the story in longhand; when I would type out the story, I would emphasis how Thomas' differences played into the students' bias.

The children, as Hansel and Gretel, were never held accountable for the murder.

Though still feeble, the emphasis on bias derived from preconceived notions of people's differences became the seed crystal of a future story.

45

Flaccid vs Irony

No time for sleep. I showered, dressed in my lifeguard garb, and decided to grab an early breakfast at Flo's. I bought the *Camden Ledger* from the outside machine. After ordering breakfast, I searched for Susan Saunders' follow-up article and again found it on page three. Susan had contacted the Whispering Pines Hotel and found that Sarah Kennedy and Matt Limekiln had indeed been registered at the hotel, stayed three days, during which time they went to the city hall, secured a marriage license, and were married in the hotel's conference room. No friends or family had attended. The young woman who took Susan's call, as it turned out, served as the witness required for the ceremony. It seemed the disappearance was, in fact, a meandering elopement—a reaction to the opposition both families leveled against the union. Susan and Roger substantiated the hotel receptionist's account in their travel to Bridgeton, talked with the families of the two students over the telephone, and ultimately, wanting to see the two alive, spoke to the nuptial pair in a nearby town.

I felt that Susan's article was a bit flaccid when compared with my story—particularly the ending; then, I realized how the story Susan had reported was rife with irony itself. Further, the theme seemed in concert with mine. Although there was no murder, because the disappearance occurred in the Pine Barrens, the bias against Pineys contributed to the worst expectations and scenarios. A social kind of paranoia. The ending of Susan's article, rather than flaccid, was an example of the irony wrought from the biases people maintained about the Pine Barrens and its residents, a fact that Susan had not ignored. The article carried the byline of Susan Saunders with Roger Axxst. No researcher was listed. Both of us seemed to have been demoted, Roger from an *and* to a *with*, and me dropped altogether.

"Good job, Susan," I said to myself through a last mouthful of French toast.

It was getting on to nine, and I walked slowly to the beach. Eddie, of course, was already there. I noticed on my way in that Roger's VW hadn't moved. Celebrating the end of the article *with* Susan, I presumed.

When we were established on the stand, eyes riveted on the beach, I took Eddie through the concerns voiced by Mike Evers about the investigation into Chris Mackee's undoing.

"Yeah, I've heard that Lifter is putting pressure on Hal Gunther to find something."

"Mackee's been saying that the two of us are responsible," I said.

"Yeah, but they'll need proof. Thank God for the garbage men who disposed of the covering cardboard that could have yielded fingerprints. I don't think there's any way to bring this back on us. But we need to be careful."

"Evers thinks that we can expect an interrogation by Gunther," I said.

"So what? Gunther's a good guy. We just stick to the truth, and say we attended a beach gathering, then went home." It sounded good to me, and I decided not to worry about it.

Something else presented itself to worry about, as Shelly Goldberg approached the stand. By this time, *The Cranberry Bog* had usurped my brain enough to exclude any functional thoughts of Shelly and the confusion she brought to my life, however, I was no closer that day than I was the previous one from being immune from the force exerted by Shelly Goldberg. Still, my blood bubbled at her approach.

"Hi, Shelly," I said. "You didn't stay to watch me surf." In my flustered condition, I took the chance.

"I'm sorry, I got called away for a family problem," she said to relieved ears. "And I'm going to have to return home for a few days. But I'll be back. The Fairfields are having a party next Saturday, and I'd like you to take me."

"Sure," my blood answered before my brain engaged.

"That's good." She followed with a brilliant smile. "I have to leave in the next hour or so. I just wanted to be sure before I left." She brushed my knee, more bubbles. "See you next Saturday," she said as she turned and sashayed off the beach.

I looked over at Ed, who sported this wide, silly smile. "You trying to commit suicide?" With that, the ever-vigilant Eddie jumped off the stand for a run.

I was left with an image of Ernest Hemingway with a shotgun in his mouth just after he blew off the back of his head.

46

Duplicity

The days passed, and I dreaded the approaching Saturday and my date with Shelly Goldberg. Out of her physical presence, my brain took priority over my body as I tried to fight down feelings of duplicity. As a writer, I'd made my peace with lying, but duplicity didn't sit well. I was glad the party at the Fairfields was on my day off and I could keep my head down, as duplicity reared its own.

On Friday, Shelly returned, as did the bubbles in my blood. She brought me another gourmet lunch, confirmed our date, and left me with the address of where she was staying. We agreed to meet there at five-thirty Saturday afternoon. As I shared my lunch with Ed, he maintained his previous goofy smile, shook his head, and *didn't say nothin'* (got that from Brer Rabbit). The bubbles receded along with Shelly's departure to her substantial beach towel, and I did my best not to look over at her.

At five o'clock, as we were taking back the stand, a young woman with a professional-looking camera around her neck approached me. She introduced herself as Kate. "Roger told me to take your picture for the *Surfing* magazine article. I'll need your board for the photo."

"I'll have to get it," I said. Roger had told me to expect a photographer, and I made the trek to the Deriksson backyard, hoping not to run into anyone.

I retrieved Tabby and was soon back on the beach. Shelly, still on her towel, looked on as I received instructions from Kate. I entered the water. Though I was nervous, I completed a few respectable rides, not pitching off until the end. Kate waved me in after three or four rides. "These are good action shots, but the magazine said they wanted one with a close-up of your face. Could you just place your board on the sand and stand on it as if you were surfing?" she asked.

I'd bathed in enough duplicity for one day and declined, saying I just couldn't do it. "Real surfers would know it was a setup." Kate smiled and said she understood, and we decided on a shot where I walked out of the surf carrying my board.

Kate said goodbye and thanked me. "I don't know if they'll use any of the action shots, but the last ones of you walking out of the ocean with the waves in the background should satisfy them. Anyway, I'll send you the prints through Roger."

After Kate had left the beach, Shelly walked over to me and asked what that was all about, and I told her of the article Roger and I had written for *Surfing* magazine.

"Wow," she said, "Roger."

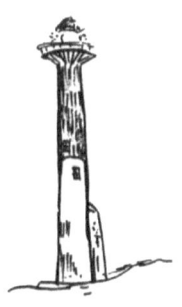

THE END

47

Ghost

Returning *my* surfboard, I also carried *The Cranberry Bog* in the string-tied file folder I used to transport my writings. Roger's VW was unmoved. Jill was off surfing at Holgate, but both Janes were home.

The jelly jar of cream sherry both mitigated and exacerbated my feelings of duplicity—certainly the theme of the day. It was a strange sensation, one I couldn't quite explain. I gave the story tentatively to Jane and sipped my sherry while she read it.

"I like it" was her pronouncement. She softened her critique, *not entirely truthful*, I thought. "It's derivative, and up until the end I didn't like it, but the ending saved it. You leave the reader with a compassion for Thomas, and a certain sympathy, but dislike, for the students. Yes, the ending saved it, turning a derivative story into one of irony. Another one for your portfolio. Bravo." It was more than a kind assessment. Again, she sat next to me on the wicker couch, her hand gently tapping my thigh. My body once more usurped my brain, like a ghost inhabiting a haunting house.

She sat next to me, waiting for my response, her hand still on my thigh, no longer tapping out the cadence of her words—still. The ghost took position over the whole house, and I bent over and kissed her. I was astonished, and waited for the slap I was sure was coming. Jane hesitated, though our lips never separated. Then she returned the kiss—long and strong—and she removed her hand from my thigh and placed it on the back of my neck, pulling me into her. Footsteps on the stairs could be heard as Jane, the daughter, descended. Her mother and I sat bolt upright, with Jane providing a little space between us.

"What are the two of you up to?" was Jane's casual greeting. I felt like I'd just been caught masturbating in the bathroom by my mother. I'm sure crimson glowed through my thin tan. Jane, however, seemed undaunted. "I've just read Jimmy's latest story, and we are just discussing it. It concerns Jimmy's take on the trip to the Pine Barrens he took with Roger."

She was now sitting on the story, due to her strategic move away from me. Standing up, she reached behind and grasped the story in one fluid motion, then handed it to her daughter. "Read it, it's pretty good."

As well as being an adroit physical move, it provided an effective diversion from my near mortification, as my heart sought to escape my ribcage. Jane seemed completely composed as she got up to top off my half-full cream sherry jar, and she asked her daughter if she'd like a cocktail.

48

Gertrude Stein vs Aunt Clair

I left Jane's early, hoping to avoid Jill's return. With Jane, the daughter, there was no opportunity to talk about the kiss—the kisses. I had no idea what it all meant, if anything. But my world was transformed into the tornado from the *Wizard of Oz*, where faces and scenes swirled around me: Jane, Jill, Shelly, Pam and Fast Eddie, Roger and Jane, the Chatsworth beer hall, the cranberry bog, Crazy Thomas, and the specter of the Fairfield party. To fill my time and put the brakes on the tornado, I stopped by Aunt Isobel's to tell her I'd be over early. She smiled with pleasure, not knowing the shady morality of the man with whom she would be dining.

As I showered, the tornado came back, and I thought of what I knew about the Fairfields. They lived in a large white house built on stilts at the north shoulder, overlooking our beach. The house had a wraparound porch. Often, when I would look over, I could see various people eating, drinking, sunning, or just observing from the deck. The Fairfields had two young daughters. Sherie was about fifteen and the target of all the younger boys on the beach. Linda was about two years younger and traveled in her older sister's wake. I'd see Sherie and her sister after beach hours walking their enormous Saint Bernard, Andy, who loved to bite the whitewater of the surf. I had been introduced to Mr. Fairfield early on by Eddie when he was acquainting me with the beach regulars. Mr. Fairfield was fairly short and stocky but not fat. He had a pleasant face and an affable personality. Eddie had told me that he was director of the Chase Manhattan Bank, which explained the white mansion on our left. I'd not met the wife but had seen her on the beach. She was dark-haired and willowy like her daughters. That was the sum of my information. I had no idea what the party was about or who was likely to attend. The fear in the pit of my stomach was that the Derikssons would be invited, and I tried not to think about it.

At Ibby's, the Beefeater's martinis, like the earlier cream sherry, softened my angst, and I settled into fried chicken, mashed potatoes, corn, and peas. More stories about France, the one about how Aunt Clair had argued about the meaning of a Picasso painting with Gertrude Stein. I had heard it before from my father, but it bore repeating. My father told it with humor, but Ibby told it with pride. I didn't tell her I was in love with the Gertrude Stein of the Jersey shore, but I shuddered. Anyway, another martini washed away the thought.

A lovely evening, I mused as I unsteadily walked the fifty yards to Aunt Clair's building. At home, to quell the beating of my heart (got that from Poe's *Raven*), I took a stab at the Jersey Devil, and after two and a half hours I had a reasonable facsimile of what was in my Jersey Devil book. I crumpled up the five pages, white-out and all, threw them away in the garbage under the kitchen sink, then went to bed. Besides, I was tired.

49

Out of the Twin Sisters

I woke up late, on the morning of the day of the Fairfield party, feeling like Gregor Samsa. As it was for Gregor, it was a difficult *metamorphosis* from the previous night to the new day. *A confirmation of duplicity*, my brain said. Countered by a weaker rejoinder from my body—*well, there you go*, both said.

I stumbled to Flo's and breakfast and another encounter with Bromo seltzer. Flo spared me of her couplet, and I left the diner anonymously, feeling a bit better. I walked home. (Where else was there to go?) On the beach, holding my sandals, feet in the surf, I thought of Karen, the only woman with whom I felt I hadn't disgraced myself. I wondered where she was now and what Beverly was doing. I wondered if she was happy becoming a detective. I wondered if I could make that happen, even in fiction.

The twin sisters of depression and duplicity wrapped me like a wet blanket as I walked to the only place I could. The beach, the ocean, the sky and clouds all became dark and disappeared. In their absence, I saw a vision of Karen, who said to me in words clear as spring water, "Jimmy, it's me who is the Jersey Devil." Then she vanished, replaced by blue sky, white clouds, water and sand. My feet were wet in the surf as I trudged home. However, my steps became lighter, for I knew just what she meant. "Thank you," I whispered.

At home in Aunt Clair's apartment, I slipped a clean foolscap into my father's ancient Underwood, not wanting to go through a transition between longhand and typing. The story was so clear: I was back in the ruin of the Mother Leeds home, but this time there were walls, white curtains, and a fire in the hearth. There was a long, narrow table, looking much like the Derickssons', covered by a white tablecloth, set with plates, cups and saucers, all glazed in a yellow and blue pattern. There was a residue of dinner on the plates, remnants of tea in the cups. A meal had just come to an end. Mother Leeds was in the brass bed facing the table, and she was giving birth to her thirteenth child as others looked on. A girl was born. She was an unusual infant. Her face was slightly contorted, and her feet were small and misshapen. Her arms were held out from her body, folded like wings, and her hands tucked under her shoulders. Her cries were harsh and deep, like that of a much older person. As the onlookers looked on, a woman proclaimed, "It's the Devil's spawn." Others echoed, "Yes, the Devil." A man shouted, "Kill it, before it grows." The refrain was taken up by others, but Mother Leeds held her baby tight, daring the others to come near. Mother Leeds had a reputation as a witch that gave the onlookers pause, and the child was left undisturbed in her mother's arms. Before the visitors left, Mother Leeds issued the prophesy: "She's got much to teach you."

Despite persistent gossip and unkind looks, the infant grew to be a little girl. Still, she had contorted features, a unique way of speaking—low and broken—slurred with an articulation difficult to follow. She also continued to hold her arms splayed out, reminiscent of wings, a maneuver she deployed to give her balance as she moved. Her mother made shoes for her small feet. Though awkward in her movements and speech, the girl demonstrated good intelligence; she could read better than ninety percent of the surrounding residents, and she cooked as well as her mother.

She continued to grow into a seventeen-year-old young woman. Her prominent breasts were the talk of the men of the town, and of meanspirited comments by the women. As it happened, as it was supposed to happen (stole that one from Kurt Vonnegut's *Cat's Cradle*), an itinerant preacher looking for a permanent gig came to town. He was adept at mining a town's gossip and fashioned his sermons around it. Quickly, he picked up on the talk about the different young woman as being the Devil's spawn. Because the surrounding land was inhospitable to farming, he married the two into a sermon. He vilified the young woman as the cause of the barren soil and called for her killing to make the land fecund once more. The words took root in fertile ears. The village formed into a vigilante mob that overpowered the Leeds cabin and killed the young woman by burning her in the family's substantial fireplace. Indeed, the only truth in the Jersey Devil myth was that she went up the chimney. The young woman's name was Karen, and her only crime was being different.

The preacher was soon caught molesting a farmer's daughter, but not before the townspeople had built him a church. Taken from his church, the preacher was hanged on a pygmy pitch pine that was tall enough for the noose. The vacant church was soon filled by a more compassionate pastor, who fanned the simmering guilt in the community concerning the murder of the young woman.

Rather than making amends to the Leeds family, the community fashioned the elaborate myth of the Jersey Devil, giving it horns and a tail, and embellishing the young woman's arms into bat wings, the small shoes into hooves, her low and broken speech into a hideous screech as she transported herself up the fireplace.

I finished the untitled story and looked at the clock in the kitchen, five after five. Just enough time for a quick shower, to dress, and to present myself in front of Shelly. Story finished, my body was back in command, as my brain slid into neutral.

50

A Bathroom Made of Glass

I wasn't sure how formal this affair was, but it didn't matter, as I dressed myself in the best I had: blue button-down Oxford shirt, khakis, topsiders with no socks, and a charcoal sport coat. I presented myself at the appointed address. Dressed in a sheer black spaghetti-strapped evening dress and Roman-style sandals tied at midcalf, Shelly Goldberg opened the door. The bubbles of anticipation now came to a boil as my brain continued to idle. Shelly took my arm, and we walked in silence toward the Fairfields' beach house. At 25th Street, my brain engaged briefly.

"Let's walk along the beach," I said. Shelly smiled. She knew what was up and followed. We went up via the stairs that provide entry onto the surrounding deck, and still we had to walk around to the street entrance. At the door, we were greeted by Mr. Fairfield. He and Shelly seemed to know each other, and he greeted her warmly with a kiss on the cheek and even remembered my name. We entered. I looked around for Derikssons but gratefully saw none. I was a bit underdressed for this crowd, but only slightly. Most of the men wore blue blazers, and all sported ties, some even ascots. There were even a few topsiders, but none with no socks, so my campiness was preserved. Other than the Fairfield daughters, we were the youngest there. I calculated the mean age of the others at fifty-seven, with a range spanning forty to eighty.

The woman all wore evening dresses of sundry years and fashion statements. Everyone held a drink, and Shelly walked me over to the bar and ordered a white wine. *Cream sherry,* I thought, but I ordered a red wine for gender contrast. "Pinot noir," I said, thinking it sounded sophisticated. (I don't think I'd ever had a Pinot; must have come from some book, or a James Bond movie.) I knew no one other than the Fairfield girls. Shelly led me over to a middle-aged guy named Hal who was a stockbroker or something. As they engaged in banter, I drifted toward the guy playing the piano, who must have been hired help. I was staring into my wine glass, elbow on the piano, when I heard, "How do you know Shelly?" I looked up to see Sherie Fairfield.

"I met her on the beach."

"Why did you come with her to the party?"

Why indeed? "Well, she asked me. How do you know her?" I asked to change the direction of the conversation.

"She sometimes helps my father with his accounts."

Really! I thought. I wondered if the depositors of the Chase Manhattan Bank knew.

Sherie continued. "Mother doesn't like her much."

Yeah, I bet. I thought.

"Do you?" Sherie asked.

"Do I what?"

"Like her."

"Yes, I like her," I said.

"Umm," said Sherie, and she melted into the partygoers, as if into a fog. I noticed that Shelly was back at my side.

"Do you know any of these people?" I asked her.

"Some of them. Most are businesspeople. I've modeled for some of them."

"Modeled?"

"Modeled for advertisements for their businesses. Hal Needles owns the local furniture store. I've done quite a bit of work for him." I must have had an edge to my voice, as Shelly seemed slightly irritated.

I thought back. Hal was the source of the cardboard for the Mackee caper—I saluted him silently with a sip of my wine. I noticed that we were receiving a number of looks from both men and women, and I saw what I believed to be different motivations behind their eyes. I thought back to the '50s song *You Don't Own Me.* Where Lesley Gore cautions *her* escort not to put her on display.

There seemed little chance of not putting Shelly Goldberg on display with this group. But who was it putting Shelly on display? And I wondered why we were there. "Come on," she said, taking me by the hand. "I'll show you the house. There are some spectacular views."

I was glad to leave the party, as Shelly took me on a tour of the three-story beach mansion. Indeed, the views were magnificent. A banquet hall assumed most of the second story, with a table that would easily seat twenty, a bar at one end, and a prep kitchen at the other. The seaward wall was all windows, and I gazed down on my beach. The lifeguard stand looked forlorn, pulled back from the ocean and on its side. The sun was setting, we'd been at the party going on two hours, and the sky was a blaze of rose and saffron. (Got that from an Algernon Blackwood short story, *The Wendigo.*) Spectacular!

Shelly continued her tour to the third floor, mostly bedrooms. She pointed to two closed doors. "The girls' rooms. They like to keep private. Only street views anyway." She took me into the master bedroom, with a bed large enough to sleep all thirteen of the Leeds children. I walked into the bathroom, and the seaward wall again was all glass. One could shower or bathe in full view of the ocean. I imagined Mr. Fairfield in the bath with a whiskey glass in hand, looking down on the lifeguard stand, the red flags, and the common folk; everything looked small from up there. "There's a door to the outside deck where you can sun yourself," Shelly said.

"You've been here—you've used this?" I asked, stunned.

"A few times," she answered. I was impressed and a bit intimidated. Shelly took my hand and kissed me. She led me back to the second floor. "I've been saving the best for last."

Back in the glass dining hall, she dropped my hand and walked to the end of the room, which ended in a wall of dark wood, maybe walnut, ten feet beyond the bar. Inserted into the wood was an almost invisible numbered pad—a combination lock of some kind. Shelly pushed four or five of the buttons, and a walnut door swung open. "Miles' private study. Ta da." *I didn't think guys like Mr. Taylor had first names.* The room was paneled in the same dark wood as the wall, and with the opening of the door, lights engaged and illuminated the interior. In addition to the wood walls and bookcases, there was a maroon carpet and drapes of the same color. The chairs and the couch sported ubiquitous rows of buttons pressed deep into the leather. The room was equipped with a music system embedded in the wall, and a phone and intercom sat on a mahogany leather desktop the same color as the furniture.

"Wow, this is the most elegant room I've ever seen," I said as I sat down on the couch, wanting to feel it on my body.

"It gets better," said Shelly, who pressed a button that retracted the curtains, revealing a now dimly lighted ocean. "Come out here," Shelly said, passing through a previously invisible door in the glass. She pushed another button that lit up the area. The surrounding deck had been partitioned by two walnut panels enclosing the space. There was a sink and faucet at one of the panels, and a small refrigerator rested on the counter. The little *room* had a single piece of furniture, a chaise lounge, the size of a double bed.

Shelly took my hand and deposited me at the foot of the lounge. Sitting near the top, she undid her sandals, pulled the spaghetti straps off her shoulders and pulled the top her black dress down around her middle. She pulled up the skirt, revealing that she wore no underwear, and reclined on chaise longue. "Your turn," she said simply.

My brain sputtered briefly to life. "I don't have any condoms with me," I said. Fact was, I had no condoms at all.

"It's OK, I have an IUD," she said. "It's a new form of birth control inserted by a physician. It's safe and effective. You'll be all right." She smiled.

"What if someone comes in?" It was my last attempt.

"I locked the door from the inside. Come on, get with it." She smiled again.

Out of excuses, I needed a new metaphor for my body's reactions. *Bubbles in the blood just doesn't do it anymore*, I thought, as I fumbled with my clothes. *Good thing I didn't wear socks*. At least my sense of humor was intact. Naked as the eyes of clam (got that from a folksong, don't remember which), I lay down next to the impeccably gorgeous Shelly. She immediately pulled me to her, and we kissed. I fumbled with her breasts, she with my penis. Foreplay was short for Shelly, and a good thing. "Come inside me," she said. She guided me into her—I'm sure she knew this was my first time. I tried to think of things that would delay me. I thought of the Jersey Devil-Karen story, but that was not much help as I soon ejaculated. But I was excited and my bubbles kept my erection alive as my motions continued. Shelly seemed unaware of my premature release, or at least gave no indication, and continued her passion. The bubbles in my blood were slowly absorbed, and we both relaxed.

"That was good," she said, I think with some surprise, as we lay next to each other. We were visible by the dim light, expertly adjusted by Shelly before we began. She got up and walked to the little refrigerator, took out a previously opened bottle of wine, and filled up our empty glasses. It was white wine, but who cared? Shelly returned to the chaise lounge. The skirt part of her dress had fallen down, but she left the top at her midriff. I took a sip of wine and fondled her nipple with my tongue—Shelly responded warmly with a sigh, and I moved to the next. The sky was now totally black, but I could hear the sound of the waves. My mind was still in neutral, my body in complete control. The wine bottle was empty, a signal to vacate our borrowed digs. We dressed and Shelly took out a hairbrush from a drawer in the counter, brushed her hair, and handed it to me. Put back together, we held hands as we descended the stairs to the ongoing party.

The partygoers had relaxed considerably in our absence. The men had loosened their ties or gotten rid of them altogether, blue blazers draped the furniture, and the women whose hair had been previously piled on top of their heads had now let it down or let it fall. Straps from their dresses had slipped down lower on their shoulders, the hors d'oeuvres were all but gone, and the bartender had vacated his post. Mr. Fairfield walked over to us. "Did you have a good time, Shelly?"

"Oh, yes, Mr. Fairfield. Quite."

"Jimmy," he said with a nod, then turned back to his other guests. It seemed a good time to leave. Shelly on my arm, I walked nervously past the Deriksson house, lit up like a jack-o'-lantern, but saw no one. We walked the short distance slowly, and I deposited Shelly at her front door with a kiss—well, kisses.

51

Line of Demarcation

I walked the short distance home, and my brain once again began to function, allowing my body to release me. I recalled how Sylvia Plath, in *The Bell Jar*, divided the world's population into two, and only two groups—those who had done it, and those who hadn't. It was Sylvia's apportioning of the world into its two respective subdivisions. I stared back from over the line I'd just crossed, and I took little joy from the long-awaited rite of passage.

But a passage to what? I wondered. A confirmation of betrayal, perhaps. I looked over to the Karen-Jersey Devil story, where I had left it. The story I had been so excited to show to Jane now looked puny and beside the point as it rested on the little desk beside the typewriter. What did the line of demarcation actually separate? I settled it between the before and after the time my integrity was surrendered. It was a harsh analysis but a fair one.

My ruminations on betrayal turned to the party and just why Shelly had been invited. A social gathering drawn from middle-aged and elderly island players seemed to be an odd milieu for a young model from Newark. Shelly engaged with a number of the men present, all of the conversations were trivial, none were substantial or marked by friendship. She had talked to not one of the women, only been the recipient of venomous looks. Why had she been invited, and what function did she provide? My role was simple. I served as a buffer, perhaps a statement. Again, though, from what? As far as the two of us, my function had been strategic, perhaps protective. Shelly's seemed to be biological, physical, a decoration or display—a trophy. I thought again of the last two lines of the Lesley Gore song. I felt a sadness that had nothing to do with my duplicity but was a purer form of concern. I hoped if I saw the beautiful Shelly in the future, she would not resemble a sports car, driven too long and too hard. I had played my part; I would probably never see her again.

52

Redemption

I woke up the next morning and resolved to work on my redemption. However, I would not speak of it—or fess up, if you will. It wasn't flat-out courage, but it was the best I could come up with. I walked to the beach, and Mike Evers was there on Eddie's day off.

"How did the party go?" he asked first thing, having been privy to Shelly's and my conversation.

"No big deal, just a lot of old island patricians and their wives—pretty boring. I was mostly there as window dressing."

"Window dressing! With Shelly?"

"Yeah, life's funny, ain't it?"

"Well, what happened between you two?" If I were to tell anyone, Mike Evers would be the last person on the island in whom I would confide.

"Nothing. We kissed good night," I said, throwing him a small bone.

"Just kissed her," Mike said in disappointment.

"Yep," I said, jumping down from the stand trying to manufacture a run, but I could find no likely recipient. The whole interaction with Mike was lame. I looked around the beach, hoping not to see Shelly. Mike was quiet, figuring I was too lame to talk to. At around lunchtime, Mike looked around for Shelly, and not finding her, he said, "Looks like no more good lunches."

"Nope, we're on our own, buddy," I said, relieved.

At around four-thirty, I felt a slap on my shoulder and looked around to see Roger. Jane was walking behind and gave me a little wave, and I smiled back. "We're all going to Holgate. Just wanted to see if you want to come. Jill's already there."

"Sure," I told him. I'd begin my redemption at Holgate. Jane and Roger went in for a swim as I finished my day.

We folded ourselves into Roger's VW, the surfboards thrusting out over the top, and drove to Holgate. I identified Jill by her corona and paddled out to her.

"Where were you yesterday?" she asked.

"Working on a story about the Jersey Devil," I said, hiding behind the half-truth. Jill let it pass. We caught the same wave and rode in parallel until I pitched off near the end and had to go chase my board.

Roger was sitting on the swells as I paddled out. "You got together with Kate, I hear," he said. "We're getting close. A week or so."

Perhaps it was my ambient dark mood, but I said, "Do you think my status as a newbie surfer getting highlighted in *Surfing* magazine will be resented by the more experienced surfers?"

"No, I don't think so. *Surfing* routinely profiles young surfers. Besides, you're getting to be a bit of a legend around here.

"What kind of a legend?" I said to his back as he slid down the next swell. Jill was back and heard part of our conversation.

"You beginning to worry about your and Roger's article and a photo in *Surfing* magazine? I'll tell you, when I got profiled, I was still fifteen, and not everybody was kind, but I got through it. So will you. Besides, you're a verified researcher for the *Camden Ledger*, so who could complain?"

She flashed me her ironic smile, punctuating her statement with her tongue. She then caught a wave, and I followed but wiped out almost immediately. I chased my board into shore and sat with Jill and her sister while Roger continued to surf.

The island was a small community, and I didn't know how much the two sisters knew about my previous night's exploits. So my words were few and awkwardly neutral. Theirs were no less cryptic, not cold but devoid of substance, and offered no clues. To dispel the awkwardness, I grabbed my board and joined Roger on the waves. Roger was nearly through, so I caught only a few rides before he joined the girls on the beach; I followed him tentatively.

53

The Oblation

I told Roger to drop me off at my apartment so I could shower and change. Then, I'd walk to the Deriksson house.

"Don't worry, we'll wait. Be quick," Roger said. I think perhaps he wanted to be sure he had a buddy when he would face the inevitable scrutiny of the Derikssons for his time away with Susan.

I really didn't want a shower but had forced myself into taking one. The motive was to pick up the Karen-Jersey Devil story as an offering to the altar of redemption. It seemed silly, but I needed a prop. I was down in close to five minutes.

"That was fast. You're sure you showered?" asked Jill as she sniffed me. "What you got in your hand?" She pointed at the vinyl folder.

"It's a new story," I mumbled.

"What's it about?" she asked.

"I want to show it to your mother first." I realized Jane was the altar. It was a testament to our growing relationship that no one questioned this de facto non sequitur.

Jill had transformed into alacrity as she bounced into the house, "Jimmy's got a new story for you," she said to her mother.

Jane greeted me with, "We missed you last night." *What's that mean?* I thought *as a chill went through me.*

As we took our seats on the couch, she handed me a cream sherry, and I handed her the story, with the working title *Karen: The Real Account of the Jersey Devil.*

"Karen?" Jane, the mother said. "The disabled woman you met on the beach? I thought she was now a detective?" She referred to the failed story. *Nothing gets by you, does it, Jane?* And with that flash, I knew that she was aware of my duplicity the previous night. She reached over and squeezed my hand to confirm it. I wondered if anyone saw the gesture. *Don't tell them what I done in Weed,* I thought to myself. (Got that from Kerouac's *On the Road,* and he got it from Steinbeck's *Of Mice and Men.*)

"She was going nowhere as a detective, and transformed herself into the Jersey Devil on a walk we had on the beach."

Jane asked no further questions and settled into the story with miserly sips of her cream sherry that lasted through the end of her reading.

She set the manuscript to her side, reached over, pulled my head around and kissed me once on the lips. "Jimmy, this is the best work you've done. How did you conceive it?" She stood up, filled her sherry jar, walked over, and filled mine.

"It was really Karen who inserted herself into the story through visions," I said self-consciously, hoping the blush from the kiss had receded back into my bloodstream. "When I drove Roger's VW back from the Leeds Point trip, she first intruded herself into the story. Then on a walk back home along the surf, she declared herself to be the Jersey Devil. From there I just ran with it."

"Wow, that's spooky!" Jill said with a tentative sarcasm.

"How was *your* time away, Roger?" Jane, the daughter, asked. I thought to change the subject.

"Got a couple of articles from it," he said uneasily.

"Co-authored, actually," said Jane. "But who is counting." I was comfortable with the family banter fully engaged.

Roger stood and picked up the story at Jane's side. "Let me read this," he said. And I was happy to provide him with some cover.

I noticed that Roger didn't play the reciprocal card and ask Jane how her trip was to Chicago and husband Charles. There seemed some definite rules as to what was in bounds and what was out. *Civilized*, I thought.

As Roger read the story, Jane said, "It's not unusual for a character to take over the narrative from an author." She gave my thigh a little squeeze but removed her hand immediately. Nobody picked up the topic as Roger read on. The story was fewer than twelve pages, but he took his time. Jane and Jane got up to fix a dinner of finger foods culled from the cupboards and refrigerator, then set them out on the narrow table that divided the rooms.

Roger finished with a "well done."

"I think I agree with Jane that this is the best so far, at least as far as fiction is concerned, though *Pablo's Cock* is a close second," he said. I felt validated and less vulnerable by Roger's statement. I took comfort that Roger had surely survived episodes of duplicity. Perhaps so would I.

As we munched our finger food and talked over a variety of mundane topics, Jill was quiet as she read the story. She talked back to the story as if it were me. *Who is Karen? Was she a real woman? How did you know her? A detective? How does my mother know about her? Why would you want her to be the Jersey Devil?* I kept a running catalog of her questions to account for them later.

Three jars of cream sherry, and I was beginning to relax. *Watch yourself*, I cautioned. Jill finished the story. "I have a few questions," she said with no shades of irony. I'd been preparing my answers.

"Karen is a young woman with a disability I observed on the beach before I was a lifeguard. I met her when I first got here, I became interested in her, but the relationship was only one way. I never could muster the courage to introduce myself. So, I just observed her, made up possible scenarios, and tried a few times to write about her. One of the stories was where she was a detective, not disabled at all, just a disguise to help her solve a murder. I couldn't escape the feeling that the plot was better in the telling than it was on the page. I shared some early versions with your mother, who remembered them.

"Why she would insert herself into a story about the Jersey Devil is still a mystery to me. I have thought about this since I wrote the story. I think she is telling a story of how someone who is different is vilified by society in its fear and ignorance. How that ignorance can be used as an excuse for depraved action and codified into a myth. I think her motivation was to identify, if not to redeem, the injustice done to those who are vulnerable and different."

I ended my sermon to astonished faces, including Jane's brilliant one.

Jill, to whom I was directing my words, her ironic smile back, said, "Will you see her again?" *Jealousy*? I thought hopefully.

I wasn't sure my oblation had brought me any redemption, but I was glad that my duplicity with Shelly had, perhaps in some small way, been redeemed in the persona of Karen.

54

Two in One

Summer was half over. The days rolled by like the swells beneath my surfboard, my disgrace remained undiscovered—at least unexposed—and the fervor around the Chris Mackee affair lingered at low tide. Still, the duplicity weighed me down, and I tried a compromise with myself. It was a strategy worthy of a short story. I came to think of Jane and Jill as different sides of a single person. The truce was a bit schizophrenic but provided some relief from the monkey that remained on my back. My relationship deepened with both women—Jill on the waves and in the sand, and Jane over stories and cream sherry.

The Jersey Devil story was not enough to put Karen down. I continued to think of her, and I tried without success to insert her into various scenarios. The detective was clearly not working. Out of ideas, I thought back to the conversation with Roger at the coffee house about *Huckleberry Finn* and Jim's statement that he owns himself being worth 800 dollars. And my query of what Jim might be worth today, and Roger's assertion that it would make a good short story. As I had nothing else, I thought I'd give it a shot.

It was a clever premise. Clever, a word that I increasingly disliked, a shyster's word or a used-car salesman's, not one for an artist. What

Alfred Hitchcock might call a MacGuffin. A MacGuffin was not necessarily a scene or a character in a narrative, but the pivot around which the plot turned. The first thing I needed to do was decide on the context—the time, the place, the situation that framed the story. I experimented with science fiction, transporting the antebellum Jim to modern times of 1967 and how he would calculate his post-slavery worth. After a few hours, the story was going nowhere, and I was frustrated. It was time to get ready for work, and I decided I'd let the story incubate for a while and see what came up.

It was a Sunday, Eddie's day off, and Mike Evers was on the stand. With nothing happening on the Mackee front, Mike was relatively subdued without a topic, left only to comment on the sea dawgs who drifted past our stand. At noon, Jill came by with a couple of lunches and the new copy of *Surfing* magazine. She handed me the magazine, wordlessly and with her ironic smile, and waited for my reaction.

"What's that?" said Evers, reaching for the magazine.

"Jimmy's and Roger's article," Jill said.

"Article?"

"Yes." Jill said. "About Jimmy becoming a surfer and how Roger helped him."

Mike had just returned from a run and was still wet, and I wouldn't let him touch it, as I thumbed through the magazine and found the article. There was a quarter-page picture of me coming out of the surf carrying my board, with the text running alongside. At the bottom of the page was a smaller picture of Roger standing beside his upright board. The second page was all text. On the third and final page was an action shot of me in the left top corner. I was glad to see it was about the size of a postage stamp, making it impossible for a real surfer to critique my form. At the bottom of the page was a larger photo of Roger, tucked inside a curl, impeccably riding a big wave. Roger had graciously given me first authorship. It wasn't necessary or expected, but it was nice.

Throughout my perusal, Mike had issued a steady stream of wows and questions that Jill answered.

He finished up with, "Jimmy, you're an Island celebrity!" I wasn't then, but by the time the Long Beach Island megaphone was through, I would be.

"Roger said we should meet here for a surf at five. I'll bring your board."

"Roger has several copies of the magazine for you," Jill said to me. "So you can give that one to Mike." I thought she knew that giving it to Evers would contribute to my notoriety.

55

Jim Makes His Appearance

As actors say, "You're only as good as last night," and I needed new material. I sat on the lifeguard stand, scanning the water for potential trouble, and searched for a new story topic. After many waves rolled by, I resurrected *What Would Jim be Worth Today*, from Roger's and my conversation at the coffee house on our way to Leeds Point.

I didn't think anyone drowned during my musings as I attempted to put together a storyline. I toyed with the idea of bringing Jim into modern times; I'd never written any science fiction. But I continued to stall over how to get him to the present day, and what he would do once there. After more waves, the idea of Jim in the present was interesting, clever even, but got me nowhere.

At five o'clock, Roger appeared along with Jane. Jill followed dragging two boards behind. I looked at Roger and the most beautiful woman in the world, and I had my story. I'd keep the MacGuffin of Jim, but the story would be about Roger. Mike and I pulled the stand back, and I gave him the copy of *Surfing*. Sitting next to Jane, he stuck around to watch us surf. Probably to verify I was authentic.

The three of us went into the water, and I felt I belonged there for perhaps the first time. Again, for the first time, I was able to jump off my board and catch it before it washed to the shore. It didn't go unnoticed as Jill said, "One article in *Surfing*, and boom, you're a surfer." We all rode in together, and I caught my board for a second time. I was unable to resist flashing Jill a goofy smile that said "see, it wasn't a fluke." I walked out of the whitewater, board under my arm, looking much like the staged photo in the article. I wrote the first lines of the story in my head.

Robb Base exited the ocean, shedding his shackles as easily as the saltwater that rolled off his back. Robb was unaware of his liberation, as it was a gentle bondage to a most beautiful woman.

I had just been given a copy of my first published article, but my excitement was equally about Jim and Roger. I guessed writing should be just like that, a constant flowing from one excitement to the next. I felt I'd just been given a glimpse into some esoteric truth. A shiver of benevolent electricity took possession of my spine.

Jane invited Mike, and the four of us walked to the Deriksson house. We went around to the backyard where the surfboards rested when not in use. In the space that Tabby, my surfboard, occupied I saw a large blue bow made of four-inch ribbon. I looked questioningly at Roger. "Take a look," urged Jill. I picked up the bow and noticed a card below it. I opened the card: *Congratulations! You're now a published Surfing author—the board is yours, Roger.* I suppressed the tears gathering in my eyes, walked over to Roger, and gave him a hug.

"You earned it," he said. "Well done. You're no longer a newbie."

I was deeply touched. I had been saving to buy a surfboard. In my conversations with Roger, he felt that I could get a top-of-the-line surfboard for between forty-five and seventy-five dollars. "But," I protested, "a top-of-the-line surfboard sells new between one hundred and fifty and two hundred dollars."

"Yeah," Roger had said, "but surfboards are like sailboats: People buy expensive ones and find out they can't sail and just want to get something out of it. If you know what to look for, you can get a real good one cheap."

So I'd been saving. I had close to two hundred dollars, as my aunts paid most of my cost of living. I had been stalling, unwilling to give up Tabby.

"Come on," he said, "let's go inside and get a drink."

We entered through the backdoor. Drinks were set by our usual seats. I saw a jelly jar filled with cream sherry at the coffee table in front of the wicker couch, and there was a cake on the narrow table that divided the kitchen and the living room; a butcher paper banner stretched the length of the table. *Congratulations Jimmy* was printed with a crude drawing of a stick figure riding a surfboard—a crude drawing for a crude surfer. Jane came over and hugged me and kissed me on the lips, and this time the tears escaped my eyelids. As we disengaged, I looked furtively to see if Richard had noticed.

We all took the seats assigned by the drinks: Jill and I on the wicker couch, Jane and Roger on their chairs at the corners of the room. Mike sat next to Jill, and Jane was at her chair opposite me. Richard stood attentively to top off our drinks as needed. I looked around the room and at various places were copies of *Surfer* magazine—it was all a bit too much.

"Roger wrote the article, too," I said, trying to shift the focus.

"Yeah, but we've done this for Roger a bunch of times. This is your first," said Jane the daughter.

"Maybe the last," Jill said with her ironic smile and tongue. I was glad for the irony and embraced it.

"Probably," I said as Richard filled my cream sherry jar. Jane beamed at me from across the room, and I tried hard not to blush.

My blush was interrupted by the ringing of the telephone. "Charles," predicted Jill.

Jane, the daughter, got up to answer it, anticipating a move into the cat's bathroom.

Rather than the cat's bathroom, Jane instead came toward me, holding out the phone. "A Hal Gunther wants to talk to you."

Hal Gunther was the person placed in charge of the Chris Mackee investigation. Things had been flowing by so smoothly over the past weeks, the Shelly Goldberg affair (call it that) not excepted, that I had almost forgotten.

"Hello," I ventured tentatively.

"Jimmy," he said, not waiting for confirmation. "Hal Gunther. I was told I could probably get you here." He didn't tell me who told him, and I didn't ask. "I'm wondering if you can meet me in two days after you end your lifeguarding day? I've just talked to Eddie Lambert. He said he can make the meeting if you can." He waited for my response.

I thought briefly of saying, *I'll check my calendar and get back to you*, but instead said rather that it would be fine with me.

"Good, I'll see you around five-thirty at Lifter's office at the township building." We then *rang off*, as they say in British mystery novels.

56

Jim's Worth

I usually don't outline my writing. I'm not that kind of guy. On a few occasions, like *Pablo's Cock*, I'll outline a story at the end. But this time I began with one. I wasn't sure why, maybe because it was about my friend, an attempt to correct misunderstandings people entertained. Maybe it was the onus to show how brave and unassuming a guy Roger was. Maybe it was because I felt that the plot was tricky; the juxtaposition of real characters, fictional characters taken out of time, hallucinations and fantasy, a coffee house conversation, and a theme of not only Jim's worth but Roger's, and more generally the worth of all of us. They were themes more ambitious than any I'd yet attempted. Anyway, I outlined the story upfront. Here it is:

The story is about Roger's relationship to Jane, and how he had let the most beautiful woman in the world slip away. The characters were renamed Robb and Sally, and their relationship paralleled that of real life and what Roger had described during the coffeehouse conversation.

Robb's character is defined by his statement: "I'm a surfer not as a diversion but as a life's work; I'm journalist not as a career but as a diversion." With his statement, Robb presents himself as a fuckup and not worthy of an adult commitment.

Sally's character is defined by a wish for a permanent commitment. This becomes an ongoing source of tension between the two, further diminishing Robb's confidence and self-worth. Sally is now a stewardess for a major airline based out of Chicago. Robb is the acknowledged best surfer on the beach

Despite her pleas, Robb had so far resisted Sally's requests to move to Chicago write for the Chicago newspapers, somewhere that offered greater opportunity for a journalistic career. Robb, a self-taught writer, knew he was not nearly ready for the big time. Besides, Lake Michigan was cold, and the waves were small and few. But Sally's urging had continued and was being made more frequently.

Clearly, Robb needs a guide to release him from his predicament.

After delivering Sally home from a dinner where they argue over Robb's fourth margarita, Robb finds a copy of the book *The Adventures of Huckleberry Finn* on the passenger seat of his VW.

At a stoplight, Rob looks down at the book and it speaks to him. "Read me," it says. Robb attributes this to his last margarita. But the presence of the book remains a mystery.

At home, Robb takes the book inside and lays it on the kitchen table. Out of spite, he makes himself another margarita. Returning to the table, he sees a Black man dressed in overalls sitting down next to the book. Robb chooses to play along and takes a sip of his drink, sure that it is responsible for this hallucination, and asks the man if he'd like a margarita. The man simply shakes his head.

A little dialogue:

Choosing to play along, Robb says, "Hi, I'm Robb. What's your name?"

"Jim."

"You from the book?"

The man nods his head. "Yas, sir."

"Welcome. But why are you here?" he asks the apparition.

"To give a little help."

"A little help?"

"Yas, sir, a little help."

"A little help about what?"

"'Bout bein' free."

"About being free from what?" Robb asks.

"'Bout bein' free from the things that keep you from bein' free."

Even though Robb knows he's responsible for 100% of the kitchen dialogue, it's getting too circuitous even for him.

"Tell me what you think I should do," he says to the Black man in the kitchen chair, who is as solid as the tequila bottle on the counter.

"Cain't tell you. It's all in the book. You gotta read it. Freedom come slow, but you made a start. I'll be around, though, to give you some help."

With this statement, Jim evaporates into dust at the other end of the kitchen table. The tequila bottle remains stable.

Robb takes the book into his bedroom and begins reading it, but he falls asleep before he reaches the second page.

In the morning, Robb wakes up hung over and goes surfing. In addition to his surfboard, Robb carries with him the book he was told to read. Though his thoughts are fuzzy, his recollection of the apparition Jim is vivid and troubling. Jim had suggested that he had made his first movement toward freedom. What was that? It puzzles him, as does what that freedom is.

What is most disconcerting to Robb is the realization that he, himself, has conjured these issues. While not believing in the reality of the vision, he is inured to the image of Jim and welcomes his return.

Robb exits the ocean, dries himself, and begins reading from page two. But he finds little useful insight from beginning chapters on attaining freedom, other than to take his surfboard down the Mississippi.

The beach has filled up by this time, and Robb spies a Black man in surfer jams observing him. Robb shakes his head, and when he looks up, the image is gone. At home and out of the sun, a new margarita is made, and the reading goes on.

The plot takes off for Robb when Jim and Huck meet on an island they'd each separately escaped to. They have a conversation about signs and what they mean. Huck observes that most signs seem to be about bad things and asks if there aren't any good signs. Jim answer that there are a few, "Like if you got hairy arms and breast it means you going to be rich." Huck looks at Jim and asks if Jim if he hasn't got hairy arms and breast. Jim acknowledges the fact, saying he's been rich and will be again. Then observes that he's rich now since he owns himself, being worth 800 dollars.

At the kitchen table, Robb reads the passage where Jim relates how he once had ten dollars and invested in a cow—"but the cow died." The runaway slave then says, "Yes; en I's rich now, come to look at it. I owns myself, en I's wuth eight hund'dollars."

Before the passage can fully sink in, Robb looks up to see Jim, bare-chested and in multicolored surfer jams, sitting at his table.

A little more dialogue.

"How's the readin' goin'?" Jim says.

"How's the swimming going?" Robb quips.

"Good," Jim says. "Went in with you." Robb smiles at the humor displayed by his conjured image. "Find anything interesting?"

"Don't know what I'm looking for," Robb says.

"Don't need to find it anyway. It'll find you." Robb is left with this statement as Jim disappears into dust at the end of the kitchen table.

"I owns myself," Robb whispers to the empty chair.

Jim will appear one last time to Robb over a beer at his residence at the Island Beach Hotel, where he nails down the significance of owning oneself.

"You owns yourself," Jim begins. "Now you beginnin' learnin' somphn'." Jim's monolog melts into Robb's. Robb melds into Jim changing places. Robb now talks to himself. "You always thought that you were a fuck-up, not responsible enough to be a good partner. In a strange way it kept you from freeing yourself from Sally, or fully coming together with her. Not responsible enough to lead a conventional life. You think of yourself as an arrested adolescent, and Sally as a mature woman—not much future in that. Though there's a good deal of truth to it. But it's more complex than that. As a twenty-five-year-old adult, engaged in activities that are not entirely adult or, at least, exclusively adult. You surf not as a diversion but as a life's work. You engage in journalism not as a profession but as a diversion, a source of money to continue your life style. You view these choices as irresponsible. Not the stuff from which good husbands are made. The fly in the ointment is the definition of responsibility. But in reality, what you've started to do *is* take on responsibility—consciously—for the decisions you've made. The fact that some people define these decisions as fuck-ups or immaturity doesn't make them less conscious, or less responsible. You need to be released, that's all—freed."

The story ends with an emotional scene between Robb and Sally at the Island Beach hotel over drinks. Robb fesses up to not being able to be the husband Sally should have. Sally admits to having an affair with a gentle, loving, and stable Chicago stockbroker named George. In the end, it's a story about realization rather than choice. (Like a still pregnant dead mother deer, I muse.) I did include, however, that Sally and Robb maintained a relationship that added color and adventure to their lives. The story closes with Sally's question: "Why couldn't you do it, just be a normal adult?"

Robb answers, "Because I owns myself, and I's worth 29,093 dollars and 63 cents. Robb, had gone to considerable trouble, calling the economic desk of the *Philadelphia Inquirer* before he finally found someone who could calculate the answer of what 800 dollars, back before the Civil War, would be worth today.

Still, I mused a paltry sum for any man's worth, as if someone's worth could be determined by another.

It wasn't yet a fully realized short story. Ultimately Robb would tell it in first person, and most of the best stuff would be in dialog outside the outline, but the plotline was the same. I worked on it pretty steadily for another two weeks, during which time the specter of Jim kept vigil, sometimes in overalls, sometimes in surfer jams, watching me from corners of the room where I wrote in my aunt's apartment, obliquely from a crowd around the lifeguard stand, or standing solitarily on the beach as I walked home in the evenings. He never spoke to me. When I finished the work and handed it to Jane, he disappeared. But he would be back.

57

Poetic Justice

Two days after the debut of the *Surfing* magazine article, Eddie and I presented ourselves at Lifter's office, vacated for Hal Gunther. I hadn't been there since our interrogation by George Mackee. Hal sat behind Lifter's desk, and Eddie and I sat on folding chairs before him.

"How you guys doing?" he said. It was to be the folksy approach. Ed and I nodded and mumbled something in return. Hal waited to see if there was more, then continued when there wasn't. "Anything you want to say before I get started?" Still folksy.

"'Bout what?" Ed asked.

"About why we're here."

"Why are we here?" Ed asked in deadpan.

"About the Chris Mackee attack." The two of us were silent. *He's too calm, he's got something on us*, I thought. I looked at Eddie out of the corner of my eye. He was cool, and I took some strength from his demeanor.

"You wish to comment on that?" Gunther said.

"An attack?" Ed questioned.

"Yes, the attack," answered Gunther, the mask of folksiness slipping down just a bit.

"Didn't know there was an attack. Just saw him drive off like a madman into holes in the sand." Ed stated this evenly. "Looked to me like he attacked himself." The interaction was all between Hal Gunter and Ed; I might as well have been a desk lamp for all the light I shed on the conversation.

"Heard there was a fire the night before," Gunther threw out as a leading question. *Now we're getting to it,* I thought.

"The night before what?" Ed asked, refusing to give up anything.

"The incident." Gunther's mask slipped down a little farther.

"Yeah, we had a lifeguard fire—have 'em regularly— where we come together and discuss things."

"It was the day Mackee had the altercation with the parent and little boy, wasn't it?"

"Believe it was, linebacker and all."

"You were in charge of the fire," Gunther said.

"I was the MC, the Johnny Carson of the fire. Nobody's in charge."

"Did Mackee come up in the discussion?"

"Of course he did. It was the talk of the beach."

"What was said?"

"The way I recall it, people were angry. Thought Mackee was an embarrassment and a danger to beachgoers. Felt something should be done about him."

"What was discussed?"

"Someone said we should go to Lifter and complain. I said I'd done that a number of times, but it did no good. There was some discussion of a strike to get rid of him. Others said Mackee was just an arrogant little prig and wasn't worth it, that it was better to leave him to the linebacker. That was pretty much it, and we turned to other topics."

"Like what?"

"Like the upcoming sale of Lifeguard Ball tickets."

"Lifeguard Ball tickets?" Gunther was puzzled. Lifeguard Ball tickets were tickets to a dance and were allocated to the lifeguards for sale to islanders. Each guard was given a number of tickets and a fixed territory in which to sell them. They were invented to help support a guard's bottom line; the individual guard could keep all the proceeds to augment his, or her, salary. Ed patiently explained this to Hal Gunther, saying, "They're really important."

Gunther was irritated by the diversion into lifeguard economics and sought to regain command of his agenda.

"Mackee is insistent that the two of you are behind the accident he suffered." Gunther stepped back from *attack* in favor of *accident*."

Ed refused to be placated. "Oh, well, if Mackee's insistent, it must be true," he answered with sarcasm. "If it was an accident, it was one of his own making. If he would have driven at a sane speed, there would have been no accident—no harm."

"The holes were disguised by cardboard."

"Yes, they were, but they would have done no harm to Chris if he'd been driving safely. Mackee's been driving recklessly for years. The incident with the linebacker's son is just the most recent episode. The township's lucky he hasn't injured anybody yet. The cardboard over the holes was probably a joke. Chris' behavior *made* it an accident."

"So you think it was a joke?" Gunther asked.

"I don't know how it was meant, only that it would have been a joke on someone driving safely."

If Hal Gunther expected Eddie to feel better by confessing to an attack, he was coming to realize he had underestimated the lifeguard. I looked over at Eddie; I knew that he was going into the Navy at the end of the summer, but I thought he should be attending Harvard Law School.

Gunther now abandoned the fallow field that was Eddie Lambert and turned his focus on the desk lamp.

"Chris says you guys baited him, causing him to drive away too fast," he told me.

"How'd we do that?" I answered.

"He says you made a mockery of your supervised drill." Ed for the first time let his cool slip and stiffened slightly. I noticed, and so did Gunther.

"Mackee has been less than complimentary about the job we've been doing, and we decided to give him an example of how good guards go about their duties," I said. "If he took that as mockery, I think he might be in the wrong business."

The policeman shifted gears. "I hear you're a writer, Jimmy." I was taken aback that he knew my name.

"I write a little," I said, feeling I was being played. Despite myself, I looked over to Ed, who had resumed his cool.

"I read your surfing article, pretty good." More play.

"I co-wrote it," I said.

"Yes," Gunther said. "Roger Axxst."

"A good deal of what I know about this case comes from Roger's articles," I said. I felt I'd just opened up a door for him. It didn't look like I'd be going to Harvard anytime soon, and I longed to be a desk lamp again.

Gunther continued. "Did you talk about the case with Axxst?"

"What case?" I attempted lamely—too late for Harvard.

"Chris Mackee's," he responded evenly.

"We only talk surfing," I said absurdly. I wasn't even getting into Slippery Rock Junior College with responses like that.

"You also were listed as a researcher in an article authored by a Susan Saunders and Roger, about two missing college students in the Pine Barrens. You must have talked about something in addition to surfing." Gunther obviously did his homework. I stayed silent, realizing when I'd been bested.

"I hear you also write short stories," he went on.

"Sometimes," I responded limply.

"You write anything about this?"

Mackee? I wanted to say, but it was clear who we were talking about.

"No."

"Why? Don't you think it's interesting enough for a short story?"

"Not really. It's just an example of poetic justice."

"Poetic justice? Like in an O. Henry story? Irony," Gunther expounded. O. Henry was the pen name of an early American writer of short stories characterized by ironic endings. I admired his style and forgave his sentimentality, as I forgave it in my own writing.

"Sounds like the perfect topic for a short story." If Gunther had actively been searching for an Achilles' heel, he had found it. The Chris Mackee affair was exactly the type of story that I ached to write. I had held back only for fear of the pitfalls of fear and betrayal. I think Gunther knew he had touched a nerve. "Poetic justice," he said, mouthing the words a couple of times as if he were chewing them. He continued.

"I hear you have a short story about an ironic cockfight coming out in the *Islander*."

"First, I've heard of it," I said. I didn't risk asking him where he got his information. I'd ask Roger that evening.

"Look," Gunther said, softening, "you're both stand-up guys. Lifter just wants to put an end to this. To save some face. If you could give it to him, there would be no repercussions. He just needs a resolution. The whole affair can be explained as you say a joke, an unfortunate joke, but a joke. I know you don't like Chris Mackee…"

Ed, who had been sitting docilely, interjected. "Nobody likes Chris Mackee, other than Lifter and his brother. You don't even like him."

Gunther smiled and lowered his eyes. "We have an informant."

"An informant to what?" Harvard Ed was back, and I relaxed into a desk lamp again.

"To what happened."

"To a joke? Who?"

Gunther considered the question. Perhaps it was only minute or two, but it seemed endless. At last, he said, "Mike Evers."

Ed laughed and repeated the name, then said, "You're just blowing smoke. Mike Evers is a gossip, but he's not a snitch, and besides he doesn't know anything about it." Eddie looked directly at Hal Gunther and held his gaze. It was as close to a confession as Gunther would ever get.

"An informant on a joke," Ed said. "That's poetic justice for you."

59

The Resurrection of Pablo

E d and I left the township building and walked to our beach; Ed veered off to his VW and I to the Deriksson house. Jill, Jane, Jane, and Roger were there and interested to know how the meeting went. I told them I really didn't know. "Eddie gave nothing away, but I don't think I was as good." Roger questioned me, and I told him about poetic justice. He laughed and said if all they had was poetic justice, we were all pretty much OK. I told them about Gunther's saying that Mike Evers was an informant. Roger laughed again. "It's just a bluff. He's a terrible gossip, but Evers would never snitch."

"He knew I was a writer, about O. Henry stories, irony and all," I said. I told them that he'd read the *Surfing* article and followed my participation on the *Camden Ledger* article. "He knows my attraction to irony, and asked me why I haven't written about Chris Mackee—it's like he can see into my head. It's creepy."

Jill and the two Janes listened but didn't contribute. Roger laughed for a third time. "Hal's an educated guy, but I don't think he can read minds."

"Then he said something I didn't understand. He said the *Islander* was going to publish what he called my ironic cockfighting story."

"Oh!" Roger said. "I've been meaning to tell you. Scott Jennings, the publisher of the *Islander*, was complaining that the paper was a little thin this week and asked if I had anything. I suggested that he publish your *Pablo's Cock* story and gave him my copy to review. Hal's good friends with Scott. They must've talked. I hadn't heard back about the story, but Scott must have decided on it. What with the *Surfing* article I thought it was sort of news. Sorry, I was meaning to tell you. Hope it was all right."

"Sure, it's fine. It's good. Thanks," I said.

"It needs an ending, though," Jane said.

"It needs an ending, though," I echoed. "Seeing they might publish it, how much time do I have—do we have?" I looked over at Jane.

"Two days. With tonight, parts of three," Roger said.

60

Skinny Dippin' & Birthdays

The day after my meeting with Hal Gunther was Jill's birthday, her seventeenth. It was a fairly modest celebration with just the family, Roger, and me. Richard drove down midweek, and we all gathered for dinner at a local seafood restaurant. I had a twinge of guilt as I dressed in the same clothes I had worn to the Fairfield party with Shelly. They hadn't even been washed, but they *were* my best. Everyone was dressed as fancy as I'd ever seen them. Jill wore white Levi's and a white tunic. Crowned by her platinum corona, she was stunning. Roger joined us a little late and was dressed in baggy shorts and a T-shirt.

Jane addressed her sister as *Old Jill* and started the family banter. Everything was cheer and goodwill, and I was happy to have been included. I allowed my extant feelings of duplicity to slip into the background.

Presents were presented. I gave Jill a necklace, with a silver surfboard on a short chain. "Put it on me," she said. I fumbled behind her but managed to negotiate the minuscule clasp.

We finished our desserts and got up to leave. "Now for our present," Richard announced. "Did you bring it?" He turned to Roger, who nodded. "We'll have to go outside," he said. We all followed Richard and were greeted by a new 50cc motorcycle. Its chrome gas tank glittered in the last light of the evening. Jill squealed and sat down on the seat and held the handlebars. Richard handed her the key, and she started the engine. "Can we take it to the movies?" she asked. We had planned to go to a showing of *The Dirty Dozen*, after the birthday dinner.

"That was the plan," said Richard, smiling. Jill said her goodbyes and hugged all there, including me. And we were off to the movies on her new motorcycle.

We both liked the movie and cheered for Jim Brown as he sprinted from the Nazi compound to the safety of the Jeep driven by Lee Marvin. I was bummed when the movie ended with John Cassavetes, playing my favorite character, being shot while escaping in the same Jeep offering Jim Brown safety—ain't that just the way with irony.

We exited the movie house. "Let's go to the beach," Jill said, holding my hand.

"Our beach?"

"No, let's go up toward Barnegat, you know step out a little. I'm seventeen after all.

"OK."

"You want to drive the bike?" she asked. I really didn't, but I felt it would be unmanly to decline.

"Sure," I said. My mother was adamant that I would never ride a motorcycle, so I'd ridden one only a few times, always in the desert or on the beach. She'd probably saved my life.

Anyway, we left the theater with me driving, the dazzling chrome gas tank between my legs. I drove tentatively, zooming down the road toward Barnegat at twenty-five miles an hour.

"Could you speed it up just a hair?" Jill urged. I could feel the sarcasm at my back and imagined her tongue at her upper lip. I sped up to thirty-five, Jill seemed placated, and I was at ease. I pushed it up to forty, feeling comfortable. "Good boy," I heard from the back of me.

We were moving into one of the few curves in the otherwise straight road and ran into sand blown across the narrow pavement, and I began to slide. I hit the brakes and the bike buckled, and we were going down the road mostly sideways as I pumped the brakes. We were probably going less than ten miles an hour when I dumped the motorcycle. We both stood up as the bike slid beneath our legs. We were OK, the bike seemed OK, its rear wheel still spinning. I put the bike in neutral, stood it up, and noticed a big dent in the glorious gas tank that looked back at me like Miss America with a black eye.

"I'm so sorry," I began. Jill shushed me. "Let's get on to Barnegat." She declined my offer for her to drive. "You're doing just fine," she said.

So we were on the road to Barnegat, albeit at a reduced speed. Jill resisted the temptation to push me on faster. "Slow down here, take this road," she said. I took a narrow sand path and stopped at the dunes. The ocean was visible, with no houses in view. "This is a good beach—private," she said.

It was still dark, the moon yet to rise. We were bare foot. Jill was in her white jeans, and I was in khakis and Oxford shirt. Our feet in the surf, we held hands.

"Ever skinny dip?" she asked out of nowhere.

"Sure," I lied, as I looked around the naked beach. Fact is, I was shy. Even after football practice, I was the last in the showers, my towel providing cover. The only exception was at the Fairfield house, and I tried not to think of that now.

Jill took me at my word, sat down on the wet sand, and removed her clothes. While we had done considerable exploring, it had been mostly shrouded. Even in the darkness, I was treated to a full view of the total landscape as Jill walked into the waves.

Quickly, I disrobed, trying to beat the moonrise, as an eyebrow of light appeared over the eastern horizon. I followed her into the surf, and she took my hand. Standing side by side, we stared out over the relentless ocean. I was embarrassed by my protruding erection that seemed to disrupt the otherwise symmetry of the scene, but what can you do? Next to Jill, with the waves rolling past our thighs, I felt relaxed, far different from the agitated excitement of Shelly Goldberg.

Jill gently pulled me deeper into the water, turned toward me, and hugged me. The cool water and warm bodies came together in a border of ecstasy never felt before. She reached down and grasped my penis, and I exploded into the sea. I wondered if my drifting semen might impregnate an awaiting oyster. I may never eat shellfish again.

We swam sidestroke, facing each other, the moon had just peeked over the eastern horizon, illuminating the water on her breasts, glowing like so many silver beads.

Jill wore her sardonic smile and nothing else as we exited, and we dried ourselves off with our clothes. Another couple had entered the beach but kept a respectful distance. We rested on the sand, holding each other in moist clothing, and I asked, "How do you think I should end the Pablo story?"

"How would I know?" she asked.

I was shocked to realize I'd asked the question of Jane. I had fused the two women, then confused them. We drove home, and I deposited Jill and her dented 50cc motorcycle, then went inside.

61

True

I thought nervously about how I had confused the two women. Was this another form of duplicity? It was certainly violated a form of dualism. I wondered if it would become apparent to Jill or her mother. It seemed unlikely. But I was beginning to respect, if not fear, the perceptiveness of Deriksson women, to feel completely at ease. I used the term *ironic* to describe one of the best moments in my life. Though a better term might have been *schizophrenic*. And I was uncertain as Jill announced that she was off to sleep, leaving me alone with her mother.

It was late, but she handed me a jelly jar of cream sherry as we sat down on the wicker couch. "What should I do with the ending of the story?" I asked. My second attempt.

"Do you know the word true?" she asked me.

"Factual," I answered easily.

"That's one meaning, but it's not the one I'm after. It also refers to consistent, in the form of alignment—a true line. A line that points not to fact but to a direction; to what it points to. It doesn't point to fact but to authenticity. Jimmy, I believe the ending to Pablo should be a true line to your authenticity, and you must decide what that is."

It seemed to be less an answer to my query and more a substantiation of the intuitive powers of a Deriksson woman about my developing character. I looked down at my arms to see goose bumps. Jane saw but did not comment. I shivered.

I looked over to the corner chair routinely occupied by Roger to see the image of Jim.

It's wasn't a solid form, as I could see the back of the chair through his body. I was not surprised as Jim had become the image of my moral compass, and I'd just been invoked to engage it.

Jane, however, broke into my ruminations. "We can get to Pablo if you want, but first I want to talk to you about your story about *Jim's Worth*." It had been a couple of weeks since I gave it to her, and I'd been anxious for a response. She asked if I'd shared the story with anyone else, and I told her not before I heard from her. "Good," she said, smiling.

"I've thought a lot about it," she said, and she put a hand on my thigh. "It's very well written, perhaps your best, and you are maturing into a writer quickly. It seems to me very difficult to meld reality with fiction and be true to each. True, in the way we have just been discussing it. But this piece is simply too good. You've homed in on your targets and shot the bull's-eyes. There's potential for hurt here. You're becoming Roger's good friend and have penetrated that friendship with insight and compassion. Pulling the character Jim from the depths of Mark Twain is marvelously creative and thickens the substance of your story." I looked over to Jim in the corner, who had solidified. "But," Jane said, "it may be too much for him to confront."

"I took the words right from his mouth," I said, defending myself.

"Yes, I've heard versions of this from Roger before. But I can tell you, Roger's not ever been so articulate or true. Even if you culled the words from his own lips, he doesn't fully believe them, nor is he ready to embrace them. He will someday, I believe, but he needs more time." I absorbed this as she went on.

"The tale is about what allows Jane and Roger to continue on. While you have inserted yourself into this eccentric family, there comes with it a responsibility to keep it together. You've been fair with Jane, though not quite as insightful. It's been quite difficult for her, and Roger plays a greater part in her life than just color and excitement. Charles, whom you refer to as George, is much more than the cardboard character in your story. You would be surprised to know what part he's played, though it's not my place to tell you."

The intimacy of the conversation, the tap of her hand on my thigh, and our physical proximity was just too much. I bent over and kissed her, and she kissed me back.

Which woman was this?

I trekked home, trying to walk a true line to my aunt's house. It was difficult to hold a true line; the wind blew strongly from the ocean, the sky had clouded over, and it smelled like rain.

62

Authenticity vs. Integrity

I now had just a day to finish the story. The ending, I thought, shouldn't take more than three paragraphs, but finding the true line to my authenticity might take longer. The decision was a distinction between clever and whatever the right word was to confront it. After some thought, I decided on integrity. Clever and Integrity measured themselves across the cockfighting ring. Jane, I was certain, had already made up her mind about how she came down on the ending. I thought she had used the word *authentic* rather than *integrity* on purpose to leave the decision to me.

I'd written before that cleverness had always been the MacGuffin, the point around which my stories turned, always thinking of it as positive. The ending of a story in which a hen defeats a champion fighting cock, with a whole town looking on, was hard to give up. I began by paying attention to the integrity of the main characters rather than myself. Pablo a poor man but one with aspirations, and taking advantage of his innate cleverness was not above its amoral application. His integrity was probably close to mine. The cantina owner, who nurtures a hatred for the brother, the owner of the fighting cock, who stole his woman, seeks only revenge. Understandable, but little integrity. Then there was El Rey del Piratas, The King of the Pirates, the champion fighting cock.

When Jane first read it, she had commented that El Rey was the only virtuous character in the story. She may have even used the term *integrity*, but I'd forgotten. Anyway, the fighting cock exhibited the only integrity in the story—refusing to attack a woman. I briefly entertained the idea of cutting off the story as he lay dead on the sawdust of the fighting ring. Making the story about his gallantry. But the story was about Pablo. Although the hero was El Rey, the story was about Pablo. There was no ducking his authenticity, wherever it rested.

I reviewed the other characters in the story: the widow Peralta, the owner of El Rey, both were cardboard characters as Jane had described George, my character for Charles, in the *Jim's Worth* story. No chance of drawing integrity out of cardboard. I was left with Pablo's integrity and my own.

Earlier, I had ceded the notion of clever in favor of out-think. I thought the latter more active and noble—just barely. Did Pablo out-think anyone, or did he just cleverly take advantage of fortunate circumstances? I left the question hanging and turned it on me.

I began by confronting that authenticity was not the same as integrity. One could be authentically compromised—authentically duplicitous. Authentically a creep. I cringed at the word, but I could hardly take on Pablo's integrity before I took on my own. What was the true line to my authenticity, the true line to my character? Did it run through the territory of integrity or duplicity? I tallied it up. A miserable list, I thought. I had fused two women that I purported to love into a single interchangeable entity. Little integrity there. How—why did this happen? Merely for convenience, to continue with both, to ease my mind? I had slept with a woman, responding only to the bubbles in my blood, after declaring I was the boyfriend of another. I had not shown the courage to introduce myself to a woman who continued to occupy my thoughts, and I wasn't sure if making her my model for the Jersey Devil went very far toward redemption. I faced a list with little integrity. The line to my authenticity seemed about as true as lightning. I left it for a while. I still had a little time.

63

An Ugly but Honest VW

It was Saturday, my day off. I hadn't done any writing, but I'd done a lot of thinking. The wind was still blowing, and the sky was clouded over as I walked almost automatically to Jill's house, hoping to catch a ride to Holgate and go surfing. Jill had already gone, and Roger was there with Jane, but rather than surfing they were off for a picnic at Barnegat. I mentioned how frustrating it was not being able to travel on my own with my new surfboard.

"You need to get a car," Roger said. I'd lost my battle with my aunt decisively early on and not returned to it. "Got any money?" he said. I had been saving for a surfboard, but with Roger's gift, I still had it all—just over 250 dollars.

"Two-hundred and fifty dollars, more with next week's paycheck," I said.

"Two-hundred fifty should be enough. Manahawkin's got a number of used-car lots with lots of wrecks for sale. Like surfboards, people get 'em for their stay and get rid of 'em when they leave. You can pick one up cheap. Jane and I won't be gone long, what with the weather. Hang in here. I'll pick you up and we can go car shopping." They both left. Jane sported a sour look but said nothing.

I was alone with Jane, the mother, who asked, "You do any thinking about your ending to the Pablo story?"

"Plenty," I answered. "But I've got more to do, and I'm not ready to talk about it."

Jane respected this and asked if I wanted breakfast. "Please," I said, grateful for the silence that continued through my eggs and bacon.

Finally, she ventured, "You know, Jimmy, many good works have been compromised by their endings." *Compromised, well, that's the word isn't?* I thought. "It's good that you're spending time thinking about it—weighing it."

I wasn't weighing anything but rather scrounging around in the trash heap of my integrity. I'd never felt so completely alone. Jane could feel the tension and chose to leave me be as she went about her housekeeping duties. It was a quite awkward time until the return of Roger and Jane.

"Let's go buy you a car," Roger said.

"Want lunch?" asked Jane. Roger had just returned from a wind-blown picnic and looked to me for an answer. I shook my head. I just wanted to get out of there.

We had to stop by the apartment to pick up my cash, totaling two hundred and sixty-five dollars. We drove off the island over the causeway in a slight sprinkle to the town of Manahawkin and its sundry used-car lots. After two strikeouts, we arrived at Claude Wainslee's, Ugly but Honest, Fine Pre-Driven Autos. We drove into the lot and stopped in front of a once-black VW beetle now made a foggy gray by excessive exposure to the elements. It glistened under the light rain. "This may be the one!" Roger shouted as he exited his car. I was envisioning red or competition orange and was put off by the elemental gray. The chrome bumpers were flecked with rust, as was the body. "It has no rear window," I said.

"It's a surfer's wagon. How else do you think you can transport your surfboard?" Roger walked around the vehicle, obviously bonding with it. "The interior's pretty good, except the back seat that has a little rain damage, but the rest of it's in good shape." He turned on the radio "Music! Rubber's not bad, either."

I was yet to be convinced, as we were greeted by a middle-aged man with a W.C. Fields nose. He wore a nametag that said Claude, old Ugly but Honest himself.

"Just took this one in on a trade," he said. "Young fella bought a station wagon for all his surfboards."

"How's it run?" Roger asked.

"Seems to run OK. Haven't checked it out, though," Wainslee answered with the honest half of his name.

"Can we drive it?" Roger asked.

"Sure." Wainslee took out a number of keys from a copious pocket, picked out one, and handed it to Roger. "Just need to leave me your driver's license." Roger complied, and we drove off the lot, with me in the passenger seat.

Roger was attentive to the sounds, to the acceleration, the brakes, how it maneuvered, how it turned. His smile broadened. "This is a good car, Jimmy. The outside's a little rough but the engine's in good shape. Probably just used to haul around his board, then sat out in the weather. I'll check out the engine when we get back, but depending on the price, I think you probably can't do much better." Roger pulled off to the side of the road and asked, "Wanna drive it?"

I drove it back, and it did feel comfortable, and I liked the pick-up. And by the time I drove it back to the island, I'd grown fond of its funky exterior.

Wainslee was waiting for us just where we'd left him, hands in his front pockets, and he gave a little hop. "How was she?" he asked, handing Roger back his license but not taking the key.

"How much?" I asked, trying not to show my increasing affection for the car.

Wainslee hesitated slightly before he said, "Quick sale—two-fifty."

At two hundred and fifty dollars, I wasn't going to have much left over for gas, selling at twenty-one cents a gallon.

"Two-twenty," I said.

He countered with a smile. "Two-sixty." Having exerted his dominance, Wainslee said, "Two hundred and thirty-five dollars."

I was still smarting from his two-sixty quip. "Two-thirty," I said.

Ugly but Honest Claude Wainslee smiled. "Done," he said, offering me his hand.

During the high-level economic negotiations, Roger had been in the back of the VW, waiting for the negotiation to finish. Then he said, "Motor's well taken care of—oil's clean." He found the rear bumper a bit loose. Wainslee noticed and said, "I saw that, too. It's just a bolt." Roger bounced the bumper a few more times, "Got a bolt?" he asked. Wainslee went inside his garage and returned with a bolt and a crescent wrench. After the bumper was secured, I drove back to the island. The rain had picked up a bit. I imagined Eddie and Mike sitting in Eddie's VW waiting for the rain to clear.

Back at the house, both Janes expressed their excitement over the purchase and the prospect of advancing my independence. Roger and I loaded our surfboards into our respective VWs and drove through the slight rain to Holgate. Jane, the daughter, rode with Roger. Jane, the mother, rode with me, uncharacteristically joining us on a surfing outing. Jill was already there. I admired my surfboard sticking out of the Beetle's rear window.

On the way over, Jane gave me another thing to think on. "Do you know who John Dewey was?"

"Didn't he run for president against Truman?"

Jane suppressed a chuckle. "No, that was Thomas Dewey," she gently corrected. I thought about hiding my ignorance with Huckleberry Finn's statement, *I don't take no stock in dead people*. But then I wasn't sure he was dead, so I stayed silent.

Jane continued. "John Dewey was an American philosopher. He

wrote a book important for writers, and other artists, called *Art as Experience*. Anyway, that's a topic for another conversation. John Dewey was once asked if he could say anything was an unequivocal good. Dewey thought about it a while and came up with just one thing. *Anything that increases one's options can be said to be good.* This car, I think, is an example of increasing your options. As is, I think, are your deliberations on the Pablo ending." (Jane was relentless.) "In your deliberation, think of increased and limited options." More insight, if not intuition. I looked down at the arms holding the steering wheel to see goose bumps rising again.

We parked in the bare lot above Holgate. The surfing was uneventful, but a first for me, with my own board and my own car. Jill returned with me, our two boards riding easily through the back window. Jane returned home with her daughter. In Roger's convertible, the single board took up less interior space. Back at the house, I excused myself early, saying to Jane, "It's not you, but me." She seemed to understand.

As I left, Roger cautioned me. "Jimmy, you have only tomorrow if *Pablo's Cock* is to be published."

64

Pablo's Authenticity

O nly one day left—one night left, really. Tomorrow was a work day, so not much writing was likely to get done. I'd left my new car at the Deriksson house, reluctant—scared, in fact—to raise it as topic with Aunt Clair.

It's hard for people who don't write fiction to understand that the characters one makes up are not solely our creations but also have lives of their own; sometimes, they can fool you. And this was the case for Pablo. I'd heard writers talk about this, but this was the first time I'd ever experienced it, where a character takes command of the story and tells the author what to do. And in this case, what not to do. But this is what the surprising Pablo did. It was not quite the same as when Jim stepped forward to take command of Roger's story as the narrator, as Jim was not really my character, but only co-opted as an image from Twain. Besides, I treated him mostly as a hallucination, as did Robb in the story.

But Pablo spoke to me, not as a hallucinogenic vision but directly to me, inside my head, to give me advice. It was as if he were saying, "If I were you, and I am you, I'd be careful not confuse your integrity with mine. My integrity is my own; it's sealed within the story—intact. It's not linked to yours. You created me and gave me to your readers. I don't need any authenticity from you."

"OK, man," I answered within my head, "the story's yours."

Pablo's voice was clear as he assumed ownership of himself, ownership within his story. Ownership of his integrity that was already present in the story. "I did what I did, and it's the readers' decision to evaluate where my integrity lies. The authenticity is defined by the story, the integrity is defined in my actions. This is true both for me and El Rey del Piratas. I have no interest in who a reader finds *is* the hero. It can be either one of us, both, or neither. The authenticity is in the true line of the story." Pablo's message was clear—once the story was written, it had little to do with me. Jane, in fact, never equated authenticity with integrity—that was me.

I took out the story and retyped the last page. I slightly rearranged the events and highlighted the reactions of the principals, so the readers could more easily see it: the joy of the cantina owner, the sorrow of El Rey's owner, the gallantry of El Rey, realizing, as Pablo had told me, that the integrity was already in the story and in its characters. Rather than adding to the ending and coming down on the side of hero or cheater, I cut the ending and left the tale with The King of the Pirates bleeding to death on the sawdust floor of the fighting ring. As I had been told by Pablo, I left it to the reader to decide who was the hero—Pablo, El Rey del Piratas, or both. In the end, I'd cut fewer than a hundred words. Pablo was left satisfied, sleeping in my brain. Maybe later he married the Widow Peralta, but I don't know—Pablo was his own guy.

65

Hurricane Watch

As a last act of the evening, I placed the finished story in a folder to give to Roger to pass on to the *Islander*. Having a previously xeroxed copy, I retyped a separate last page and went to bed trying to think of nothing.

With the morning came rain. I dropped *Pablo's Cock* with Roger, still at his room in the Island Beach Hotel. I kept the folder inside my lifeguard jersey; I wore my pith helmet, but I was soaked by the time I got there. The folder was moist, but Pablo was dry.

Roger invited me in and poured me a cup of coffee. "I'll drive you over to the beach. You can shelter in your new car," he said brightly.

Mike was there standing by the flags and the buoy that wallowed in the wet sand. Besides these forlorn figures, the beach was deserted; the sky was dark and rolling, and the waves were high. A sopped Mike, jogged over to us. "Sure glad to see you guys," he said.

"Let's go to Flo's," Roger said. "I think you can leave the beach for a while. It's safe to leave the flags and the buoy, just move 'em back. No telling what the tide will do with a sky like this."

At Flo's, we sat at the counter, Mike and I dripping rainwater off our linoleum stools onto the floor. "What do we do if rains all day?" I asked the two experienced lifeguards. Roger answered.

"You need to stay at the beach until a supervisor comes and says you can go. A supervisor usually knows where his guards shelter in the rain. Yours, however, is indisposed, and Eddie's car would be the sheltering place, so you've struck out twice. I'd drive your VW to where you can see the beach when a supervisor arrives. I would think today it won't be long."

The clock behind Flo's counter read ten o'clock, and Roger drove us to my car outside the Deriksson place. "I'll drop your story off at the Rag and maybe see you later. Jane has some things to do today, so we've made no plans."

I explained to Mike about my purchase of the car, as I positioned it on the sand that marked the entryway to the beach, giving us a good view below. The tide was creeping up steadily. The rain was coming from the ocean, so the open back window was no problem as the rain dripped into a growing pool on the already compromised backseat. We sipped on the to-go coffees we'd brought from Flo's. Before we finished, a Scout carrying Supervisor Dan parked at the buoy. We left the protection of the VW and jogged over. "Weather's bad, and not getting better soon, so you guys are off for the day," was Dan's welcome message. He drove off. I picked up the rain-and-sand-soaked flags, Mike, got the buoy, and we loaded them into my VW. I took Mike home and returned to the Deriksson house.

When I arrived, I found Jane in a near hysteria. She hugged me at the screen door. "It's the cat. He's been in a fight. He's hurt badly." She spit out the staccato sentences between sobs. She pulled me into the living room, where the cat—I would never learn his name—rested languidly on the braided carpet. I could see blood streaking his orange fur; he moved not a muscle, and his breath came irregularly in shallow gasps. "Jane's gone with the car, visiting friends, and I can't reach her. Can you take me to the vet in Manahawkin?" she asked, and I assured her that I could. She hugged me again.

"You're soaked. You need to change." She went upstairs, returning with a gray cotton sweatshirt and gray cotton sweatpants, white socks, and black Converse tennis shoes. "Richard's, he never uses them. You can change in the bathroom. I'll get the cat in his carrier."

I put on the dry clothes in the bathroom named in honor of the victim, trying to keep my feet out of the litter box in the confined space allocated to the cat's business—that and Jane's phone calls with Charles.

The rain had gotten stronger, and the wind had picked up as we drove off the island. Only four blocks wide, the drainage was minimal, and the streets were under about a foot of water. The stalwart car raised wings of water out to each side as we cut through the flooded streets. The causeway, built high over the ocean, allowed us to leave the flood behind.

It took only minutes to reach Manahawkin, and a few miles more to the vet. "Will they be open on Sunday?" I asked.

"Yes, they maintain an emergency room that's open all the time. I called my friend who'll come to meet us. We're good friends. We went to high school together," Jane said as I pulled into the parking lot.

Inside. we were met by a middle-aged woman who looked to be a contemporary of Jane's. We bypassed the receptionist in favor of an exam room. Jane's friend, whom she introduced as Sandy, took the cat out of the carrier and stretched the flaccid feline on a stainless-steel table. The cat seemed exhausted but was breathing normally. *That's good*, I thought, but what did I know?

"He'll live," Sandy said as she took her stethoscope from the cat. She reached across the table and grasped her friend's shoulder. Jane expelled a long breath and tried to smile.

Sandy gave the cat an injection. "Vitamin D. I'll need to do some tests. You go somewhere and relax. Have a cup of coffee, maybe something stronger," Sandy counseled her friend. "Call me in a couple of hours." Jane nodded. There were tears in her eyes.

Back in the Volkswagen. "Where to?" I asked.

"I have another high school friend, Lucy. She owns an inn just up the coast. We can go over there and have a drink and a little something to eat.

"It seems the cat will be all right," I said.

"Yeah." The tears returned.

We drove to a little inn on the water. It was not on the open shore but on an estuary-like thing. It was in no way similar to the Oyster Creek Inn, not in geography or architecture, but I was reminded of it. The Sandpiper was a single-story, modest but artful structure made from wood and natural stone. In fact, it was several self-contained buildings. The largest formed an office and restaurant. Smaller freestanding cabins were stung out on either side of the restaurant, like wings along the water, four cabins to each side.

We entered and were seated at a table with a view of the estuary. The open ocean could be seen in the distance. A waitress approached our table. "Lucy!" Jane exclaimed, and the woman returned her surprise. "What are you doing waiting tables?"

After greetings and introductions, Lucy said, "Waitress called in sick at the last minute. I think it's the weather."

Jane ordered martinis up for both of us. Lucy looked at me with some scrutiny but returned with the drinks.

"What are you doing here, particularly on a day like this?"

Jane gave a synopsis of the ongoing cat drama.

"Wow," Lucy said. "I just heard they closed the entranceway to the island. There's a hurricane watch in effect." Jane looked at me, took a sip of her martini, then asked Lucy, "Are any of your rooms available?"

"There's just one left." Lucy looked at me again. "It's just got one double bed, but there's a couch that makes into a bed."

"Do you take cats?"

"For you, we take cats." Lucy smiled.

"We'll take it," Jane said.

Jane ordered crab cakes and additional martinis for both of us and asked if there was a phone she could use. Lucy came back to the table with a telephone with an exceptionally long cord and a local phone book. First, Jane called Sandy and found that the cat needed stitches in several places and significant wound cleaning and antibiotics, that she was resting and heavily sedated. Sandy suggested that the cat stay at the hospital for a day at least, and Jane was relieved. Next, she reached Jane at home and told her of our exile from the island. I asked to be handed the phone to talk to her. I asked if she could ask Roger to alert my aunts to the situation. "Roger's been to my Aunt Clair's apartment," I said, and I gave her the number of the buildings and the apartments. I also asked her to make sure to check in with my Aunt Isobel, feeling that this just might be an example of something Clair would think not to tell her. Jane assured me that she and Roger would touch base with both.

After the call, Jane relaxed into her martini and crab cakes, and I followed. "What did you do with the ending of the Pablo story?" she asked casually over a bite of crab.

I took a sip of my elegant drink, feeling underdressed in Richard's track suit. "I didn't finish it at all. Actually, I cut the ending." She shot me a concerned look as the rain assailed the windows. Her concern dissipated as I recounted my inner conversations with Pablo and my decision to leave the ending with him. I finished with, "It's between the integrity of Pablo, El Rey del Piratas, and the readers. The story ends with El Rey del Pirates dying on the sawdust of the cockfighting ring."

At first, she smiled, then the smile dissolved into tears. Between the cat and me, we were the origin of a lot of tears.

I sipped my second martini up, ever, as Jane dried her eyes with a napkin. "I must confess that I was worried as to what you would do, not sure which ending I was hoping for. Lots of trepidation, no clear conviction. I know you were going through lots of anguish deciding. Never once did I come up with the solution you found—that found you." She smiled and more tears appeared in her eyes. This time, she let them stay on her cheeks, and she reached across the table and took my hand and squeezed, not letting go. With my free hand, I drank from my martini glass. I now had an erection that the tracksuit did little to disguise. Out of the corner of my eye, I saw Lucy coming toward the table, and with one look at the scene she retreated, deciding not to intrude.

We finished our crab cakes and martinis, and if anything, the rain had gotten more furious and the ocean closer. Lucy walked over again, carrying a key. "Number eight, the last one to the left—to the north."

Jane went into her purse. "I'll get this," she said ostensibly to me.

"Don't worry," Lucy said, "we can settle up when you check out."

66

Summer Dress in a Hurricane

It was getting onto three p.m. as we entered our room. As we'd been told, there was a double bed and a sleeping couch. There was also an enormous picture window overlooking the lagoon or estuary, which now roiled like a pot of boiling water. The window was divided into five elongated wooden frames—I took to add stability to oncoming winds. If ever they were needed, it was now. The view through them, however, was dramatic.

Jane lay down on the bed, and I sat on the couch and looked out the segmented picture window that dominated the room. After a while Jane said, "Jimmy, why don't you come and lay next to me." I gave the thin cotton sweatpants a skeptical look but complied. I wished I were in a tight pair of jeans. As we lay side by side, she reached over and took my hand.

"I'm really proud of your ending. It was the act of a truly mature writer. Did you actually hear him speaking to you?"

Although it was yesterday, it seems a long time ago. "It's strange. But yes, he actually did speak to me, but I can't remember what he sounded like, only his words—it's strange. But he was definitely there."

Jane squeezed my hand and turned toward me. The cotton sweatpants did nothing to shield my growing embarrassment. I gave up the ghost (whatever the hell that means) and turned to meet her.

This time, she took the initiative and kissed me, placing her free hand around me pulling me into her. She adjusted her position to accommodate my erection. The panels of the picture windows shook in their frames—at least I thought it was the windows. "Take off your pants. You don't want to spot up your only trousers," she said with a little giggle.

"I have no underwear," I said. Jane had provided me with a pair with the other clothes, but I balked at putting on something as intimate as Richard's underwear. It just seemed wrong, and I'd left them folded on the toilet of the cat's bathroom.

"All the more reason," she said with another chuckle. I complied, wondering if my whole body could blush.

We stayed hugging each other for what seemed a long time, with my penis held between her legs. Even though her dress was in between, I could hardly stand it. It's amazing what restraint you can call forth sometimes, and I tried to relax in her arms with only mild success. After what seemed like forever, she pulled up her skirt, shed her underwear, and brought my penis in contact with her pubic hair, while gently moving her hand up and down. I released all over her. She rolled onto her back and allowed me to see my handiwork. It was like snow on the back of a midnight-black wild horse. We stayed that way for what must have been an hour, softly tasting each other.

She lay back, and I looked down at her black horse, and the snow had melted.

She got up and removed her one-piece muumuu that I realized was more of a summer dress. "I've got to take a shower." She moved naked across the room, and I glimpsed a view of her daughter Jane in years to come. *Hold on, Charles*, I thought.

67

Piña Coladas

Jane exited the shower, still toweling off. I picked up my sweatpants and saw no spots and said so. "Don't put them on till you shower," Jane cautioned.

"There are spots on the bedspread, though," I said. "Think Lucy will notice?"

"I don't think Lucy cleans the rooms, even for a sick maid in a hurricane. Besides, I believe she's already noticed. Come on, take your shower and we'll go back over for cocktails and dinner—that is, if the chef hasn't called in sick."

We battled our way through rain and hurricane winds and entered through the front door. Lucy was now behind the bar, and the other occupants of the rooms were scattered around the restaurant. "Your kitchen open?" Jane asked in an exaggerated Jersey accent.

"Yeah," said Lucy, "Night chef called in, but the lunch chef was still here, couldn't get home. Told him I'd take him home after dinner. We've got a Jeep, so you're OK."

We sat down at the bar. This time, Jane ordered piña coladas. Lucy looked at me again as if arriving at a decision, but high school friendship won the day, and both were delivered. My first colada, and it didn't even taste like alcohol. We ended up drinking three. At piña colada number two, Jane, after reviewing the menu, asked if the fish and chips were good.

"Sure," answered Lucy, "if you like frozen fish and chips."

"Love 'em," Jane responded. The fish and chips came, and I said they were pretty good. Though I was no expert, as I pointed out to Lucy.

"It's the sauce. We make our own sauce."

Jane ordered piña coladas number three, and Lucy questioned if we'd be all right, this time looking only at Jane.

Jane answered again in a thick Jersey accent. "Sure. We've only a short walk through a hurricane."

I can't taste the alcohol, but it can taste me, I thought as I began to feel the effects.

We made it back to our room through the deluge. "Take off your sweatshirt and pants," said Jane. "Fold them and keep them nice for tomorrow."

What about my shoes and socks? I wanted to say. Instead, I went with, "OK if you take off your dress." Jane disrobed completely, and we both slipped inside the sheets. Unlike before, things were calm—easy. Jane put her head on my shoulder and her arm around my waist, and I was only half aroused. It felt so nice. Maybe it was the alcohol, but I think it was more than that. It felt natural. Jane's breathing fused with the sounds of the hurricane wind outside, and we fell asleep in each other's arms.

68

Amazing

I t's amazing what you can get used to, and how fast you can get used to it. Things you thought were impossible become commonplace in no time—it is truly amazing. It was like that with Jane. All you needed was an injured cat and a hurricane, then you'd be laying naked next to the love of your life, all seeming natural. That was the bliss I experienced for two days in the hurricane on the Jersey shore.

I went to sleep that first night calm and at peace with myself and everything else in the world, but I woke up the next morning excited—agitated—and physically engaged. Jane was still sleeping with her back turned away from me, and I hugged her from behind until she started to wake up in little jerks. She turned toward me, and we kissed and petted. I had thought petting was just a teenage thing, but Jane was quite proficient. We did the wild horse and snow thing, and I was quite satisfied.

We went to the restaurant for breakfast and were informed by other cottage residents that the island was still closed to incoming traffic and still under a hurricane watch, but no evacuation had been called for. The wind was still high. But the rain seemed to be less than the night before. We didn't see Lucy, and Jane paid for breakfast. She asked for the telephone and called home and talked to Jane, who said everyone was fine. My aunts had been notified and weren't overly concerned; they were used to such weather. The winds were high, the streets were still flooded and only passable in a few places, and there was a heavy rain—not much need for lifeguards. Jane next called the vet and was told that cat was resting comfortably. But that there was no need to pick him up that day. We were unencumbered with no pressing responsibilities. There was a little shop tangential to the restaurant and office that sold sweatshirts, cups, and sundry clothing—T-shirts and such, all with a sandpiper logo. I looked hopefully for underwear but found none. Jane bought us plastic slickers, and we walked out in the rain to the banks of the lagoon. Sea birds plied the banks for whatever it was that they ate. Intermittently, we held hands and kissed surreptitiously a few times.

It was an intimate moment, and I asked an intimate question, hoping it was not too impertinent. "Do you resent Richard for pulling you away from your early aspirations of being a writer? What with family duties and all—children." Rather than taking offense, she became thoughtful and didn't say anything for a long time, maybe ten minutes. I thought maybe she was thinking of something else, when she said, "No, I don't think so, though I've thought a lot about it. Who I resent, really, if anyone, is me. Me, for not continuing with it. For what I sometimes believe was an easy way out."

I thought back to her earlier lesson of the difference between having and making.

"Like not having time to do something or not making time to do it?"

She smiled. "You remember. You are a good student. Yes, it's just like that. Still, sometimes I sit down before a piece of paper with a pen and an idea and think of writing something. Then I think it's too late, then I think, I'm just too late, then I think I'm taking the easy way out again. Though you, Jimmy, have infected me."

69

Puzzle Pieces

We returned to the room. Jane was restless, prowling around the room and picking up things. From the little kitchen: plates, cups, salt and pepper shakers. She opened a drawer and pulled out silverware, corkscrews, knives, can openers. She scrutinized each and set it back down. She seemed to be orienting herself to a foreign, unfamiliar place.

I'd been orienting myself to something new, something exhilarating, something in my own mind that was natural. However, Jane, I realized, was in a land unknown in her experience, a place where she had no bearings. A place where she was rearranging puzzle pieces from different puzzles, and some of the pieces were upside down. Still, she forged on with the unfamiliar picture, assembled from pieces that didn't exactly fit.

"I need to see my cat," she said. I took a coffee cup that she had set down, and happy for something to do, I started bailing out the lagoon that was now the backseat of the car.

During our drive to the veterinary hospital, I asked, "Do you want to call Sandy?"

"No, it doesn't matter," she answered.

The receptionist disappeared at Jane's query and returned with

Sandy. I kept my distance, not wanting to intrude. The three disappeared inside. I took a seat. Sandy returned and motioned me to follow, leading me to a row of cages. Before one, Jane held a somnolent cat. It seemed she was drawing strength from something familiar to her from her pre-hurricane time little more than a day ago.

Both cat and Jane were immobile. The receptionist left, but Sandy waited patiently for her friend as Jane gathered strength. After what seemed a long time, Jane looked up at me and smiled. "I'm all right," she said, and Sandy seemed to understand, and for that I was relieved.

As we left the building, Jane held my hand. "Let's get us some clothes."

A number of stores are closed, but we found an open Penny's, where she bought a colorful red and yellow summer dress, I got a pair of Levi's to corral my frequent erections and underwear to do the same, and a pair of rubber flip-flops. I'd grown a certain affection for the sweatshirt; Richard's shoes and socks were adequate, if I needed them. Before we checked out, Jane selected a colorful yellow and black Hawaiian shirt with palm trees. "Wear this!" she commanded, and we exited the store wearing our new purchases.

I was relieved for the protection offered by the jeans and underwear. Jane, in her red and yellow summer dress, acted as if she'd had an injection of energy. She actually twirled on our way to the car. "What next?" she asked me. I'd not a clue and said so.

The wind was howling, and the trees were bent over like croquet wickets. "Let's take a drive," she said.

"A leisurely cruise through a developing hurricane?"

"Exactly," she said. "Drive along the shore, if you can."

There were lots of fallen branches blocking the roadways, a few powerlines were down, and we zigged and zagged our way along the coast. The waves were majestic and huge. We found an open 7-11 and bought hoagies. We parked as close to the shore as we could get and watched the giant waves roll in through the rain. We ate our hoagies with the large bottle of Coke we shared between us. Intermittently, we kissed and petted like a high school couple at a drive-in. Indeed, the feature through the windshield was the ocean; as the waves seemed to get closer and larger.

A nearby tree branch snapped and landed near the car—a sign that it was time to leave. While it was nearing only five o'clock, the sky was dark when we arrived back at the inn. We parked near the front door of the restaurant and went to the bar in our new threads.

Lucy was behind the bar. As it turned out, this was her usual place. Guess she wouldn't be cleaning our room. "You've been shopping," she said. Jane gave a version of a curtsy and sat down at the bar with me at her right elbow.

"Margaritas," said Jane, changing it up for the evening. *Margaritas, the only Mexican food east of the Mississippi*, I thought. Lucy didn't even give me a look as she placed two lime-colored drinks in front of us.

"The dinner chef is here, and I recommend the real seafood. The hurricane is blowing out, I hear they're going to open up the island tomorrow if it continues," Lucy said.

"That's good news," Jane said flatly. I wished the hurricane would never end. We were still full from our 7-11 hoagies, and we had two more margaritas before we ordered.

"How did you like the books I lent you?" Jane asked me. I was embarrassed and had to admit that I had read neither *White Lotus* or *The Child Buyer*. I had begun *The Child Buyer* but put it aside in favor of my own writing. It had also seemed a little farfetched. But I didn't say that.

Jane proceeded to tell me about their author. John Hersey began as a journalist and was credited as the originator of the new journalism that reported the news as stories. *Hiroshima*, about the bombing of Japan, and *The Wall* about the Warsaw ghetto, were among his first.

From there, he moved naturally into fiction, and most all of his writing had a social theme. *White Lotus* is about the enslavement of a young American woman by the Chinese after their victory in a war over America. She's taken to China to live out her life as a servant, but she becomes involved in a resistance movement. Some feel it's analogous to the slave experience in this country.

"That's the way I read it, too," she said, "but I'm giving too much away. *The Child Buyer* is my favorite of his, and it's not all that farfetched as one might think." Jane again showed the ability to peek into my mind.

She went on. "*The Child Buyer* is an exposition of the effect of commodifying people—turning them into things. Reify, I think, is the word. It's also a warning to take things seriously in their infancy. Read it. I think you'll derive something from it," she said. I picked up on how she didn't say I would like it, but that I'd derive something from it. Jane was a constant amazement. Then she shifted gears.

"I always saw Roger as a young John Hersey, turning his journalism into fiction. He hasn't done it yet, and I'm beginning to lose hope, but still I'm hopeful. I think you got him right in your story *Jim's Worth*, in your character, what did you call him? Robb? Yes, Robb. I think you nailed him. It was the work of an insightful friend, though you should never show it to either Roger or Jane. Invoking the character of Jim from *Huckleberry Finn* was a clever mechanism."

She'll never know how clever, I thought, as Jim would not leave me.

"The character you missed, worthy of a story of his own, is Charles. Though you'll probably never get to know him well enough to write it, but there's a good story there."

Jane ordered the fourth margaritas and with them dinner, a tandem order of soft-shelled crab, another first. "Very good choice," Lucy said. Our margaritas came with only a slight glance at Jane from Lucy.

The ever-observant Jane noticed. "I'm only walkin'," she said in thick Jersey. Lucy smiled.

The soft-shelled crab became a favorite on the spot.

Wisely, we left the car in front of the restaurant and walked the hundred or so yards to our cabin. The rain had all but stopped, and the wind had mitigated its fury. The hurricane was coming to its end.

Maybe it was the four margaritas, maybe it was a growing familiarity, but I shed my clothes and slipped into the newly made bed naked. I waited to see what Jane would do.

Jane, too, slipped into bed sans her yellow and red summer dress, and under the influence of four margaritas, a hoagie sandwich, and soft-shelled crab, we went back to kissing and petting. With a temerity that surprised me, I kissed her nipples. After a while, she reached down and took hold of my *member* and placed it on her wild horse, and I attempted to enter her. "Not yet," she said, "not yet." A puzzle piece yet to be added to the picture.

70

The Benefits of a Good High School

The view out of the five vertical panels that framed the picture window showed blue sky, a calm lagoon, and small waves in the distance. The trees had resumed a vertical position, no longer trying to break through the earth and dance. And the long-legged seabirds gently speared the shore. The hurricane days were over, and an ominous normalcy had usurped their place. Time to go home.

I was a bit fuzzy when I awoke, but there was no hangover headache. Jane was already up and making coffee. She handed me a cup as I stood staring out the picture window, trying to clear my head.

"I was up early and called home. The watch is over, and the island's opened up. The cat's also OK to be picked up." I nodded and sipped my coffee.

Jane's wet hair told me she'd showered. "I'll shower and get dressed," I said.

After a fairly silent breakfast, we went to the little kiosk in the reception area. "Checking out of number eight," Jane said to the girl on duty.

She checked a large book and said, "No charge."

"There's been some mistake, we had the room for two days and ate a number of times at the restaurant." *Not to mention about a hundred cocktails*, I thought.

"No mistake, ma'am. Lucy told me that there was to be no charge for your stay," the young employee said. The checking of the book had been mere theater.

"Can I talk to Lucy?"

"She's out."

"Well, thank her from the bottom of my heart for what was a lovely stay. Tell her I'll be in touch." The girl said she would be sure to tell her. Jane took a twenty-dollar bill out of her purse. "For the maid."

"Lucy was adamant there was to be no charge," said the loyal and literal employee. I was fearing an oncoming pissing contest between the two women at the slim kiosk, but Jane turned and left with a thank you.

At the vet, Sandy brought out a much-animated cat and handed him to Jane. He meowed at Jane's petting and baby talk. Sandy put him in the carrier we brought and handed the carrier to me. I wanted to ask the cat's name, but I'd noticed before that if you don't know someone's name after a significant period of time, it's awkward to ask. Rude, even. I wondered briefly why that was.

"Thank you, Sandy, for all your trouble," said Jane.

"No trouble," said Sandy, and the two women hugged.

"Sandy said no charge on this one," said the girl at the receptionist's desk.

"This is just too much!" Jane said, taking the carrier from me.

On the way home, Jane sat with the cat on her lap, the carrier resting on the drying backseat.

"I guess it pays to go to high school with the right crowd. Nobody at my school would have anted up for a gumball," I said. Jane smiled but said nothing.

We worked our way to the causeway around broken tree limbs

that still littered the streets. The island seemed relatively intact, save for branches and garbage leftover from the flooded streets. Roof tiles and cedar shakes seemed to be the most common damage. We moved easily to the house. Jane carried the cat, I the empty carrier.

Inside, Jane was glad to see us and hugged us both. Jill and Roger had gone surfing.

"I want to hear about everything," the daughter said. I was in a sweat to get out of there, not wanting to be part of any conversation. I refused an offer of lunch saying I needed to see if I still had a job. I went into the bathroom and changed into my now dry lifeguard togs, then quickly left.

71

Caterpillars

I walked the short distance to the beach to find Ed and Mike manning the stand. "Welcome back. You enjoy your vacation?" Ed said. It wasn't really a question. Besides, what could I say?

"You got my message from Roger?"

"Yeah, I passed it on to Lifter."

"What did he say?"

"He said to alert him when you got back."

Mike spoke up. "He said I was to go to another beach if you came in today. Bataglia's alone until I get there. You here now?" I assured him that I was, and he left for Gino Bataglia's beach a quarter of a mile away.

I looked over the beach. "Where's the buoy and the flags?"

"Probably still with you. Mike said you put them in your car when the two of you left."

"Shit! They're on the screened porch at the Deriksson house. I had to take Jane's cat to the vet and we got caught off the island when the hurricane came. Want me to go get them?"

I was grateful Ed had no further questions about my lockout. "No, it's pretty calm, don't think we'll need the buoy, and the people are pretty compliant. And Chris Mackee probably won't be by." He chuckled. "I can get them at the end of the day."

There were few beachgoers, and the water looked like glass. I hoped Jill and Roger were getting some surf after their two-day hiatus. I would find out later that Roger had defied the hurricane sanctions and surfed the big waves more than a few times. My hero.

At the end of the day, Eddie retook custody of the buoy and flags, and I went into the house. Jane caught me before I made it through the porch. "Just a few lies," she whispered. "The important one: You had your own room, and play down the alcohol." I nodded, and we entered the living room.

Jill and Roger had yet to return, and we were back to the pedestrian cream sherry, and I welcomed it as I would an old sweater. I was feeling comfortable when Jane, the daughter, said, "There's something I don't understand. Why is there a pair of men's underwear folded on the back of the toilet in the cat's bathroom?" We both stiffened and feigned ignorance, leaving it a mystery. Jane was denied any follow-up by Jill and Roger's arrival.

Jill was excited and hugged and kissed her mother, then bounced over to me and kissed me squarely on the lips in front of everyone. "Let me go upstairs and change. We can go for a walk, and you can tell me about your hurricane adventures," she said, smiling her ironic smile by touching her tongue to her upper lip. Jane refilled my cream sherry jar that had been spilled by Jill's advances.

I listened to Jane's account of our time away. Huckleberry Finn would have been proud, as Jane told the truth mainly, embellishing real events, downplaying others, leaving others out completely. I was uncomfortable and tried my best not to squirm, but it was artful storytelling—perhaps it wasn't too late for Jane to become a writer.

As a part of world religions class in high school, I attended a lecture by a Buddhist monk. At the end of the lecture, the monk was asked a question by a female student who was a lot smarter than

I. She asked the monk what individuals in the *great chain of being* would look like if you could view them over time.

The monk laughed, as he did frequently: "Caterpillars," he answered. He explained that if you could observe the whole, you would see a line of connected beings starting with babies followed by toddlers, children, teenagers, young men or women, all moving progressively into middle and old age, getting ever older, until the line would start again with a baby. "An individual viewed over time would look like a seemingly endless caterpillar, each segment attached to the one before and the one after in a progression with a head, and two legs, four limbs for the babies. Death would be marked by a baby replacing an old adult in the chain." The monk laughed again. "What we see as an individual is really a chain of connected beings, an endless caterpillar. The individual is just a snapshot in time."

As Jill and I walked along the beach, I imagined I was walking with a two-segmented caterpillar. Unlike the monk's caterpillar, mine was made up of two separate individuals—two separate women. I realized I was neck-deep in some metaphysical shit. Still, I walked along and held her hand. Later, the caterpillar and I would neck and explore each other on the sand.

When we returned to the house, I went inside my car and gathered up the cotton track suit, socks, and Converse shoes and gave them to Jane. I never knew what happened to the underwear.

72

Reification

I was caught with my pants down with regard to Jane's query about the two books she had given me at the start of the summer. I had read neither *White Lotus* nor *The Child Buyer.* I had previously started *The Child Buyer*, was a dystopian tale about the purchase of gifted children to serve a corporation that took over the parenting of a young child in order to shape it into the perfect corporate asset. The narrative is told in the form of a government hearing to determine the fate of a particular male child. The plot seemed farfetched, and I had lost interest, but Jane said it was her favorite, so I was obliged to read it. Besides, it was only a third of the length of *White Lotus*, so I could partly account for myself sooner.

As I read the chilling book, my admiration for it and its author grew. The tale is made more chilling through its use of the mundane context of a government hearing as the baseness of human intention and action is disclosed. By the end of the book, I was a John Hersey fan. Jane had used the word *reify*, and I had to look it up.

To represent something abstract as a material or concrete thing, to give definite content and form to a concept or idea. But I was confused by the definition and Jane's application of it to the story. Abstraction? Abstraction of what? My puzzlement continued until I thought of a child as an abstraction—the process of childhood.

Taking the process of childhood and turning it into a concrete thing. Thingifying it into a commodity (Jane's word); the selling of a childhood so that it could be turned into a thing useful to a corporation—a new form of slavery. I thought of Jim. What could be more insidious? What could be less human than turning a human childhood into a thing? A better plot and context than I'd ever come up with. As the legislature ceded to the arguments of the persona of the child buyer, it presaged an ultimate trajectory of an amoral, materialistic society. Bravo! Good for you, John Hersey, and good for you, Jane. We have met the enemy, and it is reification.

73

Omnipresence of Metaphor

I finished *The Child Buyer*. It was late night after dinner with Aunt Ibby. I lay on the couch in Aunt Clair's living room under the breeze provided by the open windows under which the couch was placed. I wore nothing but my lifeguard trunks, and the air from the windows and the rough fabric of the couch were the only respite from the relentless humidity that seized the island after the hurricane. Even so, I found my body in little puddles of sweat anywhere I happened to come in contact with an object like a chair, bed, or couch.

I looked at the cover of the small paperback, which depicted a sitting child looking up at a hulking man in an overcoat and hat lurking over him. I shivered. I took the book over to the little desk with my father's portable Underwood and placed it so that the disturbing image was kept fresh as I typed. I wrote an account of my impressions, pretty much as I've written them here. I read it over and felt it was an accurate response to what I thought. I folded it longways and placed it between the middle pages of the book. I'd give them to Jane after work the next day. It was pretty well past two o'clock, and I turned in on the couch, touching as few parts of my body as I could. Sleeping in the bed was impossible. You didn't want to wake up to find yourself in a wet shroud.

After work, I walked to the house. Jane was alone. I presented the book and my account of it to her, much like a fourth-grader would ceremoniously surrender a book report to his teacher. She poured our jelly jars before she sat to read it. "You're understanding well" was her only comment.

"The children are all out," she said. "Let's take a ride."

"Where to?" I said when we were seated in the VW.

"Drive up north toward Barnegat."

I drove off and waited for what was to come next.

"We need to talk about the hurricane," she said. I'd been dreading this conversation. Still silent, I waited.

"Ours is not a typical relationship," she said, expelling a dry chuckle. "Not that I'm sorry for it." I exhaled relief. "Jimmy, you've awakened things in me I thought were dead." Here, she hesitated. "At least long buried. It comes to me as quite a surprise, and I continue to unearth new things daily. I feel younger, invigorated in ways I haven't experienced for some time. Sandy and Lucy could see it, and it's why they extended us so much courtesy. I didn't need to explain to them. They could see it in my eyes. But Jimmy, I fear I might be stealing your youth." I began to disagree.

"Hush," she said. "Let me say what I need to say. Like I said, I'm not sorry. I couldn't quit now even if I wanted to, but I *don't* want to. What I know and need to tell you is this can't last, and soon you'll have to let it go. You don't have to believe it now, but just like a story you know can't end up happily ever after, you have to expect the ending's coming. It may seem unfair that we've met our soulmates out of temporal sequence for a happily-ever-after story. That's the bad news. The good news is that we met at all. It's like your dilemma with the two possible endings of *Pablo's Cock*, either a hero or a cheat. Our story can end in sadness and regret, or it can end happily, although the happiness will be bittersweet, a more complicated, but interesting ending. In Pablo's story, you came up with a creative third ending. Offering up Pablo, and letting the reader decide. But, Jimmy, in our story we *are* the readers—and not the writers—we're not the ones who determine the story's end—only how we receive it."

I pulled to the side of the narrow road, put my arms around her, and kissed her deeply and long. The cars behind slowed down to pass.

Resuming our way, I asked the question that had been on the forefront of my consciousness. "What did you mean by, not yet?" After the heavy conversation, the adolescent query caused us to laugh.

In between her giggles, Jane said. "Well, Jimmy, you've got a birthday coming in two weeks."

We continued on and parked in the long shadow of Barnegat light. We walked down to the beach, holding hands, and sat on the sand. The sun was low in the sky, not quite ready to set. Sometimes, everything's a metaphor.

74

Jim Again

On the way home, I glanced in the review mirror to see Jim in the backseat, sitting behind Jane. I wasn't all that surprised; he'd said he'd be back. He was bare-chested and wore his colorful surfer jams as he sat on the damp seat. "Tell her 'bout the *humbling part*," he said.

Of course, I knew just what he meant. He was my vision after all. He referred to the part of the book where Huck fools Jim into thinking a storm that had separated them was all a dream. Huck is feeling clever—that word again—when Jim begins to *'terpret* the symbolic meanings of the various events, that Jim now believes has come as a warning. Huck, basking in his trickery, says, "I understand your meanings, but what's the meaning of these." Jim looks up to see the residue of the storm, leaves, broken branches, a broken oar that litter their raft, and realizes he'd been the butt of Huck's Joke.

"What do dey stan' for? Dat truck dah is *trash*; en trash is what people is dat puts dirt on de head er dey frens…"

Huck says, "It was fifteen minutes before I could work myself up to go and humble myself to a nigger, but I done it, and I warn't ever sorry for it afterward, neither."

The scene came early in the book, but I'd always thought that it was the climax of the story and that Twain should have found a way to put it toward the end.

The message was clear. I looked back to the rearview mirror and Jim was gone.

"Jane, I have to tell you, I slept with Shelly Goldberg. It was the night of the Fairfields' party."

"Yes, I know, or at least strongly suspected," she said. "I saw you and Shelly walking back from the party. I knew before that, though. I saw the way you looked at her on the beach."

I slowed down and looked at her. *When?* I wanted to say. I hadn't seen her on the beach anytime Shelly had been there. But I stayed silent. Jane wasn't finished.

"I organized a little party that night mainly for Jill. I invited some of Jill's friends, even Fast Eddie. He came with his new girlfriend. I told her that I'd invited you, but you had an engagement with your aunts, that you couldn't get out of—I passed along your apologies." She flashed an ironic smile worthy of her daughter. "While confession may be good for the soul, don't ever tell Jill. For one thing, you'd expose me as a liar." I remembered the house all lit up and looking festive as Shelly and I walked home.

"You're not angry?"

"Jimmy, you're young, Shelly was obviously willing. Besides, as beautiful as Shelly is, she needs a lot of support. I hope you were able to provide her with some." I nodded. Boy, insight *and* compassion.

75

Another Picnic

The summer rolled by like clouds over the horizon, an uncoiling of a watch spring toward its inexorable end. I spent a good deal of my day off selling Lifeguard Ball tickets, and it turned out I was pretty good at it. At two dollars and fifty cents a pop, I made over 175 dollars. Eddie sold just twenty-five dollars, and it seemed unfair to me. If you considered the proceeds of the tickets as a tip for service, the fact that I made seven times what Ed, the far the better lifeguard, did was to my mind a travesty. After a little thought, I suggested that we pool the money between us and split it down the middle. Ever bound to an internal integrity, Ed refused, and though I tried, he would not compromise.

Jane and I continued to drive the VW to Barnegat Light, my pole star, and *neck* on the beach. I liked the old-fashioned term, rather than *make out*. It seemed more innocent—if not more honorable.

I began to work on a final summer story about a young lifeguard who falls in love with an older woman. Often fiction can embellish reality, shine it up, so to speak, but sometimes it can dull it down. My story was of the dull-down variety. I ripped it into four pieces and placed it in the wastebasket in the kitchen and showed it to no one.

Jill and I continued to take nighttime walks on the beach and surf at Holgate. Sometimes we met Roger there. Jane was in Chicago visiting Charles and attending to airline stuff, so Roger didn't come by as often. Jill and I enjoyed our time together, and I was mostly a gentleman. On my birthday I would be two years older than her, again. Two years mean a lot when you're nineteen and seventeen. I just couldn't coordinate my love life within proper timeframes.

The summer for lifeguarding ended the last week of August, extended a week from the previous year to protect the hangers-on who didn't have children to get back to school. In addition to ending with the Lifeguard Ball, there was a day of lifeguard competition where the various lifeguards competed in athletic events, like timed buoy rescues and races of various distances. Chris Mackee was back. Rumor was that Lifter was refusing to pay him for his time away unless he worked the last days of summer. The investigation into the perpetrators of the *attack* had gone nowhere. He routinely drove by our stand, speeding up his modified sane pace as he passed us. He did stop, however, to record what, if any, events we wished to participate in.

Ed said, "The digging-holes-in-the-sand one."

Mackee turned his back on Eddie and asked me. I suppressed a chuckle and looked at the events on his clipboard. I didn't want to wimp out in front of him. The buoy rescue event was a team of two people. "Want to do the rescue event?" I asked Ed.

"Already done it. Just want the sand-hole one," he said, taking the opportunity for another dig. I wasn't particularly fast, but I was a strong swimmer, and I signed up for the half-mile race.

"That's a long-distance race," Mackee said as he left with a snicker.

"Careful with those holes," said Ed as Mackee's wheels spit sand on his departure. He slowed down considerably, though, as he approached the jetty. Ed laughed uncontrollably, and I joined him.

On my day off, before the last week of *lifeguard summer*, Jill organized a potluck with the surfers at Holgate. Jane, the daughter, was still away in Chicago, but Roger was there, and so was Andy, my first surfing mentor. I knew almost all of them, though I'd done most of my surfing at 29th Street beach. Everyone seemed happy to see me and slapped me on the shoulder or shook my hand. Some congratulated me on the *Surfing* article, and a few even mentioned the *Pablo's Cock* story in the *Island Rag*. What with the hurricane and all, I had forgotten all about it. "I haven't seen it yet," I said. "Hope I can still find it."

"I saved you some copies for your portfolio. Hope it'll fit," Roger said with a slap on my shoulder.

The whole Deriksson family came sans the Chicago daughter—Jill, Richard, even young Jan came with a few of his friends. Ed had to work, but Mike Evers showed up, having taken the day off. Fast Eddie and Pam were there, and Pam came up and kissed me on the cheek, while Fast Eddie shook my hand. I remembered that it was Pam's picnic that set the stage for everything that followed. I thanked her, and she smiled.

I hadn't surfed in the previous two weeks, but I didn't embarrass myself. Roger was complimentary, and I began making plans to transport my board back to Arizona. Andy and a few other surfers came up to say kind things about my surfing. Debbie came up to talk. It had been her who'd lent me her surfboard that first time, but it was Roger's compliments that meant the most. We all ate, drank, laughed, told exaggerated stories, and surfed until we were sated with it all. Someone, as someone did at the first picnic, suggested that we retire to the Island Beach.

Jan and his friends decided to walk home. The rest of us filled the Island Beach bar. Tables were pushed together, and about twenty of us sat around. I sat located between Roger and Jill, Jane sat across the table and kitty corner from us, Richard at her side. I kept looking at her, afraid Richard would notice. I was reminded of trying not to look at Shelly Goldberg sitting on the buoy, unable to help myself.

76

Lifeguard Games and Ball

Two events dominated my last week of the lifeguard summer, as I began to think of it: the Lifeguard Ball and the Lifeguard Games. I spent an inordinate amount of time worrying about the long-distance swim, thinking it might have been a mistake and a win for Chris Mackee. Nothing to do but swim it out, I told myself.

The day arrived, and the Deriksson family and I sat on the beach. Jill, by my side, offered encouragement, optimism, sarcasm and ironic humor, and ultimately distraction.

The half-mile swim was set for the middle of the events since it would take some time, and the organizers wanted it completed by the end of the day and the trophy awards. I wasn't worried about trophies, just survival. About the time my event was to start, supervisor Dan came by. "No need to race," he said. "You're the only one who signed up for the event." I expelled the stress that had been building up in me like phlegm for days. I was glad it was Dan, and not Chris, who delivered the message. Perhaps it was my win after all. I sat with Jill and enjoyed the last half of the competition. At the awards ceremony, there was one trophy left. Lifter, who was handing them out, was confused until Dan alerted to the half-mile swim situation. Lifter called me up, handed me the trophy, and shook my hand—we were friends again. I walked back to our towel, and Jill squeezed my arm. "My hero," she said.

The Lifeguard Ball was two days later, marking the end of lifeguard summer. Few people other than lifeguards and township employees showed up, though many more had bought tickets. There was a local band, made up mostly of lifeguards, and Gino Bataglia and Amy Trinket were among a few others I knew vaguely. Amy sang well, and the band was pretty good. I walked over to Art Lifter and thanked him for the trophy. He left me with wisdom of "Life's about showing up.," he said. Sounded good to me.

I stumbled through a few dances with Jill, and we left for the beach. We walked by Ed and his girlfriend, Linda, who were busy making babies before he went into the Navy. We gave them a quarter-mile of distance before we lay down ourselves. I'd drank a good deal of cream sherry preparing for the ball, and I cautioned myself to behave, which I did—mostly.

The Ball, I couldn't help but feel, was an anticlimax to an end of an eventful and near perfect summer. I wasn't sure what I wanted. Fireworks? A full moon, maybe. But lying with Jill in the sand to the sound of breakers made up for it.

77

Two Days Before Not Yet

During the week that followed, Jane and I, as much as we could, necked in the shadow of Barnegat Light, while Jill and I continued to surf at Holgate. The caterpillar remained structurally intact. Jane, the daughter, had returned from Chicago, and with her came more of a presence of Roger, making it harder for us to schedule the necking time.

Jane remarked, "Jimmy, since I've met you, I've become a terrible liar." Indeed, I was honing the art myself. My birthday was less than a week away, and Jane and I had planned to spend the night at the Island Beach Hotel the night of my birthday on the fifteenth. It took some deception. I had been scheduled to leave the day after my birthday. The bus stopped a block away from my aunts' apartments in the early morning and would deliver me to the Philadelphia airport in time for a night flight back home.

Demonstrating my lying élan, I told my aunts my father had asked if I could leave a few days early for a family gathering, that I would have to leave on the morning of the fourteenth, two days before my original departure. We could celebrate my birthday on the night of the thirteenth. Since it was my father, it was all right with them. If need be, I could make up a story for my father of why I thought I needed to leave early—the police and the Chris Mackee affair, maybe.

On the evening of the thirteenth, we had my nineteenth birthday celebration at Aunt Ibby's apartment. A dinner of soft-shell crabs, mashed potatoes, succotash, and cornbread, all my favorites. There was even a cake with my name on it. Many stories of France were relayed, and some I heard for the first time. I loved it, and my aunts were in heaven. A lot of Beefeater and Almaden Mountain Red Burgundy went down that night; I wouldn't have to worry about my aunts getting up early in the morning to say goodbye. It would be just me. They gave me the same present they had given me since I was three years old, a card with a ten-dollar bill in it. I loved it, even teared up a bit. I went back to Clair's apartment and packed my two suitcases. True to my word, I had bought a travel bag for Tabby's trip to Arizona. I had left her bagged at the Deriksson home. The next night, we had planned a goodbye dinner at the Island Beach, with the entire Deriksson family and Roger. I had let it be known that I would be leaving on my birthday, one final bit of deception, clearing the night for Jane and me. Roger had said he would bring Tabby to the hotel.

I looked around the apartment, gathered my portfolio of writings, made thicker with a few copies of the *Island Rag* Pablo story. I had Jane's copy of *White Lotus*, still unread. Feeling I was all done, I thought of the story of the young lifeguard and middle-aged woman I'd ripped up and thrown away. I looked in the wastebasket, and it was still there. I removed it and placed it on the writing desk beside my father's Underwood, secured in its case. Then I went looking for scotch tape. It was a number of drawers before I found a roll. It was old and yellow, maybe as old as the Underwood, but it would serve. I meticulously pieced each page back together, all eleven pages. I was glad to have used page numbers. I put it carefully in the portfolio. I'd maybe get back to it later. I put the portfolio of writings along with Jane's copy of *White Lotus* in one of the suitcases. I was ready to leave.

I slept better than I thought I would, waking up at six with only a mild hangover; I wondered how many times Steinbeck had woken up with the same. My chicanery had been efficient, and I had parked my VW around the corner, two blocks away. Hell, I was a veritable Huck Finn as I carried my suitcases easily to my car; the typewriter made it only a little awkward. I drove to the Island Beach Hotel and parked behind it. I had a reservation for two nights, so I just checked in and went up to my room. I lay down on the bed and was asleep until I was wakened by a knock at the door. I opened it to find Roger.

"What time is it?" I asked.

"About ten. Come on, Jill's waiting in the car. I brought your board," I had been asleep for three hours. I was still groggy as I put on my lifeguard togs, but I felt great as I walked barefoot to the car.

We surfed for better than two hours, then went to Flo's for a late breakfast.

Jill said, "Mom's really looking forward to tonight, I can tell." I dared not speak of what I was looking forward to. I felt a twinge of guilt—an impotent twinge, it was.

"When do you leave the island?" I asked her.

"I start back at school in a week. We'll be leaving sometime before that. I begged mom to stay here and let me finish school in Camden, and she said she'd like to but Jan's too young. Maybe in two years, she said. In a year, I'll be living here on my own." *On her own*—I experienced another twinge, but like Jane's analogy of a short story whose end you know is coming, I let the thought dissolve.

The dinner was quite the festive event, and everyone seemed joyful. Jane, Richard, Jill, Roger and Jane, even Jan came and seemed talkative. "Where will you surf in Arizona?" he asked.

"Nowhere in Arizona to surf," I said. "But California is only six hours away." The statement made me sad. I was sorry I hadn't gotten to know him better.

Over dinner, we laughed a lot, loudest at remembrance of the Chris Mackee incident, though we looked around to see if anyone was listening. The ominous cloud, however, had lifted.

I had insisted that there were to be no presents, so of course everybody brought one. Even Jan gave me one of his toy soldiers. Jill handed me a small but heavy package. I opened it to find a chrome gas cap taken from the gas tank of the 50cc motorbike I had dumped. I remembered the dent in the gas tank. All the assembled laughed. With her ironic smile, she said, "I've replaced the tank."

"It was beautiful. You can make a necklace out of it," I said.

The laughter was short-lived as I reached into my pocket and handed Jill the keys to my VW. "I've already signed over the title and given it to your mother." I looked over to Richard. "Roger's determined the vehicle is safe." Jill smiled broadly, no longer ironic. She got out of her chair and kissed me on the cheek.

Roger gave me a wooden tiki he'd brought back from a trip to Hawaii, a carving of a surfing god, meant to be worn on a leather thong. He tied it around my neck, and I fought back tears. Richard gave me a copy of the book *Waves and Beaches*, with an inscription. I had already bought the book early in the summer, and I was afraid to read the inscription, but I looked at the page with my eyes thrown out of focus. I didn't read it till I got back to Arizona. In the end, it was a kind memory we both shared.

I opened Jane, the daughter's, wrapped gift. It was soft. I was afraid it was Richard's underwear she had found folded on the back of the toilet in the cat's bathroom. A white T-shirt with the large red letters *LBI*.

"Jimmy, I'm glad you're leaving tomorrow as I'll not be here on your actual birthday," Jane, the mother, said. "Lucy's arranged for me to visit Manahawkin and to stay the night at the inn, and you'll be gone before I'm back." It was delivered artfully, and all part of the plan. I unwrapped the little package, a paperback of *The Child*

Buyer. Again, I fought back tears as I thought of our conversations.

"Thank you," I said. It carried this dedication: *To my inspiration.* "I will treasure this," I said. I felt I was losing the battle with my tears, and I removed the copy of *White Lotus* from under my seat and handed it to her. "I didn't take time to read it, but I will," I said, remembering her lessons of take and make. She, too, had tears in her eyes.

"Keep it," she said.

"No, I know how much books mean to you. I'll get another copy. I insist." She simply shook her head. I ended up carrying it back to Arizona.

Dessert, a few more glasses of wine, and we all said goodbye at the door to the hotel. Lots of hugs, some kisses, but Jane and I were restrained in our embrace. Richard shook my hand and said, "See you next year?"

Then they were gone.

78

Happy Birthday

I woke up on my birthday in the Island Beach Hotel with nothing to do till I was to meet Jane at five o'clock. Jill had my car, her car now, so I walked to the beach down from my aunts' apartment. I wore the LBI T-shirt given to me the previous night and a wide straw hat to hide my face. I looked like a tourist—perfectly incognito. I took the long way around. It was a bit of a walk, but what else did I have to do?

I walked slowly up to the shore of my first beach, feet in the surf, like a salmon returning to his place of birth, and found myself thinking of Karen. I searched the now reduced number of beachgoers, looking for her. I practiced how I would greet her: *Hi, Karen, I'm Jimmy, you don't know me, but I know you, I'm very glad to meet you. I'm Jimmy and I've been wanting to introduce myself to you for a long time. Hi, Karen, I'm Jimmy, how do you like being the Jersey Devil?... a detective?* Ridiculous! Still, I observed everyone I passed. I thought of how the straps of her bathing suit were tied in the back. She couldn't have tied them herself. Who tied them, and why? To preserve her dignity? The thoughts, rather than sad, gave me a warm feeling. Could she get out of her suit by herself? Probably not, so who untied it? Was the process of tying and untying an assault on her dignity? I found there were tears coming, and I changed the topic from the straps to an internal conversation of just why this young woman had become so important to me.

My musings about Karen had brought me to my destination. I looked to the entry to the beach. Two blocks beyond resided my aunts. I fought down the duplicity as I shed my LBI T-shirt and took a swim. I watched two children of about seven or eight years old playing in the surf, unconsciously adopting a lifeguard's vigilance. I wondered if they were twins. Either they attended a private school that started later than the beginning of the third week of August or had bohemian parents who disregarded the stricture of starting dates. I favored the latter.

I left the two children and walked to Flo's for breakfast. It was a risk, but a small one, and I chose to take it. At the diner, no one seemed to recognize me—thanks to the disguise offered by the LBI shirt and straw hat. Thank you, Jane. I'd bought the *Camden Ledger* and thumbed through it over my hashbrowns, eggs over easy, and sausages. Nothing about haps in the Pine Barrens. It seemed a long time ago.

I walked back to the hotel, taking my time, stopping to sit on the sand and to take an occasional swim. Still, I looked for Karen. I came to think that her lesson was that sometimes you have only one chance to do the thing that, if not done, you'll regret for the rest of your life. Awkward, but a form of closure, and I took it.

I reached the hotel a little before three, took a shower, dressed in my underwear I sought to dry off, which was not easy given the humidity. I didn't have a watch, so when I thought it was nearing five, I walked down to the bar. I chose a booth in a back corner of the room, ordered a beer, and asked the waitress the time. She said it was just past four-thirty. *Not bad*, I thought. I still marveled at Island Beach's lack of an ID policy. If Jan had ordered a beer the night before, would they have served him? I looked up to see Jane entering.

Jane ordered a piña colada, and I followed. "Aren't you afraid Roger might see us? He has a room here." I thought to ask, surprised that I hadn't thought of this before. (In every mystery novel, the criminal makes just one mistake.)

"No," Jane said, "he and Jane are off on a holiday." *Holiday. Good word.*

Our piña coladas came. Then Jane delivered the thunderclap. "Jimmy, after much soul searching, I can't consummate our relationship." The bolt of lightning ran through me. Still, I was silent as Jane continued.

"It's not for Jill, and not for Richard, though there is the potential for much hurt there. It's a more selfish reason that I choose not to honor my birthday promise." She smiled an ironic smile, not quite reminiscent of Jill's. "I became enamored of your youth and promise and found I was unable to refrain from inserting myself. The hurricane gave me, us, an opportunity for intimacy, an intimacy I never anticipated or thought possible. I said at the time that you awakened things I'd long thought dead. And you have. I've called you soulmate. And you are.

"If we follow through with our plan, *my promise*, it will be closure to a summer infatuation between a middle-aged woman and a young man, and it will end there. Our connection is deeper than that. Though we may never see each other again, I want what we have to be consummated through the years by the effect I have on your future life, on your judgments—on your behavior—and on your writing. I want to play a part in your decisions, in your future, if you will. And I'm selfish enough not to give that up for an evening of something ephemeral. I want our relationship to last, to continue to grow."

By the time the waitress delivered our second piña coladas, there were tears cascading across my face. The waitress quickly set down the drinks and left. Jane took my hand across the table as my tears continued to flow. As I regained some control of myself, Jane took a napkin and wiped my face—we finished our drinks. "Let's go out to my car," she said. I told the bartender on our way out that I'd be back, and he nodded.

The parking lot was empty, and we sat in the backseat of her car. We kissed, and I could feel the summer draining off the seat in a puddle on the floor around my feet. I had been expecting a bittersweet ending, but not this one. But it felt surprisingly right, surprisingly soft, surprisingly warm.

"You said I awakened things you thought were dead. Will you begin writing again?" I asked.

"I don't know." There were tears in her eyes. "Maybe."

"You've become an excellent liar, an important skill for a fiction writer." At that, Jane smiled.

It was a long goodbye. Nothing was hurried or urgent. Cars now pulled into the parking lot, and it was time to part.

I walked through the hotel door and saw Tabby in her travel bag. Roger had leaned her upright against the wall the previous night. The hotel said it was OK to leave her there till morning. I felt astonishingly calm and at peace.

Jane was absolute magic.

79

Nothing More to Write

In the morning, albeit after sleeping in a fetal position, hugging a pillow through the night, I went downstairs to call a cab. After some discussion, we placed Tabby through the two open back windows, sticking out three feet on each side. The driver loaded my suitcases into the trunk, while I carried my portfolio and the Underwood in the front seat. It was just past six o'clock, there was little traffic, and the surfboard caused no trouble on the short ride to the bus station. The bus would transport me back to the Philadelphia airport and to a former life, but not the same life, and not the same guy.

On the way, thoughts of the summer seemed to dissolve in my bloodstream—Karen, Shelly, Jill.

Jane...

Jamey Gittings is a fiction writer who splits his time between Arivaca, Arizona and Big Sur, California. Gittings was a problematic high school student who ultimately annexed a Ph.D. degree in areas of behavior disorders, mental retardation, and behavior psychology from the University of Arizona. He has founded a school for youth and adults with disabilities, worked for the United Nations, the Government of Afghanistan, and with the Government of India on projects focusing on disability, gender equality and international development. Jamey is the author of three previous novels.

For additional information,
please visit: jameygittings.com
or
To contact Jamey directly:
jameygittings@gmail.com

www.ingramcontent.com/pod-product-compliance
Lightning Source LLC
Chambersburg PA
CBHW050024120726
47903CB00006B/1905